MAKING A
KILLING IN
DIAMONDS

MAKING A KILLING IN DIAMONDS

THE DIAMOND DISTRICT MYSTERY SERIES, BOOK FOUR

ROB BATES

Kenmore, WA

CAMEL PRESS

A Camel Press book published by Epicenter Press

Epicenter Press
6524 NE 181st St.
Suite 2
Kenmore, WA 98028

For more information go to:
www.Camelpress.com
www.Coffeetownpress.com
www.Epicenterpress.com
www.robbatesauthor.com

This is a work of fiction. Names, characters, places, brands, media, and incidents are the product of the author's imagination or are used fictitiously.

Cover and interior design by Scott Book and Melissa Vail Coffman

Making a Killing in Diamonds
Copyright © 2025 by Rob Bates

Library of Congress Control Number: 2024952548

ISBN: 978-1-68492-322-9 (Trade Paper)
ISBN: 978-1-68492-323-6 (eBook

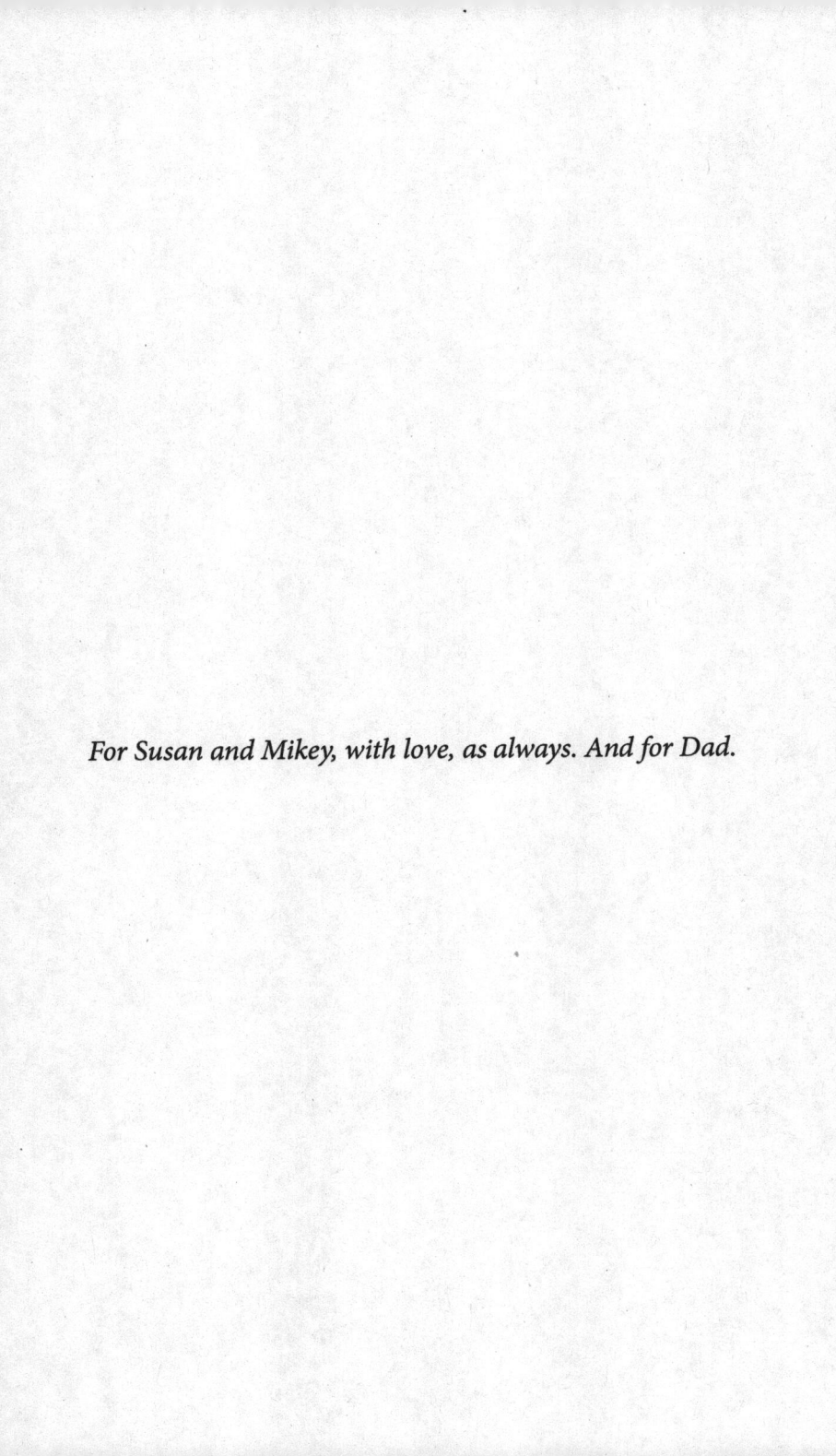

For Susan and Mikey, with love, as always. And for Dad.

AUTHOR'S NOTE AND ACKNOWLEDGEMENTS

WHILE THIS BOOK DEALS WITH REAL-LIFE issues, it is a work of fiction and should be viewed as such. Lab-grown diamonds do exist, and are a real force in the industry. However, as far as I know, there is currently 1) no way to produce a lab-grown diamond that is not detectable by advanced equipment (which means they can all be distinguished from natural diamonds), and 2) no way to produce high-quality lab-growns as quickly and cheaply as they are produced in this book.

The story also includes some techniques and "experiments" which may or may not be feasible or scientifically possible. The people, companies, labs, publications, and hotels in this book are all fictional. There's even a fake country.

For those who want to learn more about the (actual) diamond industry, I'm compiling a list of resources on my website, robbatesauthor.com, which will include links for those interested in exploring the industry's ethical issues. And if you get stuck on the industry or Yiddish terms, there's a glossary in the back.

Now to the thank yous. My deepest gratitude goes to my family—to Susan and Mikey, of course, as well as my father, Susan B., and Michelle. Thank you to my friends and colleagues, both inside the industry and out. And I'll give one more shout-out to the real Max and Mimi, wherever they are.

I would also like to take a moment to remember and thank my (now former) agent, Dawn Dowdle, who died in 2023. I'll always be grateful to her for taking a chance on me. This book is dedicated to her, as well as to Hedda Schupak, my former editor at *JCK* who died the same year.

And heartfelt thanks to Jennifer McCord, my editor at Camel Press, for her dedication to making this book better. And one more tip of the hat to my writing group colleagues for helping me get this book in shape, and having the patience to read it twice.

Finally, whoever you are reading this—whether this is your first book of mine, or you've read the first three—I thank you for giving my work your time. I appreciate it more than I can say.

Rob Bates
New York City, 2025

CHAPTER ONE

MIMI ROSEN WAS STEPPING OUT OF her comfort zone and learning a new skill. She was expanding her horizons, and hating every minute of it.

Mimi's official title was chief marketing officer for the Max Rosen Diamond Company. Which sounded impressive, except in the three years Mimi had worked at her father's office in New York's Diamond District, she hadn't done much marketing.

But now the company needed business—badly. Sales had fallen, because of the increasing vogue for lab-grown diamonds. These were gems created by machines, rather than in nature, which sold for far less than mined stones. Traditionalists—a club Max proudly belonged to—saw "synthetics" as cut-rate copies riding the coattails of the industry they'd worked hard to build. Yet, even Max would admit—begrudgingly, with a scowl—that they'd eaten into natural diamonds' market share.

Max made it clear that selling lab-grown diamonds was out of the question, so Mimi searched for a way to boost business. It might be time to try TikTok. Many fellow former journalists were creating online videos. That sounded like fun.

Which was why, on a beautiful Sunday in early March, Mimi was holed up in her apartment, hunched over her computer, creating her first TikTok—and not finding it fun.

Mimi planned to film herself reciting "five fascinating diamond facts." Almost immediately, her perfectionist tendencies took over. She agonized over whether she was using the right background, the right music, the right text, the right font. One button beckoned her to add emojis, which she didn't understand. *Why would anyone want emojis on their video? Aren't they annoying enough in texts*? She struggled to master the editing software, which sent her scrambling to online tutorials.

"Making TikToks shouldn't take long," said the chipper host of one. "I usually put mine together in ten minutes."

Mimi wanted to punch her.

Six hours and one sore neck later, Mimi finished her first creation. She'd labored on it so long she could see its shadows when she closed her eyes.

Mimi took a break, microwaved a pre-prepared dinner of chicken-something-or-other, and watched it again. It wasn't bad. The editing was professional. The content was solid. There was one problem: her.

Just looking in the mirror made Mimi self-conscious. Watching herself on video felt excruciating. Mimi had just started wearing her brown hair long, after a year of wearing it short. Having to stare at her image made her continually rethink that choice. She was also forty-two, and worried how she'd look on an app where everyone appeared half her age. Happily, she saw TikTok had a wrinkle-removing "beauty filter." This amused her, since she kept reading that TikTok prized "authenticity." *The hell with authenticity*, she decided, and applied the filter.

There was no improving her delivery, however. It felt forced and phony. Unless TikTok invented a "sincerity filter," it was obvious she didn't find her "five fascinating facts" all that fascinating.

Her father, on the other hand, would be perfect for TikTok. He owned the company. He'd spent his life in the diamond game. He was passionate about the product.

He would *not* want to do it.

MONDAY MORNING, MIMI ARRIVED AT THE office early, to get a head-start on what promised to be a long process convincing her father to appear on TikTok. As expected, he told her "no" the minute she proposed it, like he always did when Mimi asked him to try something new.

"I don't need to do videos," Max said, with a dismissive wave of his hand. "I have a very good reputation. Everyone knows me. So business is a little slow."

"Dad, business hasn't just been slow lately," Mimi said. "It's been dead."

"Don't worry. Everything's fine. The only way I'm leaving here is feet first."

Mimi smiled, more out of obligation than anything else. He'd made that joke for decades.

"We're in the standard springtime lull," he said. "People are enjoying the nice weather and not buying diamonds."

Mimi was tempted to mention that she'd worked for his company for three years, and it had never experienced this "standard springtime lull" before. Instead, she gave him a long list of reasons why he should appear in the videos, but he was only truly convinced by her capper: "It won't cost anything." Even Max couldn't argue with that.

"All right," he declared. "I'll give it a shot. But that's it."

They agreed to start filming after lunch. Mimi felt like she'd scored a real victory, yet she was surprised how quickly her father capitulated. Obviously, everything *wasn't* fine.

WHEN THE TIME CAME TO FILM, Max remained confused about what he was supposed to do, despite Mimi explaining it to him countless times. She sat him on a chair in front of one of the office's better-looking wood panels, away from its sea of paper-strewn desks.

Mimi removed the loupe that usually dangled from her father's neck and brushed down the two islands of white hair that framed his bald head. She centered his *yarmulke* on his scalp, and made sure his glasses weren't off-kilter. He was wearing his standard out-fit—a white button-down shirt and brown slacks.

To help with "lighting"—basically, pointing a lamp at Max—Mimi recruited Channah, the office receptionist who was one of Mimi's closest friends. Channah happily agreed. But then, she did most things happily these days. She'd been married for a year, and as she put it, the glow hadn't worn off. Mimi had a hard time getting used to the obvious *sheitel* that now covered her head, but otherwise, she was still Channah—good-natured, full-figured, and apple-cheeked, her face dotted with brown freckles.

Mimi enlisted Zeke, Channah's husband, to act as cameraman. The month before, Zeke had lost his job at a tech start-up which was developing an AI that could write code; the owners told him he'd done such a good job, he'd be replaced by his own program. "In a way, it's flattering," he shrugged.

So Max hired him as "director of computer operations"—even though there's a limited amount of computer operations a three-person company needs. Basically, Max was subsidizing Zeke—and by extension Channah—until he got a new job. Mimi knew that was a terrible business practice, especially with the company on the ropes, but she was in no position to object; her father had done the same for her after she'd lost her journalism job.

Zeke set out to redo the company's website. Max was fine with that, since no one visited it anyway, and it kept Zeke busy, and prevented him from droning on about tech subjects Max had no interest in. Max also gave Zeke small tasks to do, like packing boxes or paying invoices. Zeke tackled them all with gusto, even if they weren't what he earned his master's in computer science for. Then again, Mimi did those same jobs when she first started working for her father, and she had twelve years of journalism experience.

Now, Mimi had given Zeke a job he was actually interested in, and he approached it with characteristic zeal. He spent a good ten minutes deciding where to place the camera (his phone) and asking Channah to adjust the "lighting" (the lamp).

"My God," Channah whispered to Mimi, laughing. "My husband's turned into Stanley Kubrick with a *yarmulke*."

"Zeke, this doesn't have to be perfect," Mimi said. "The most important thing is that Dad says something interesting and provocative."

"Oh yeah," Max interjected. "And what interesting and provocative things do you want me to say?"

Mimi had a ready answer. "I want you to talk about lab-grown diamonds."

"*Oy*." Max glanced up at her. "I don't want to talk about those things. I'm sick of that subject."

"Dad, you talk about them constantly," Mimi said. "You might as well try and get business out of it."

"I wouldn't know where to start," Max said.

"Try this." Mimi pulled out a list of tips she'd found online. "First, introduce yourself. Second, give your credentials. Then, say what you plan to talk about. State your opinion on the subject, and provide your reasons for that opinion. The entire video shouldn't be more than two minutes. We'll film you for five, and edit out any rough spots.

"Just pretend you're talking to me. It'll be fun." She nodded to Zeke. "All right! Let's go!"

Max looked straight at the camera. "Hello, whoever is watching whatever this is. My name is Max Rosen." He punctuated his intro with an awkward smile. Mimi made a note to edit that out.

"I've been in the diamond business for a long time. Over fifty years. I think I know a thing or two about a thing or two."

Feisty, Mimi thought. *Good. He's getting warmed up.*

"I'd been asked to talk about synthetic diamonds. Some people call them lab-grown diamonds, but they're not grown in labs, they're made in factories. I call them Frankenstones. They're this monster the industry created that is now on the rampage.

"People ask me if I would ever sell synthetics. I say, 'no.' Natural diamonds are a treasure of nature, created by God. They're billions of years old. These new fake diamonds were produced last week by some *schnook* in a factory—no different than any other trinket.

"Synthetic diamonds are not rare or valuable, and the technology to produce them keeps getting cheaper. Every week, they are worth less, and soon that will be their value—worthless.

"I can't in good conscience sell an item I'd never buy myself. I prefer inventory that goes up in value, not down. I've dealt in real diamonds for years, and rarely, if ever, have I lost money on them.

"And by the way, this isn't just about diamonds. They want to make lab-grown flowers, lab-grown vegetables, and lab-grown fruit. Suddenly, objects created by God aren't good enough. We have to produce everything in a lab. Why would you need lab-grown fruit? I've eaten regular bananas for seventy-six years. Trust me: they're fine."

Okay, Mimi thought. *Now, he's getting* too *warmed up*.

Max wagged his finger at the camera. "This is what's wrong with the world today. Everything's electronic. My grandkids are always staring at their phones like zombies, playing these games where they blow people up. I ask them: 'what's the matter, there's not enough violence in the real world? You need to make terrible things happen in a fake one?'"

Mimi had cringed throughout her father's tirade, but that was the last straw. "Okay, Dad. Stop!"

"Why?" Max's head jerked back. "That was going well."

"You were way off topic," Mimi said. "You weren't talking about diamonds. You were talking about video games."

"But it's all related! The same people are behind all these things." He turned to Channah. "What do you think? I was making sense, wasn't I?"

"I liked the part when you talked about bananas," Channah giggled.

Zeke fiddled with his glasses, then scratched his beard. "Mr. Rosen, I think you were a little harsh in your assessment of video games."

"Enough!" Mimi snapped. "Let's get back on track! Dad, I know you feel strongly about this topic, but we can't use any of what you just said. You were way too angry."

"You said I should be interesting and provocative."

"Yes. But not crazy." She imagined her father going viral—in the worst way: "Watch this INSANE old man rant about diamonds!"

Mimi took a calming breath. "Let's try again. Understand that not everyone feels the same way you do. Don't just rant. Persuade."

They filmed take after take. They all came out the same. No matter how many times Mimi asked her father to soften his language, he still sounded like an old man complaining about modern technology. Maybe because that's what he was.

"Dad," Mimi said, "you're too agitated."

"So? Everything I said was factual."

"Not really," Mimi said. "Lab-grown diamonds are considered real diamonds. It's in the name. 'Lab-grown diamonds.' They're not lab-grown tomatoes. They look the same."

"Yeah, and chatbots sound like real people," Max said. "That doesn't mean they're the same. Besides, gemologists can tell a synthetic from a real stone. That means they're different."

"Well, like it or not, a lot of my friends are buying lab-growns," Mimi said.

"Mine, too," said Channah. "They say they're doing it because they're eco-friendly, but I think they just want a bigger rock."

"That's another thing!" Max raised his voice. "They keep saying synthetics are eco-friendly. You're replacing a mine with a highly industrialized factory. How is that eco-friendly? To grow these diamonds, they need temperatures as hot as the sun. You know how much electricity that takes? You think that's good for the environment?"

"Dad, the video's over. You can stop ranting."

"I'm just getting started. These companies make me sick. Like that big one, Diamond Superior. You hear these people talk, you'd think they were curing cancer."

"They're taking advantage of the industry's bad reputation," Mimi said. "You talk to people outside the industry, they think every diamond's a blood diamond."

"But that's not true!" Max said. "A lot of diamonds help people.

If everyone stopped buying diamonds, millions of people would be out of work."

"Yes, I know that and you know that," Mimi said. "But consumers don't. They believe all diamonds are bad. And in marketing, perception equals reality."

"Forget marketing; I'm talking facts," Max said. "I'm surprised you're defending those *ganefs*. Weren't you the one who lectured me about how we have to take care of all those poor people that depend on diamond revenue? Do you think wiping out their livelihoods will help? How about your co-op in Africa? What will happen to those people when they have no source of income?"

Mimi had worked with the co-op for two years, after meeting Sulaiman Kamora, a Reverend from a small mining village in the African Democratic Republic. They'd worked out a deal where Max would sell its gems direct to the market, and Kamora's community would net a greater share of the profits. After a few big sales, the village had built a well, which provided a welcome new source of clean water. Mimi's dream was for the locals to earn enough to construct their first health clinic. She was extremely proud of the co-op; it had been written up in several trade publications, and she carried pictures of it in her purse to win new supporters.

"Dad, lab-grown diamonds won't destroy our business. They'll find a place in the market, and everything will go on as usual." Mimi didn't know how true that was, but didn't feel like hearing her father rant all afternoon.

LATER THAT AFTERNOON, MAX CALLED MIMI over to his computer.

"So you don't think lab-growns will destroy the business, huh? Look at this."

It took Mimi a moment to grasp that Max was still trying to win the argument they'd had hours ago.

He pointed to a story from industry news publication *JN*.

Diamond Superior announced Monday it can produce lab-grown diamonds that are completely indistinguishable from natural gems—even by top grading labs using the most advanced equipment.

Speaking from his company's production facility in Santa Mira, Calif., Diamond Superior CEO Eugene Thorble said the Chrysalis diamonds will be unveiled during a presentation at the upcoming Jewelry Expo, which starts Wednesday at the Omnichannel Hotel in New York City.

Thorble said the Chrysalis formula—named after the process by which a caterpillar turns into a butterfly—can transform any carbon-based object into a lab-grown diamond completely indistinguishable from a mined stone. He expects to start selling the diamonds within the next month.

"This is a technological milestone," said Thorble, a billionaire whose previous company, Sustainabills, produced a cryptocurrency tied to carbon credits. "For a long time, gem labs could distinguish a lab-grown diamond from a mined stone.

"We have tested our new production against every detection device on the market," Thorble said. "We believe this will spell the end of the mined diamond industry once and for all."

MIMI CLICKED ON THE ACCOMPANYING VIDEO. Thorble appeared about thirty—annoyingly young to be a billionaire. He sported a beard, a sharp nose, and a squiggly mouth, which made him resemble a perpetually pissed-off pigeon. His voice was nasal, verging on screechy. The only time he displayed anything close to happiness was when he described the chaos his new diamonds would unleash.

"We have sent three of our diamonds to Michelson Gemological Associates, the best lab in the industry," he proclaimed, holding up a grading report. "They identified all three as mined stones, which they are not. They were produced by us."

Mimi's head sank into her hands. That was the lab started by her childhood friend, Paul Michelson. He prided himself on scrupulous accuracy. This must be humiliating for him.

"We are currently producing thousands of Chrysalis diamonds,"

Thorble said. "In a few weeks, we will flood the industry with them. No one will be able to tell them apart from mined stones. Traditional diamonds will lose all their value overnight."

"Turn that off!" Max roared. "I can't bear another second." He slapped his palm on his desk. "I told you! Those lab-grown idiots want to wipe out the entire industry."

Mimi had no response. She found Thorble's comments disconcerting, to say the least; if what he said was true, it would mean not only the end of her job, but her father's company and their co-op in the ADR.

Then again, this guy didn't exactly radiate trustworthiness. "Dad, you know how tech companies like to exaggerate. Like that woman with the blood tests. They're probably just saying that to get investors. Don't worry."

"Sure, tell me not to worry," Max said. "My net worth is tied up in my inventory. This changes everything. If labs can't tell the difference between my real diamonds and their fake ones, all my inventory will be worth nothing, and that means I'll be worth nothing, too. This company will have to close and we'll all be out of work."

As Max got more and more worked up, the veins in his neck bulged and saliva gathered around his lips. Then, mid-rant, something changed—his voice became rawer, and his words kept getting interrupted by coughs, which started out normal, then veered into a wheeze.

"Dad, are you okay?" Mimi asked.

"I'm fine," Max rasped, gripping his shirt. "Just some heartburn. I must have eaten something bad." He sank into his chair. Beads of sweat dotted his forehead. This wasn't heartburn.

Mimi called to the reception area. "Channah, come here. Now!"

Channah ran to the back. "What's the matter?" When she saw Max, her eyes bulged. "Oh my God. I'll get some water."

"I'm calling an ambulance," Mimi said.

"Don't!" Max barked, but then he doubled over. "You know what, maybe you should."

Mimi was already on the phone with 911. She gave the operator the office address, and begged them to come as soon as possible.

Max sat, flushed and sweaty, gulping down the water Channah gave him. His *yarmulke* had fallen off, exposing his age-spotted scalp, which made Mimi turn away. She was so used to seeing his skull covered, it was like seeing him naked.

After a few minutes—which felt like forever—Mimi heard a siren, faintly at first, and then louder as the ambulance roared onto Forty-Seventh Street. She peered out the window and saw a fleet of blue shirts enter the building.

"The medics are coming," Mimi shouted to her father. "They should be here any second."

Max didn't respond. He clutched his chest and crumpled to the floor.

CHAPTER TWO

THE EMTs SWARMED INTO MAX'S OFFICE. One knelt over him, and asked if he was conscious. Max croaked that he was. The EMT strapped an oxygen mask on his face and checked his vitals.

He said that Max was having a cardiac episode, and needed to be taken to the hospital immediately. He and his comrades lifted Max onto a gurney, which they wheeled out to the hall. They rode the emergency elevator down to the street, where an ambulance was double-parked outside.

Max was hoisted into the ambulance. Mimi climbed in with him. The doors closed, leaving Mimi, her dad, and another EMT sitting in the back. Mimi held her father's hand as the ambulance roared through mid-afternoon midtown Manhattan. Max muttered something under his mask, and Mimi put her head down to hear him. He was moaning "Esther, Esther"—the name of his late wife.

THE AMBULANCE ARRIVED AT NEW YORK-PRESBYTERIAN Hospital, and Max was immediately taken in for examination. Mimi waited in the reception area, her mind going to dark places. Mimi's relationship with her father had weathered many ups and downs, but she loved that man, and wasn't ready to lose him. Yet, as her therapist told Mimi after her mom died, there's never a good time to lose anyone.

Nearly every chair in the waiting room was occupied, but Mimi was too antsy to sit anyway. The walls were covered with blaring televisions, meant to distract the people waiting; judging from all the somber faces, they didn't help. This was a place where lives were changed, not for the better.

Mimi walked out the front door, joining a scattered group standing on the street, most of whom were smoking. What happened suddenly hit her, and she began to cry. A woman opened her purse to hand Mimi a tissue, but Mimi put up her hand to indicate she already had one. The woman turned away. Everyone else stayed focused on their phones.

When Mimi's tears ran out, she called Michael Matthews, the burly ex-cop she'd been dating for the last two years. Michael had recently taken a temp job managing a local jazz club. He never liked being called at work; he was always too busy. As a result, Mimi never contacted him there, which was a problem, since he was rarely anywhere else. Today, he answered Mimi's call, no doubt sensing it was important.

"My father collapsed on the floor of his office," she said, catching her breath, "and now he's in the hospital."

"Jesus!" Michael exclaimed. "Is he all right?"

"I don't know," Mimi said, her voice quavering. "They're examining him now."

"That's crazy." Michael was now giving Mimi his full attention. "How are you doing?"

Mimi gulped, then said the first thing that came to mind. "I'm scared. Really scared." She squeezed her hands and held her breath, so she didn't dissolve into tears again.

Michael uttered a few more "I'm sorry"s, and "that's awful"s, but as a former homicide detective, he knew there wasn't much you could say to comfort a distraught family member.

"I'll find someone to cover for me tonight," he said. "I can be at the hospital around six."

"Okay," Mimi said in a voice barely above a whisper. "Thanks."

"Keep me posted," he said. "And hang in there. Don't worry.

Hopefully, it'll be okay. I love you, babe." Michael always sounded awkward saying "I love you." He generally uttered it quickly, under his breath, making it sound tinny and mechanical. That time, he pulled it off better than usual.

As painful as the afternoon had been, Mimi particularly dreaded making her next call, to her sister Brenda. Mimi's older sibling lived in Lakewood, New Jersey, not far from Mimi, but their lives were very different. Brenda had followed their father's prescribed path: she had married early, lived in a religious community, and observed all the Jewish holidays and traditions. She had five children, and one grandson.

Mimi was raised in that world, but was no longer a part of it. She and Brenda didn't see each other much, and only called each other for emergencies, like now.

Brenda answered with an anxious "hello." She, too, knew something was up.

"I don't know if it's anything serious," Mimi said, "but Dad just collapsed in his office."

For the next three minutes, Brenda badgered her for details.

"The EMTs said he was having a cardiac issue," Mimi said.

"How did this happen?"

"He was upset about something with his business."

"He collapsed because of his business?" Brenda's tone could cut glass.

"More about the industry overall, not his company in particular." Mimi's body tensed. She knew what was coming.

"Can you please tell me why that man is still working?" Brenda said, shifting to older sister voice. "Maybe years ago, he made a decent living, but now he's just *schlepping* in from Queens so he can *kibitz* with his friends. I don't understand why they don't all just get together and play cards or something instead of wasting so much time and money."

Mimi wanted to respond, but every time she tried to talk, Brenda steamrolled over her. The afternoon had been crazy stressful, and this wasn't helping.

"Dad needs to understand, the world has changed," Brenda continued, as if she was a sudden expert on modernity. "When we were growing up, he made a good living, because all his friends were in the industry. Now his friends are dying, and his company is nearly dead, too.

"You may not notice it, because you see him every day, but lately, when he comes to visit, he looks so tired and unhealthy. He's too old to work like he did twenty years ago. I tell him that all the time. You should, too."

Mimi wondered if Brenda was being territorial here. Mimi wasn't as religious as her sister; in fact, she wasn't religious at all. She fought frequently with her father growing up. But now they saw each other five days a week. They had formed a bond that was stronger and different than what they had before, which Brenda couldn't match. Of course, this wasn't a competition. At least, it shouldn't be.

When Brenda finally took a breath, Mimi jumped in. "You know what Dad will say. He doesn't want to sit around all day. He wants to keep busy. He has an active mind."

"That's why he should move in with us," Brenda declared, and she was off again. "We'll give him plenty to do. Honestly, we could use the help. We have one grandson living with us, and another on the way, God willing. Not that I expect him to be Mr. Super Diaper Changer or anything, but he can play with the baby, read to him, make sure the nanny's doing her job when I'm at work.

"And you know, it won't be such a big change. He comes here for the holidays, so it'll be like a really long visit. We just remodeled the basement, so he can live down there. He can have his TV, his computer. Everything's online today so he can still see his friends on Zoom."

"Dad hates Zoom," Mimi interjected.

"He'll get used to it," Brenda responded. "If he doesn't like talking on the computer, he can make new friends. There's plenty of seniors at our *shul*. They have a club for older people. The point is, every time he visits here, he's happy and smiling, like a different person. And then he goes back to that big empty house and he's miserable."

"He's never told me that," Mimi said.

"Of course, he'd never say that to you. But think about it. How could he not be unhappy? Our whole family used to live in that house. Now it's just him. He needs to sell that place, close his company, and get on with his life. But you know him. He won't ever stop going into that disgusting dirty office and that old dying business."

Mimi couldn't deny her father's office was a mess, or that its décor was frozen in the 1970s, or that its business had seen better days. But working there had taught Mimi so much—about herself, about her family, about business, about everything. That office held a whole world.

"What does he say when you tell him this?" Mimi asked.

"That he has a staff to support—meaning you and his receptionist. I couldn't believe it when he told me he'd hired the receptionist's husband, because the guy lost his job. I said, 'what are you, an employment service? You don't have to give a job to every *schnorrer* who comes knocking on your door. You're not running a charity.'

"And Mimi"—Brenda pivoted back to older-sister mode—"you're supposed to be his office manager. You're supposed to stop this lunacy. Everyone who works there can find other jobs. I mean, if he closes the business, you could find something else, right?"

"Sure," Mimi said, though now that she thought about it, she wasn't sure that she could. She'd spent the last three years working for her father. That wasn't the ideal path back to journalism. She could probably write content for websites, but those jobs were notoriously low-paying and unstable, and she hated the word "content." As her old editor once said, "content is something you put in a box."

She had hoped her detective agency would provide a new path. When Michael retired from the force last year, he invited Mimi to help him start a P.I. firm devoted to solving crimes in the Diamond District. That was a testament to Mimi's success solving murders—which always surprised Michael (and sometimes Mimi). She'd only investigated her first case because she knew the victim— her cousin, Yosef, who was also Channah's fiancé. Two cases later, the skeptical cop she knew as Detective Matthews was not only her boyfriend, he wanted to work with her. Mimi had always wanted to be an investigative journalist, so the P.I. firm was a dream come true. She cut back her time at her father's company to four days a week, so she could devote the other day to the detective agency. But the new venture never really took off. After a few frustrating months, Michael started a temp job at a local jazz club, and Mimi went back to working for her father full-time.

"I can't tell Dad what to do," Mimi told Brenda. "It's his choice."

"Talk to him," her sister demanded. "At his age, he shouldn't be dealing with so much stress. And he definitely shouldn't be collapsing from it."

Mimi was far too drained to discuss this. "All right, Brenda. Let's talk later."

She hung up and headed back to the hospital.

AFTER A HALF HOUR, THE DOCTOR called Mimi in from the waiting room. Max was sitting on an examining table, dressed in a hospital gown, his feet in orange hospital socks. At first, Mimi was taken aback by how frail he looked, but then he smiled at her, and that made her smile, too.

"I've examined your father," said the bespectacled young doctor. He was wearing the standard white coat and sitting next to a computer. "He has developed an irregular heartbeat, likely aggravated by stress. Fortunately, today was just a flare-up. But it's something we'll need to monitor, because we don't want this to escalate into something more serious. He'll need to watch his diet, and, as much as possible, minimize stress. I've prescribed medication to lower his blood pressure."

"Just what I need." Max's face sunk. "More pills."

"I'm also prescribing Valium," he said. "You should take one whenever you feel overwhelmed or anxious. Now might be a good time to start." He nodded to the nurse, who handed him a pill and a cup of water.

"I don't want pills to calm down," Max said. "I'd rather stay myself."

The doctor smiled. "Mr. Rosen, I've just met you, and I can't imagine you being anyone else. I also recommend a lifestyle change. You said that you own a diamond business. I imagine that's stressful."

"No kidding," Max grumbled.

The doctor put his finger to his chin. "I just read about these new lab-grown diamonds. They say they're good for the environment."

"What are you crazy?" Max snapped. "How could something produced in a factory be good for the environment? They're made with methane, which is a fossil fuel you get drilling for oil, and then it leaks out—"

"Dad!" Mimi interrupted. "Take a Valium!"

Max swallowed the pill, as a frown cut across his face.

"Mr. Rosen," said the doctor, "your business is clearly making you anxious. I know being a business owner is not easy, especially at your age. You need to prioritize your health, particularly your heart health. How long have you been working in the diamond industry?"

"Fifty-two years," he said.

"And you still do it full time?" he asked.

"Of course," Max said, a note of pride in his voice.

"Okay." The doctor stood up. "For most people, five decades is enough. You're seventy-six. Maybe it's time to retire."

Max's face grew a full shade whiter. "You want me to stop working?" He looked like he'd just been asked to cut off his arm.

"It's your choice, Mr. Rosen, though it's something you might want to consider. You're not a machine. In the end, we all have to answer to our bodies." He rattled off checkout instructions, shook Max's hand, and left.

"How do you like that?" Max asked, his brow full of lines. "That guy thinks I should retire." No doubt he'd heard that from Brenda. It was different coming from a doctor.

Mimi at first felt angry. How dare this arrogant young man, at the beginning of his career, tell an old man to retire, especially when that old man enjoyed his work? Max loved the diamond business. He relished making deals and *schmoozing* with his industry friends. When he heard a juicy piece of industry gossip, he treasured it, like it was a diamond itself.

Still, Mimi couldn't ignore what the doctor just said. And she couldn't blot out the sight of her father falling to the floor.

While Max changed back into his clothes, Mimi called Brenda to tell her their dad was okay. Brenda was so relieved, she spared Mimi another lecture. They both agreed Max would spend the next few days at Brenda's house.

When the Uber arrived to take Max to Brenda's, Mimi expected him to argue that he needed to go back to the office. Instead, he got in without protest. Maybe he'd been sobered by the doctor's warning. More likely, it was the Valium.

Max's car sped away, leaving Mimi alone on the street with the afternoon sun pouring down on her. The last few hours had been a nightmare, but at least her father was okay. She was about to call Michael when she received a text.

"My name is Kabir Mehta. My company is KM Diamonds. I have a big case for your detective agency."

Mimi was way too frazzled to discuss a new case—especially since most of the inquiries the agency received turned out to be nothing.

"I'm sorry," she wrote back. "We're not accepting new clients."

"You must speak with me," responded Kabir, who apparently didn't take no for an answer. "It's about an important issue—the Chrysalis synthetics from Diamond Superior."

Mimi stopped in her tracks. "What about them?"

"The formula to make them was stolen from us."

Mimi spent a few seconds staring at the message, before writing, "I'll call you."

CHAPTER THREE

MIMI SETTLED ON A BENCH AND phoned Michael. "My father's okay," she said. "He was just discharged from the hospital. You don't have to come."

"Hey, I'm happy to hear that," Michael said. "You had me worried there. Listen, I've already arranged for someone to cover for me tonight at the club, so why don't you come to my place around seven? We'll have dinner, and you can stay over. It sounds like you've had a rough day."

"I have," Mimi smiled. "That would be nice." It would be especially nice because she hadn't stayed at Michael's place since he began working at the club.

"Oh, one more thing," Mimi said. "I just got a text from a diamond dealer. He has a case for the detective agency. It's related to these synthetic diamonds that are big news in the industry."

"You know my schedule here," Michael said. "I'm way too busy to talk to him."

"I'd still like to meet this guy. By myself, if I have to."

Michael groaned. Mimi wasn't sure if she was supposed to hear it, but she did.

"If you want to talk to him on your own, fine," he said. "Just make sure he doesn't have a problem with me not coming."

"Why would he?"

"The agency's main selling point is my experience at the NYPD. I'm also the one with the license."

That was true. Michael automatically qualified for a New York State private detective license because of his law enforcement experience. Mimi had to work for a P.I. firm for two years, then take a test. She understood the reasoning behind that policy, even if she wished Michael didn't constantly remind her of it.

After she hung up with Michael, Mimi called Kabir Mehta, the agency's would-be client. She made sure to note that she could come to his office, but Michael Matthews could not.

"Who?" asked the heavily accented voice on the phone.

"Michael Matthews," Mimi said. "He was the NYPD liaison to Forty-Seventh Street. He's the person the detective agency is named after."

"I've never heard of him," Kabir said. "I am calling for you. You were recommended to me by Paresh and Swapna Mehta. Paresh is my cousin. He and his wife said you are very sharp."

Mimi remembered Paresh and Swapna from a past investigation. They were nice people.

"That's sweet of them to say," Mimi said. "How are they?"

"Their business is down, like everyone's," Kabir responded.

I wasn't really asking about their business, Mimi thought. *But fine.*

"I pray you can help us," said Kabir. "The fate of the industry could depend on it. Can you come to our office and talk? Right now, if possible."

Mimi checked her watch. It was nearly four o'clock. She wasn't due at Michael's until seven. She considered returning to her father's office, but that would mean spending the afternoon with Channah and Zeke, rehashing every moment of one of the worst days of her life. Or, she could distract herself by hearing about a potentially big case.

It wasn't a hard choice. "I'll be right over," Mimi said.

A half hour later, Mimi was back on Forty-Seventh Street, visiting KM Diamonds, located on the ninth floor of one of the block's oldest buildings. Its lobby had recently been remodeled, though its ground-floor "security" was little more than a guy thumbing his phone, and its elevator was the size of a bathroom stall.

Every office door on the ninth floor was painted the same shade of brown—except for KM Diamonds'. It had big glass front doors that opened to a lobby twice the size of Mimi's bedroom. The KM Diamonds receptionist told Mimi that the meeting wouldn't be held there, but at Pure Green Diamonds—the closet-sized office next door.

Pure Green's office consisted of little more than a safe and a desk. Its walls were bare, except for a clock which showed the time in both Mumbai and New York. Mimi didn't see a security camera—a standard feature of diamond offices. Since the company was only selling low-cost lab-grown, Kabir Metha probably didn't care if it was robbed.

Kabir was tall and heavy-set, with curly gray hair and thick eyebrows that hooded questioning eyes. In person, he was just as brusque as on the phone. He barked out an introduction to his nephew, Hrundi, who sat next to Mimi on the other side of the desk.

The nephew looked up from his phone, which had a Batman sticker affixed on its back. He extended his hand to Mimi and said with an easy smile, "call me Andy." Hrundi-slash-Andy vaguely resembled his uncle, but he was smaller and slimmer, and his accent was far less thick. While Kabir wore a button-down shirt and slacks, Andy was dressed casually, in short sleeves, jeans, and sneakers.

"The reason you are meeting with me and Hrundi is extremely sensitive," Kabir said, pointedly not using his nephew's chosen name. "The information I am about to provide could ruin our company. You must promise you will not disclose it to anyone."

"I may discuss it with my partner, Detective Matthews," Mimi said. "But I won't tell anyone else. You have my word."

Mimi raised her hand. Kabir nodded, and Mimi put it down. That was something Mimi liked about the diamond business. Any other industry, she'd have to sign a stack of non-disclosure forms. Here, her word was enough.

"A few months back," Kabir began, "Hrundi wanted to start a lab-grown division. I know other Indian companies were getting into it, so I gave him seed capital to buy some growing machines. And now we have, what, ten of them?"

"Sixty-eight," Andy said through gritted teeth.

"Hrundi insisted we hire this scientist, Dr. Raj Shranka. Write that name down."

Mimi did.

"He cost a lot of money and I didn't see why we needed someone who cost that much, but Hrundi insisted."

"People think growing diamonds just involves turning a machine on and off," Andy said. "The actual process is highly technical. Everything must be perfectly calibrated. The scientists call their growing methods 'recipes,' because they're like chefs. If they get one ingredient wrong, they ruin the meal.

"I've always been interested in science," Andy continued. "When I was setting up the company, I reviewed the literature, and came across Raj Shranka. He was still at university, so he wasn't on anyone's radar, but his research was far ahead of everyone else's. We made him a nice offer to come work for us. And, honestly, considering what he achieved for us, we got a bargain."

As Andy spoke, his eyes shone and a grin played on his face. He had real enthusiasm for this subject. "Most Indian growers use the same methods and machines. Raj built us a totally new apparatus, way ahead of anyone else's. Other companies take ten days to create a diamond. We make ours in less than two hours, and not only are they nicer than our competitors', we produce them for only a dollar a carat. Other companies' costs run about twenty dollars a carat. That adds up when you're churning out thousands of diamonds. We sell them wholesale for one hundred dollars a carat, and we could probably get seven hundred if we sold them retail. That's bigger margins than Tiffany gets!

"The office here is small, but our operation in India is huge and it's getting bigger. Our sixty-eight machines produce as many diamonds as our competitors, who have operations the size of football fields. We have only been in lab-grown six months, but we're on the cusp of becoming the biggest company in the business. We're easily the most profitable."

Andy looked at his uncle for approval, which he didn't get.

"Yes, the business has made lots of money," Kabir grumbled. "Why don't you tell how we're about to lose even more?"

Andy winced. "A few weeks back, Raj developed a formula that could produce diamonds which were indistinguishable from natural gemstones."

"What does that mean?" Mimi asked. "I've always heard that gemological labs have machines that can detect synthetics."

"They do," Andy said. "Or at least they did, until now. Raj figured out a way to fool them."

"So there's no way to tell those diamonds apart?" Mimi said.

"It's not clear," Kabir said. "When I heard that Dr. Shranka had created synthetics that couldn't be detected, I called him and said this could be very dangerous for our industry. He told me he believed his diamonds could be differentiated, but only with a method the labs aren't using currently."

"And what's that method?" Mimi asked.

"We don't know," said Andy. "It was in his notes. But they're missing. Like him."

"He's missing?" Mimi asked.

"Yes," said Andy. "And we think he sold his formula to Diamond Superior."

"We don't just 'think' that, Hrundi," Kabir said. "We know it. Four days after Shranka disappeared, Diamond Superior announced their formula. It sounded exactly like the one he came up with. Which would be quite a coincidence, and I don't believe in coincidences.

"That formula is ours. Shranka came up with it at our company, using our equipment. He signed a release giving us exclusive rights to his work."

Mimi scrawled in her notebook. "Did you patent it?"

"We were looking into that," Kabir said. "But this all happened very quick."

"You still might be able to take legal action against Diamond Superior," Mimi said.

"We would rather not," Kabir said. "We don't want this public. We are clients of Vanderklef. They cannot know our company developed the formula that might kill the industry."

Mimi's father often talked about Vanderklef. At one time, the diamond miner controlled over ninety percent of the world's diamonds and was considered such a monopoly that its executives weren't allowed in the United States on antitrust grounds. In the years since, Vanderklef's market share had fallen to thirty percent, and while it was still an enormously powerful company, it was no longer the all-controlling entity it once was. Many in the industry still viewed the company with a certain reverence, even awe, remembering the days when it held an iron grip on everything from marketing to supply. Some even expressed nostalgia for that bygone era, like residents of a former dictatorship who longed for the days when the trains ran on time.

"When Raj first developed the formula," Andy said, "he suggested we tell Vanderklef that if they didn't buy it from us, we'd sell it to one of the big synthetic manufacturers, like Diamond Superior. That was a company he mentioned specifically."

"And you didn't want to do that?" Mimi said.

"Of course not," Kabir snapped. "My company has been a client of Vanderklef for thirty years. We have made a lot of money from their boxes."

That was something that amazed Mimi—the big miners sold unfinished diamonds, known as "rough," in Ziploc bags packed into plain wooden boxes. Yet the gems in those baggies could be worth millions.

"I have no reason to antagonize Vanderklef," said Kabir. "How much would we get for that formula? Ten million dollars, maybe."

"That's a lot of money," Mimi said.

"In good years, we make triple that from Vanderklef," said Kabir. "Though, obviously, that was a lot of money for Raj Shranka."

It's a lot of money for me, too, Mimi thought. *It's a lot of money for most people.*

"I told Raj we'd decide how to handle the formula," said Andy. "But we were still concerned he'd do something on his own."

Kabir picked up the story. "We'd arranged for Shranka to give a presentation at the Jewelry Expo this week at the Omnichannel Hotel. That was before he came up with this formula. We seriously considered not letting him come. But he promised to use his speech to tell people how to detect these diamonds. I said fine, though I wanted to keep an eye on him, to make sure he didn't try to sell the formula from under our nose. Hrundi, tell the woman how well that worked."

Andy winced again. "We arranged for me and Raj to share a suite at the Omnichannel. We came in last week so Raj could create educational materials for our sales force.

"The first night was fine. Raj spent hours in his room, playing with his diamond-growing machine, creating different stones. It was like a hobby for him. He thought it was fun.

"Then on Thursday, he stayed in all day, making a video about his diamond-growing method. That night, he looked over the list of conference attendees, and noticed that John Charles Harrington, the CEO of Vanderklef, was attending. He asked me, 'what's the harm of asking him if Vanderklef wants to buy the formula?' He said he'd approach them on his own, not as part of our company. I told him that would be extremely foolish. Vanderklef is smart, they have spies everywhere, they would know he was working for us. We argued and he agreed not to say anything.

"Then Raj asked if he could take a walk on the streets of New York since he'd never been here before. I said no. He was acting strange and I could sense in my stomach something was off with him. He went back to his machines. I could hear him in the next room, cranking out diamonds.

"Then about 10 p.m., I was in my room playing a video game. He snuck up behind me, conked me on the head, and knocked me unconscious. When I came to, he was gone."

"He banged you on the head?" Mimi was shocked. "With what?"

"I don't know," Andy said. "I didn't see him coming. I had headphones on and was engrossed in a game."

"Like a nine-year-old," Kabir scoffed.

"Please, uncle, don't give me a hard time. I feel bad enough."

"I'll decide when you've felt bad enough," Kabir growled.

Mimi jumped in to change the subject. "Andy, are you sure it was Shranka who hit you?"

Andy gave a weak shrug. "He was the only other person there."

"So you haven't heard from him since Thursday night? That's four days ago."

"Correct," said Kabir.

"And you have no clue as to his whereabouts?" Mimi asked.

"We said, he is missing," Kabir yelled. "That means we don't know where he is!"

Before she came to the office, Mimi had Googled Kabir Mehta. Reporters inevitably portrayed him as a good-natured, religious, humble mogul-next-door. None hinted at the intense, ill-tempered person standing before her.

"If you don't mind, Mr. Mehta," Mimi said, closing her notebook and placing it on the desk, "I would appreciate you treating me like a human being. And I would prefer you treat your nephew that way, too."

Andy flashed a conspiratorial smile.

Mimi knew her comment might cost her the case, but she wanted the rules of engagement spelled out ahead of time.

Kabir's nostrils flared, and he paused before answering. "I am sorry. I put my heart and soul into this company, so my family wouldn't have to struggle like I did. I have hundreds of employees. They all have families and are depending on me. I don't want it to end like this, simply because we trusted the wrong person."

"I understand," Mimi said. "My father's in the business. He's worried about the Chrysalis diamonds, too. But what do you want me to do?"

"Find Dr. Shranka," Kabir said. "Find out how to detect these diamonds, before they destroy the business. And if you do it discreetly, without Vanderklef discovering we were involved, we'll give you twenty thousand dollars."

"Twenty thousand?" Mimi tried not to gasp.

"Not enough?" said Kabir. "How about thirty?"

"That's fine," Mimi said, staggered at the number—even coming from a man who'd just bragged he sometimes made one hundred times that a year.

"That's fine," Mimi said. "But this could take a while. We'd also like a stipend."

Kabir stroked his chin. "How about one hundred dollars an hour?"

Mimi was thinking of asking for two hundred dollars a week. She hoped she didn't sound too enthusiastic when she blurted, "great."

"Do you have any pictures of Shranka?" she asked.

Andy handed her a copy of Raj Shranka's passport. It listed his age as twenty-five. From his picture, that looked about right. His face was round and unlined, covered by boxy glasses, and topped by straight black hair.

"Is this what he looks like now?" Mimi asked.

"Pretty much," said Andy.

"Let me know if you find other photos. Does he have a wife or significant other?"

Kabir and Andy exchanged puzzled glances.

"I don't think so," said Andy. "He was very quiet. He didn't talk much about his personal life. I doubt he had one."

"How about his family?" Mimi asked.

"I don't know," Andy said. "He never talked about that, either."

"And he's based out of India?"

"Yes, Mumbai, like us," Kabir said. "But we believe he's still in America. He's here on a work visa, and they'd notify us if he left."

"Does he know anyone in the States?" she asked.

"Not that we know of," said Andy.

Mimi chewed her pen. There weren't many paths to follow. "Is there anything notable about him? Any interesting physical characteristics that aren't obvious in this photo?"

"Not really," said Andy.

She glanced at her notes. "You said he made a video for your sales team. Do you have a copy of that?"

"It may still be at the hotel," Kabir said.

"Can I inspect the room?" Mimi asked.

Kabir turned to Andy, and they had a short dialogue in Hindi.

"I believe so," Kabir said.

"I don't think you'll find much there," said Andy. "He took his laptop and all his notes."

"She should still look at it," said Kabir. "The Omnichannel is just a few blocks away. Hrundi isn't staying there anymore, but we still have control of the room, because they wouldn't let us cancel. Hrundi, give her the key."

"I don't have it," Andy said, patting his shirt.

"You lost the key?" Kabir hollered. "Call the front desk, have them make a copy."

Andy rummaged through his pockets. "Hold it. I have it." He slid it toward her.

"Okay," Mimi said. "I'll go there now, do a quick inspection, and maybe my partner can come and examine it tomorrow."

"Good," said Kabir. "It's important that we settle this as soon as possible." He stood up and marched to the door. "Hrundi, get this woman everything she needs." He aimed his finger at his nephew. "And do not screw up again!" he screamed, then stormed out.

"I won't," Andy whispered to his uncle's back.

Mimi turned to Andy. "Is your uncle always like that? He was very hard on you."

"It's fine," Andy said with a shrug. "I don't let it bother me. I caused a major problem. I *should* feel bad."

"You trusted someone that you shouldn't have," Mimi said. "It happens. Don't beat yourself up about it."

Andy's head bobbed. "I know. But I understand why he's upset. My uncle's accomplished a lot in his life. He and my father grew up in a shack with no indoor plumbing. My uncle worked hard to get where he was. He was my hero growing up. I felt lucky when he let me work at his company—even though, as you can see, it's not always easy.

"That's why I wanted to do my own thing, and start a lab-grown division. It was perfect for me. I'm a huge tech guy. My uncle isn't big on change, so it took a lot of convincing for him to agree. And it was doing really well. For the first time in my life, I thought my uncle might be proud of me." His shoulders slumped. "Then this happened."

"Sorry. I'll do my best to find Raj Shranka."

"You can try," said Andy. "But honestly, I doubt you'll find him. Raj is way too clever." Andy leaned toward Mimi and lowered his voice, even though they were the only two people in the room. "Don't tell my uncle I said this, but I don't blame Raj for disappearing. To do what he did—create a lab-grown diamond that's undetectable—probably angered a lot of powerful people. I'm sure many of them want him dead."

CHAPTER FOUR

MIMI ENTERED THE TWO-ROOM SUITE ANDY Mehta and Raj Shranka shared at the Omnichannel Hotel, not sure what she was doing there. Finding Shranka felt like a big job. The detective agency had trouble locating missing diamonds. This was a missing person. He could be anywhere. Even if she found him, how would she convince him to give up his detection technique? It's not like she could torture the guy.

Mimi wasn't even sure how to search this oversized hotel room. She had read a few books on how to be a private detective, and they all said the best place to look for clues was the garbage. She checked the trash cans. They were all empty. That made sense. This was a hotel. Housekeeping had probably cleaned them out.

Shranka had also left behind most of his toiletries and wardrobe. "Why wouldn't Shranka take his clothes?" Mimi jotted in her notebook. "Maybe he left in a hurry. Or he figured he'd get millions for his formula, and could buy some clothes."

Mimi rifled through his clothes. She even checked his underwear. Her big discovery was it was gross checking someone's underwear.

Shranka's personal effects were unremarkable. There were razors, shaving cream, toothpaste—all standard for a man attending a conference. There were some strange black marks in the bathtub, and Mimi wasn't sure what to make of them. She discovered a big heavy metal cane; that was probably what Shranka knocked Andy on the head with. She also found a round metal device about the size of an air conditioner, a camera mounted on a tripod, a 3D printer, some scientific journals, and several bottles of chemicals. She took pictures of all of it.

Every window in the room was open, including one near the fire escape. She noted that, too. Then, tucked in the corner, she found his stash. It was a box of diamonds. Not just any diamonds—they all appeared to be D Flawless, as good as diamonds get. Mimi had never seen an actual D Flawless before—and given these were probably synthetic, her father would say she still hadn't. Even so, they were lovely. Light continually moved through them, sporadically bursting into color like fireworks. Their surface was so clear it glowed.

She found one exception—a lime-green stone that was the apparent runt of the litter. Natural green gems were extremely rare, and, while this one was probably lab-grown, its color was striking and otherworldly; Mimi couldn't stop staring at it. She dropped it, and a handful of the D Flawlesses, in a plastic bag for safekeeping.

Mimi removed the camera from the tripod, to see if there was anything interesting on it. After a few frustrating minutes navigating its menu, she found the training video Shranka made for the company's sales staff. She pulled up a chair and watched.

The video began with Shranka sitting in the hotel room, in the same chair Mimi was in now. The metal device stood on a table to his left.

"I am Dr. Raj Shranka," he said, "the chief technician of Pure Green Diamonds. Andy Mehta asked me to explain how diamonds grow, in as simple terms as possible."

Shranka looked much as he did in the passport photo, except he was wearing a white coat, and his hands were covered by yellow rubber gloves. He was an awkward on-screen presence, continually avoiding the camera's gaze. His demeanor bounced between intense concentration and vague distraction.

He spoke softly, and at times, Mimi strained to hear him. Yet, his voice had a soothing quality and his accent was so refined, it was almost musical. "Before we start," Shranka said, "I will provide background on lab-grown diamonds. The science behind them is fascinating."

In Mimi's experience, when someone called a subject "fascinating," that meant it was boring. Dr. Shranka, however, did his best to keep things interesting, which Mimi appreciated—though some of the more technical aspects sailed over her head.

"For centuries," he began, "people believed that diamonds were magic, and had mystical powers. So it was quite shocking when, in the late 1700s, an English chemist burned a diamond and discovered it was composed of one of nature's most common elements—carbon.

"Once it became clear that diamonds were nothing more than carbon bombarded with intense heat and pressure in the Earth's mantle, scientists attempted to create them above the Earth. The problem is creating diamonds requires *a lot* of heat and pressure. You need as much heat as the sun, and pressure equal to eighty elephants stepping on your toe. Which would definitely hurt." He smiled. "Some of the early inventors worked in their basement, and had accidents when they tried to grow diamonds. I even caused an explosion once. But that's a long story."

Which I'd like to hear! Mimi thought.

But Shranka was already discussing something else. "In the 1950s, General Electric produced the world's first verified synthetic diamond. It caused headlines around the world. The industry panicked. The head of one major jeweler bought a sporting goods chain, because he was convinced his business was over. But those original diamonds were ugly and more expensive than standard gemstones. It wasn't until recently that scientists developed machines that could regularly produce beautiful gemstones at affordable prices. I'll show you how we do it."

He laid his hand on the gray machine, stroking it like it was a puppy. "This diamond growing machine is proprietary to KM

Diamonds. There are two ways to grow diamonds: high-pressure-high temperature, which we call HPHT, and carbon vapor deposition, or CVD. I've developed the first technique that combines aspects of both."

He lifted a clear thin plate from the table with his rubber-gloved hands. It held what looked like a clump of pepper surrounded by a circle of salt. "Nothing grows without a seed," he said. "To create diamonds, you must first laser-slice a diamond into a seed as wide as a human hair. Then, you place it on a piece of crystalized carbon.

"The carbon can come from anywhere. There's businesses that create memento diamonds from the ashes of dead animals and even dead people. I'm a Jain and a strict vegan, so don't worry, I won't hurt your animals." He smiled. "I get the carbon for these diamonds from peanuts. So when you look at a dish of peanuts, you see a snack. I see a diamond mine." He smiled again.

Mimi smiled with him. "His jokes are corny," she wrote. "But what do you expect from a scientist?"

He turned to the machine and slid the plate of carbon inside, then lowered the metal dome over it. After tugging on the cover to ensure it was shut, he pushed a button. The machine hummed to life.

"We're going to bombard the carbon with heat, pressure, and hydrogen. And it will melt, attach itself to the seed, and form a diamond." He held up his watch. "It's now twelve o'clock. The entire process takes two hours. See you after lunch." He switched off the camera. The video turned black.

Mimi moved to the next installment. "Hi, everyone." Shranka said. "It's me again. It's now two o'clock, two hours since we last talked. While the diamond's been growing in the oven, I've monitored its progress on my laptop. Because I use chemical super-accelerants, our diamonds form faster than others.

"I love watching a diamond grow. It reminds me of being a child when my mother would bake poori bread, and she'd let me peek into the oven to watch it rise." He held up his laptop, which showed a dense collage of charts and numbers. He pointed to a video feed, which showed a small square object continually swelling in size. "That is our diamond." A bell rang. "Our bread is ready."

He placed his laptop back on the desk, donned a mask, and switched off the machine. Opening the lid released a huge cloud of steam, which he swatted away. He removed a tweezer from his front pocket, and plucked a small glowing object from the machine. He held up a bright orange square to the camera. "This is the 21st century version of diamond rough."

The glowing cube looked different from any uncut diamond Mimi had ever seen. It was not, like most rough, a jagged rock wrested from the bowels of the Earth. It resembled a floor tile that was the color of fire.

"When this cools off, it will be gray. When I said that science recreates what nature does, that's not entirely true. Sometimes it gets us just shy of where we need to be. Usually the diamonds look gray and need a touch-up, which means we have to subject them to other chemical processes to get the color right."

His gloved hand glided over the knobs on top of the machine, like they were piano keys. "These knobs add non-carbon atoms, which alter the diamond's appearance. Most of the time, they make the diamond whiter. But there are chemicals that can turn the diamond pink, or other colors. Whatever you like." He bowed his head. "I'm at your service."

As awkward as he was, Mimi found Shranka likable. He was a natural teacher. She wished he'd stayed in academia and worked as a professor—instead of what he apparently became: a crook, and a violent one.

Mimi clicked on the next video. This time, Shranka was sitting beside another machine. "Let's talk about how we cut our diamonds. Since lab diamonds form so predictably, I have developed a way to cut them using 3D printing. In just a half hour, this device can change that little orange square we just created into a polished diamond that looks no different than one you see at your local jewelry store.

"It's often said that natural diamonds are so rare, that if you gathered every diamond ever mined, they'd only fill a double-decker bus. But look here." He bent down, and picked up a box—the same one Mimi had just found in the corner of his hotel room. He tilted it sideways so viewers could see it was packed with white diamonds. Mimi looked for the green, but it didn't seem to be in there.

"This equals what a regular mine produces in a month. And they're all D Flawless. The most perfect diamonds in the world. You rarely find diamonds like this in nature. Soon, we'll be able to produce thousands of them a day."

He put the box on the floor and plucked a diamond from his coat pocket. "I have other things I'm working on—special experiments I call 'my children.' The interior of this diamond has been inscribed with a hologram." He displayed it to the camera. Inside was a miniaturized video of Dr. Shranka, waving "hello." Shranka waved back. "Hello, me in a diamond." He smiled and placed it back in his pocket.

"But that's not my only child. I've created what may be the world's first mutant gemstone—it's half-diamond, half-emerald. I've infused diamonds with a chemical that lets you track their location. I have also—" He paused. "I'm often asked: will there ever be a lab-grown diamond that cannot be differentiated from a natural? Currently, grading labs with the right equipment can distinguish a manufactured stone from a natural, because the two have distinct growth patterns. A natural diamond grows chaotically, while a man-made diamond's growth is strictly controlled. It's like if you split a person in two, you'd see a big mess of veins and bones. But if you took apart a robot, it would all be even.

"The chemical accelerants I use grow diamonds so quickly, it's difficult to distinguish them from diamonds formed in nature. So perhaps, with a few tweaks, it might be possible to create stones that could fool the advanced equipment on the market. In which case, the labs would need a new technique. This is all hypothetical, of course."

He said this with a sly smile, and it was the only sign of darkness Mimi saw in him. Because, she knew, he wasn't speaking hypothetically; he *had* developed a diamond that could dupe those machines. "I will discuss that issue in detail in my presentation at the Jewelry Expo. But for now, thanks for listening."

Mimi watched the video so many times she almost had it memorized. Aside from that telltale smirk, nothing else he said raised suspicion, and even that felt in line with his off-kilter sense of humor.

Overall, Shranka came across as both a scholar and a gentleman. That didn't jibe with the person who, a few hours after he filmed that video, would assault his boss and steal valuable info. But as even he admitted: sometimes it's hard to tell an imitation from the real thing.

Mimi left the Omnichannel Hotel at quarter-past-six, her purse bursting with souvenirs, including the video camera and several Shranka-created diamonds—a handful of D Flawlesses and that very strange green. Michael lived in Brooklyn, about an hour away, so she had little chance of getting to his place by seven. She texted him that she'd be late, blaming it on the subways—always a good excuse.

On the ride over, Mimi searched Google for information about Dr. Raj Shranka. He didn't have much of an Internet or social media presence, and just about all of it was related to his studies or papers.

She did find a photo of him on the Instagram of his sister Vashti. He was standing, awkward and stiff, with his arm around her. Vashti Shranka looked stylish and fashionable, and far more confident than her gangly sibling.

"This is my cool brother Raj," she wrote. "Grab him, ladies. He works with diamonds, and is a real gem himself."

Mimi quickly fired off a message to her. "Hi, Vashti. I work for a detective agency based in New York City. I am trying to find your brother, Raj."

"Leave me alone," came the quick reply. "I'll tell you, like I've told all the others, he doesn't want to work for you."

"You don't understand," Mimi said. "I'm not trying to offer him a job. I want to find him. I work for a detective agency."

"Hired by a lab-grown company, I'll bet," Vashti wrote back.

That was true, so Mimi dodged the question. "I am not trying to recruit him. I'd just like to talk to him."

"Yeah, right. All the lab-grown companies have been trying to hire Raj. He keeps telling them he's not interested. So now they're pestering me. I don't know how many times I have to tell you people—stop!"

"You don't understand," Mimi wrote. "Your brother is missing. Have you heard from him in the last four days?"

"No," Vashti responded. "But why would I? He's in New York, at a Jewelry Expo."

"I'm in New York right now," Mimi replied. "And I swear to you, he's missing."

"Is this a joke?" Vashti said. "Or some kind of scam? If so, it's extremely sick and inappropriate. Leave me alone."

"Please, understand what I'm telling you," Mimi pecked furiously on her phone. "Last week, your brother was in a hotel suite with Andy Mehta of KM Diamonds. He disappeared with some proprietary technical information. Since then no one's been able to find him."

Vashti didn't get that message. She had blocked Mimi.

CHAPTER FIVE

At first, Mimi felt strange entering Michael's modest two-story house in Brooklyn. She hadn't been there for so long.

Within seconds, she felt comfortable and at home. Everything was the same, except Louie wasn't there. Michael was spending so much time at the club that he didn't have time to take care of his beloved Maltese, so his daughter was dog-sitting the little fellow. Mimi wondered if Louie missed Michael as much as she did.

Mimi's lateness had given Michael time to shower and shave. He even surprised her by wearing the nice blue button-down she'd bought him when they first started dating. They lounged on his leather couch, and she rested her head against his broad chest. He smelled nice. They considered going out to eat, but were too tired to do anything but order delivery from the Mexican restaurant down the street.

Topic A was, of course, Max's afternoon fall.

"I'm glad he's getting treatment," Mimi said. "But it's scary. I don't know what will happen if—" She struggled with thoughts she didn't want to verbalize.

Michael put his arm around her. "When my mother was sick, a friend told me, 'if the worst is going to happen, nine times out of ten, you know ahead of time.' Which turned out to be true, in my case. Of course, it was still a shock when it did."

"I know you're worried," he continued, "and that's natural. But from everything you've told me, your father's not dealing with anything life-threatening. And if he is, there's probably not much you can do about it, unfortunately."

That was typical Michael advice: smart, to the point, and a little too blunt.

"Let's talk about something else," Mimi said, as she fingered the buttons on Michael's shirt. "I met those people who called about a case."

"Already?" Michael tilted his head.

"They told me to come over right away. They want us to start investigating immediately."

The buzzer rang. It was the delivery guy. Michael got the door. He handed the messenger a five-dollar tip and returned with a bag of food dangling from each hand. He plopped them on his brown circular dining table.

"Anyway, the case is fascinating," Mimi said, as she moved from the couch to her usual seat at the table.

"Okay," Michael responded, with either mild surprise or mild disinterest; Mimi wasn't sure which. He was far more engaged in unpacking and distributing the night's dinner.

Mimi plowed on regardless, relaying everything she knew about Raj Shranka, the missing scientist who'd invented a formula for undetectable diamonds, then disappeared after giving Andy Mehta a conk on the head.

"KM Diamonds said they'd pay the detective agency one hundred dollars an hour, and if we find the guy and his formula, we'll get thirty thousand." She lifted her margarita in a plastic cup.

"Nice," said Michael, sipping his beer. "That's about thirty thousand more than we've earned so far. But if we find him, do we have a guarantee they'll pay us?"

"No," said Mimi. "But you know the diamond business. Deals are done on handshakes. Your word is your bond."

"Yeah. And when I was on the force, I took in plenty of people who took advantage of that system. Honestly, at this point, I'm beginning to doubt the agency will amount to much. A lot of people in the Diamond District still hold grudges against me."

"What are you talking about?" Mimi smiled. "Everyone there loves you."

Michael didn't return her smile. "They loved me when I busted the crooks who robbed their stores. They weren't so fond of me when I'd take in one of their jeweler friends who was caught buying stolen goods. Then they'd beg me to go easy on the guy, he just made a mistake. Of course, they never asked for mercy for the so-called animals who robbed their stores. Yet, if that pal of theirs wasn't acting as a fence, those other guys wouldn't be sticking guns in their faces." He rolled his eyes skyward. "They never wanted to hear that. But that's okay. Certain enemies, I'm proud to have."

"Think of it this way," Mimi said. "You always said the detective agency was one big case away from really making it. This could be it."

"Eh." Michael wrinkled his nose. "This whole thing stinks. They're saying this scientist assaulted someone, then stole his formula. But they don't want to tell the police. That's a red flag."

Mimi was surprised that Michael had actually listened when she recounted the case.

"I've explained that," Mimi said. "Kabir Mehta doesn't want Vanderklef to know that Shranka developed the formula while working for him. Vanderklef is still a very powerful company. Besides, we're a detective agency. Isn't that one of the main reasons people come to us, they don't want the police involved?"

"Well, yeah, but—" Michael emitted a growl, from deep in his throat. "God, I forgot how difficult you are to argue with."

"You know far more about law enforcement matters than I do." Mimi always made sure to stroke Michael's ego before she disagreed with him on anything related to the detective agency. "But we should take this case. If we solve it, we'll make thirty thousand dollars."

"That's *if* we solve it. We don't know if we will."

"We should at least try. This case could make our reputation. Can you tell me why we shouldn't take it?"

Mimi looked at Michael, demanding a response. But she knew the answer.

MICHAEL HAD RETIRED FROM THE NEW York City Police Department the year before, following two decades on the force. Being a policeman was such a big part of Michael's identity that Mimi wondered how he'd handle civilian life. She soon found out: not well.

Michael was as dedicated a detective as anyone could hope for. He cared about the people he dealt with: the victims, the witnesses, sometimes even the criminals. "When I started out," he said once, "my captain told me that when you arrest someone, you change their life. I've always remembered that." When Michael was wrestling with a difficult case, it would eat at him, and he'd go nights without sleep, poring over evidence until he was sure he was doing the right thing.

All this led to what he called "vague burnout." And so, last year, he took advantage of New York's generous police pension, which lets officers retire after twenty years of service and receive half their salary, plus benefits, for life.

Michael's departure from the force was a long melancholy affair, garnering him a plaque, a citation, and many drunken toasts. Through it all, Mimi played the role of proud girlfriend, gazing at him fondly through the endless rounds of praise. It was all very gratifying, yet at the same time, rather obvious—of course Michael was an excellent cop.

After leaving the force, Michael threw himself into building the detective agency. He spent a few chilly afternoons handing out fliers on Forty-Seventh Street—like the hawkers he used to hate. He didn't get the response he expected. He barely got any response at all.

The agency did attract occasional clients looking for stolen heirlooms—all referred by Michael's buddies on the force. In one case, Mimi and Michael located the pilfered loot; in the other two, they didn't. Mimi didn't find those cases all that interesting, though Michael said they were the bread and butter of P.I. firms. Yet, he didn't act excited about them either, letting Mimi handle the eBay searching and pawnshop scouting.

Once it became clear the detective agency wasn't going anywhere, Michael fell into a funk. His once-frantic life had become quiet and empty. One day, Mimi called him from work and became intrigued by a sound in the background. "What are you watching?" she asked, then listened closer. "Is that the Home and Garden channel?" Michael got so rattled, he sputtered an unconvincing denial and hung up. Mimi never mentioned it again.

Michael was happy he could spend more time with his sixteen-year-old daughter, Catherine, who was headed to France that fall for her Junior Year Abroad.

"How does she feel about the extra Daddy time?" Mimi asked him once.

"She's a teenager," Michael responded. "Mixed."

He also took care of his mom, who had been diagnosed with cancer right before he quit the force. She died two months later. Michael handled it with his standard stoicism, but it was still a blow.

Michael had hoped to devote some of his post-police life to music; he'd long played clarinet in an amateur jazz band, which gigged once a month at a club in Queens. He always lamented he never had time to truly master the instrument. For the first few weeks after he left the force, he happily practiced an hour a day. Then, his band called it quits. The other members had become too busy—though Michael now had plenty of time. He always knew the group would end one day, but it was another blow.

One night, when Michael sounded down, Mimi prodded him to find a new band. He belonged to an online society of New York jazz aficionados, but he never went to their regular meet-ups, because he "didn't want to hang out with a bunch of geeks." Mimi urged him to try it, just once.

Michael came back from that first meeting, walking with a bounce that had been missing for months. "I don't know what I expected," he said. "But the people were great. I learned a ton. I have so many new records to buy."

He'd since become a regular group attendee. While the get-togethers always brightened his mood, that still left the rest of the month. Then, about ten weeks ago, a group member, who owned the club where Michael's band used to play, offered him a temporary job as club manager.

"He's opening a place in London and needs someone to watch over things in Queens while he's gone," Michael told Mimi. "He thinks I'll be good because I have a take-charge personality.

"It sounds like a lot of grunt work," he added. "Honestly, it could be a nightmare. But it's just for three months."

Mimi wasn't thrilled that Michael would be focusing on something other than the detective agency—though she had to admit, at that point, there wasn't much to focus on. "Give it a chance," she told him—even though it *did* sound like a nightmare.

TWO MONTHS LATER, MIMI WAS EATING Mexican food in Michael's living room, hearing him say the club job was so all-consuming he couldn't help with a promising new case.

"I'm just very busy," he said. "I know I haven't been around much lately, and I'm sorry about that. But this job will be over soon, and then things will get back to normal."

Mimi intertwined her hand with his. "That'll be nice."

Michael let their hands stay together for a second, then reached for a tortilla chip. "Honestly, I'll miss working at the club. It's been a lot of work but honestly, I kind of—" He used the chip to scrape the last drop of guacamole from the bottom of the plastic cup. "Like it."

Mimi was shocked. It had been so long since Michael liked anything.

"I always enjoyed playing in the band," he said. "But I knew I wasn't talented enough to do it professionally. This lets me feel like I'm part of the music scene in some small way. Granted, it's a job. There's a lot of stress and aggravation, but it's nothing compared to being a homicide detective. I don't go to sleep seeing dead bodies before my eyes, so that's a plus. And I love the music, though I'm usually too busy to check it out. Maybe this is just the honeymoon period, but for now it's good."

That was as close to a rave as Michael got.

"I told the owner, if a similar job opens up, I'd take it in a heartbeat," he said.

"What similar job could you get?"

"I don't know." He leaned back on his chair. "I've been playing with different ideas. Like maybe I could get some money together, and start my own club. I've only been on the job two months and I've learned so much, and I have so many ideas how things could run better. I feel like a new world has opened to me." He chugged the last of his Dos Equis.

Mimi was happy to hear the renewed energy in his voice—though she wasn't sure where she fit in his "new world."

"What about the detective agency?" Mimi asked.

"When the job is done, we'll start it up again, see if anything happens with it. Though, honestly, I doubt it."

"But something *is* happening," Mimi protested. "This case."

"And if the clients can wait a month, we'll take it."

"They can't, though. The Chrysalis formula is being introduced in the next few weeks. They want us to start right away. I'd really like your help with this."

"I'm sorry, I'm just too busy," Michael said, annoyance creeping into his voice.

Mimi swallowed hard. She still harbored hope for the P.I. firm. It would be a good fallback if her father's business closed—which was now a real possibility. "I thought we were building this agency together. You and me. As partners." The minute that left her mouth, Mimi regretted it. Michael was happy with his new job. She should be happy, too.

Michael took her hand. "We *are* partners. I just don't have time for this case."

Mimi was quiet for a moment. "Then I'll handle the case myself."

"I was afraid you'd say that," Michael said. "I know I can't stop you from getting involved in an investigation. God knows how many times I've tried. I'll just give you my standard warning: be careful. This scientist guy could be dangerous."

"Shranka? I saw a video of him. He looks harmless."

"Looks can be deceiving. This guy knocked someone unconscious. I don't want to ride to your rescue again."

"Please. 'Ride to my rescue.' When have you done that?"

"Three times! At least."

Mimi's fists clenched. "You're exaggerating."

"Let's not discuss this right now. I'm wiped." He methodically packed the remains of the meal into a bag, rose from the table, and tossed it in the trash. Then he slipped off his shoes, and parked himself on the couch, resting his black sock-covered feet on a nearby stool.

Mimi moved to the couch and leaned against him, tucking her left leg under her waist. "I understand you're busy. But can you give me tips on how to approach this case?"

"Sure," he mumbled, not disguising his lack of enthusiasm. "First off, finding this guy will be difficult. Usually, when someone's on the run, they hide out with their girlfriend or family. That's where we check first. But you said that everybody he knows is in India. So that avenue's closed.

"One possible tactic—and I would be careful with this, because it poses certain risks—is what we call 'smoking them out.' If this guy truly made a breakthrough discovery, he probably has an ego about it. That's human nature: you do something big, you want credit for it.

"So, just spitballing here, if you get this Diamond Superior company to deny that he invented this formula, that might aggravate him enough that he'd publicly rebut them. But don't let that come from you, because if you anger this guy, he might do something crazy."

Mimi fished her notebook from her purse, and jotted that down.

"Let me see the pictures you took of his hotel room," Michael said.

She handed him her phone, and he paged through the photos—quickly, at first, then he started taking more time with each one. His detective brain was kicking in.

"The problem is," he said, "that room gets cleaned every day. So the scene's been tampered with. Since it's already been compromised, have the client ship any remaining items to my home, and we can go through them if we need to."

He paged through more photos. He stopped at one of the chemical containers. "It says 'sulfuric acid.' Do they use that in diamond making?"

"I think so. For touch-ups."

Michael put the phone down. "Let's say you're right, and this guy Shranka is harmless. His sister said that other companies want him to work for them. So was Andy sure it was Shranka who knocked him out?"

"I asked him that. He said he didn't see Shranka do it, but didn't think it could be anyone else."

Michael nodded. "If Andy doesn't know who knocked him out, it's possible that someone else could have done it, and kidnapped the doctor."

"Yeah, I guess," Mimi said, mulling this over. "But how did those other people get in the room?"

"I don't know. Maybe they snuck in. Was there a fire escape outside?"

"Actually, there was a fire escape near one of the windows. And all the windows were open."

"So that's one possible entrance. There's no signs of a break-in, though the maid service might have cleaned that up." He thought a bit. "Find out who else was staying at the hotel."

"But how do I do that? Call the hotel and ask if they've hosted any kidnappers lately?"

Michael's lips bent into a smirk. "You're the one who wants to be a detective. Mind you, this might be a dead-end. It's just something to consider."

"Okay," Mimi said. "Can I show you the video that Dr. Shranka made?"

"Sure," Michael said, though he didn't seem that excited about it.

She held up her phone so they could both watch. The video had just begun when Michael's phone buzzed. He glanced at the text, then muttered, "hang on a second." Mimi paused the video, while Michael wrote back. He sat and waited for a reply, stared at his phone, then sent another text.

"Christ," he said. "There's a problem with a bathroom sink at the club. It's leaking all over the place. Give me a few minutes." He took out his laptop. "Gotta find a plumber." He spent the next ten minutes phoning different services. When he finally got a plumber to come, he called the person who was supposed to be covering for him, and offered to come if they needed him. After a few more calls and texts, he told Mimi he had to pop over to the club, but he'd only be gone for an hour, maybe two.

Mimi said, "fine." When Michael was on the force, he'd get similar calls, and he always promised he'd be back soon. Then Mimi wouldn't see him for the rest of the night.

MIMI WENT TO BED A FEW hours later. When she awoke the next morning, Michael was in bed next to her, snoring. His shirt—the nice blue button-down she'd bought him—lay crumpled on the floor. She had vague memories of him tiptoeing into the bedroom late at night, trying his best not to wake her.

Mimi went downstairs and found a note waiting for her in the kitchen. "Hey babe," it began. "I'm really sorry about last night. One of the bathroom sinks got stuffed up. We ended up having to call two different plumbers. It was a nightmare. But at least everything's better now. I love you." He signed the note with a heart.

"P.S.," he added, "we can talk later about that case with the Crystalline diamonds."

Mimi moaned. It was *Chrysalis*, not crystalline.

CHAPTER SIX

NEW YORK IS A CITY OF extremes, which extends to its temperatures—it has sweaty summers and chilly winters. Springtime, though, was the fleeting moment when nature got it right—when the elements worked together to strike a near-perfect balance. The warming temperatures always reenergized Mimi following the sluggish weeks of winter.

After Mimi left Michael's that morning, she took the subway to Forty-Seventh Street, happily gulping down fresh air as she walked to the office.

When she arrived, Channah was sitting at her usual spot at the front desk, and Zeke was parked next to her, gabbing away. With Max gone, he'd probably be there all day.

While Max wasn't in the office, he still made his presence felt, continually calling and emailing. The doctor told Max to only contact the office if there was an emergency. What the doctor didn't realize was, to Max, everything was an emergency.

"Dad," Mimi yelled, after she'd spoken with him three times, "you need to stop calling! The doctor told you to relax."

"How can I relax?" Max almost screamed. "That Chrysalis announcement yesterday turned the industry upside down. I don't know why I'm sitting here. I should be in the office."

"No, you shouldn't," Mimi said. "The doctor told you to take a week off, and you agreed. And honestly, maybe it's time to, you know—" Mimi tried to phrase this delicately. "Wrap things up."

"Oh God. Have you been speaking with your sister?"

"Yes, but it's not just her. The doctor said the same thing. You saw what happened yesterday."

"Yeah, I saw it. It happened to me, remember? And don't worry. I'll be fine. I don't need to retire. If I did, who will support you?"

Mimi gripped the phone. "Dad, I don't have to rely on you."

"Oh, really? I don't see your detective agency making millions."

"We just got a big case." That came out more defensive than she intended.

"Don't tell me about it. I'm stressed enough as it is." Max always called Mimi's investigations "my main source of *tsuris.*"

"Dad, you need to take it easy, and stop calling. Enjoy your time at Brenda's. Seriously, if you call again, I'm not answering. You need to relax. Take those pills the doctor gave you."

"I've already taken three," Max said.

"Did they work?"

"Does it sound like it?"

WITH THE ADVENT OF SPRING, MIMI and Channah resumed their regular lunches at Bryant Park. Most days, they were joined by Zeke. Today, with Max out of the office, Zeke stayed behind to answer the phones. Mimi was grateful for the alone time with Channah. It had been a while.

"So Michael's no longer interested in the detective agency?" Channah said. "That's so weird. It was his idea!"

"I know!" Mimi said. "I mean, I'm glad that he likes his new job, but—" She plucked some noodles from her takeout container, and twirled them around a white plastic fork. "Whatever. It's always awkward when you mix your business and personal life."

Channah nodded. "Yeah."

"You and Zeke work together now. Is that a problem?"

Channah shrugged. "It's okay."

Mimi's eyebrows knitted. "Just okay?"

Channah giggled and covered her mouth. "Honestly, it's more than okay. It's fantastic. Zeke and I come in together, and we talk on the subway, and then I see him at work, and we have lunch, and we're together all afternoon, and then we commute home together, and we're together all night. It's like heaven!"

Channah gazed dreamily at the sky, until a realization crossed her face. "But I know that's not true for everybody." She reddened. "I hope I didn't upset you."

"No, no, Channah. It's fine. I'm glad things are going well."

"They are, *Baruch Hashem*." Channah's head bounced from side to side. "Except for the kid thing."

The "kid thing" was something Channah had made fleeting references to, but since Zeke was always around, she and Mimi never had a chance to really talk about it. In Channah's religious community, procreating was considered a *mitzvah*, and married couples tried to have kids immediately after the wedding. That was Zeke's preference. Channah, however, wanted to wait.

"What's happening with that?" Mimi asked.

"Right now, I still feel we should hold off. It's not that I don't want a baby," Channah said, like she needed to explain herself—though as far as Mimi was concerned, no explanation was necessary. "I'd love to have a child. Maybe I'll have eight, like my parents. I'm sure I'll like being a mom. My sister loves it." She grinned. "Most of the time."

"How old's her little boy now?"

"Which one?"

"She has two? Didn't she just—"

"Yeah. She had one after the other. That's what I'm up against." Channah rested her face on her palm. "Don't get me wrong. I love my nephews more than anything. Sometimes I can't believe how beautiful they are.

"I *do* want children," she reiterated. "But not right now. After everything I've been through, I want to take some time and enjoy life. I'm twenty-six and I've never done that. It would be nice if Zeke and I shared some time together, just the two of us.

"I'd love to travel. See the world. Experience something different, besides New York. I've never been outside the city, my whole life. I'd at least like to see New Jersey." She laughed.

"Unfortunately, with Zeke out of work, we have no money for a vacation. But that's another reason not to have a baby. We can't afford it. We're both working for your father. You know I think he's a wonderful man, but he doesn't pay that well. I hope that doesn't offend you."

Mimi chuckled. "It's fine. He doesn't pay me well either." She poked at her food with her fork. "What does Zeke say?"

"He wants kids, but knows not to push me. The big problem is my parents. They think it's a psychological thing, like when I took a long time to get married, because I was still mourning Yosef, *olev ha-shalom*." She paused. There was always a heavy silence when Channah mentioned her late fiancé. She swallowed and went on.

"But I'm glad that I waited, because I got married when I wanted to, not when everyone else wanted me to. My parents are convinced I need professional help. They're having me see a therapist. Which has been helpful. I've been through a lot. But as far as the kid thing—" She laughed. "Boy, did that backfire."

"How?"

"The therapist is totally on my side. She said having children is my decision and I should wait until I'm ready. So that's what I'm doing." Channah popped a piece of sushi in her mouth. "What about you, Mimi? What do you want? With Michael?"

The question startled Mimi, and she froze.

"Should I not have asked that?" Channah asked, alarmed. "I don't want to be a *yenta*."

"No." Mimi was lost in thought. "It's a fair question. I don't really have an answer."

"But you two are good, right?"

Mimi shifted uneasily. "We're fine. Lately, he's been working all the time and I don't see him that much. So that's not great. But marriage isn't a big issue for us. He lives at his house, I live in mine, and we see each other nights and weekends. Or at least we did, before he took this job."

"Obviously, he's been divorced, and so have I. That makes you kind of skittish. We've never even discussed marriage."

"Why not?"

"I don't know. He never brings it up. And I don't either, maybe because I won't like what I hear."

Mimi hadn't liked what she heard last year, when she asked Michael if he'd be open to her moving in with him. It was right before the lease for her apartment came up for renewal; she believed she'd outgrown the place and wanted to live someplace else. She also wanted a sense of where she stood.

"We can't do it," Michael said. "My place is too small for two people." And while his house wasn't exactly spacious, it was roomy enough that Mimi stayed over most weekends. She spent a lot of time ruminating over his answer, before deciding to just drop the whole thing.

Mimi re-upped her lease, expecting—or maybe just hoping—that would be her last renewal. Now, her lease was about to expire again, and she dreaded raising the subject with Michael.

"Well, your father's certainly not afraid to bring up you two getting married," Channah said.

"Yeah." Mimi rolled her eyes, exasperated. "That's so annoying."

It was almost a ritual: whenever Michael came into the office, Max would ask if he wanted to buy an engagement ring. It was a joke, but at the same time, not.

"How does Michael react when he says that?" Channah asked.

"He smiles and nods, like my father's a silly old man. He takes it in stride, like he takes everything. That's something I've always liked about Michael. He's been through so much as a cop, not much bothers him. He doesn't constantly fly off the handle like the people I grew up with. But sometimes—" Mimi paused. "It would be nice if he showed more emotion."

"You know what my therapist said?" Channah said. "When you go through a big trauma like I did, it becomes harder to trust people. When Yosef died, I learned bad things about people I thought I knew. It took me a long time to get over that."

Mimi nodded. "My investigations have definitely made me less trusting. I've never had so many people lie to my face. And I was a reporter! You'd think I'd be used to that."

"Right," Channah said. "Now think about Michael. You've only done a few investigations. He's done hundreds. He's spent his entire life dealing with bad people. I'm sure that affects him. It has to."

Mimi pursed her lips. "Maybe that's it. There's a trust problem. And I don't know how to get around it."

"That he doesn't trust people?"

"Yeah." Mimi thought a bit. "I also don't know if I trust him."

CHAPTER SEVEN

When Channah and Mimi returned from lunch, Zeke was sitting behind the reception desk, his face drawn. He leapt out of his chair the minute they walked in.

"Mimi, I warn you, you're about to see something you might not like," he said. "You need to prepare yourself."

"What is it?" Mimi asked.

"Your father's here."

It took Mimi a second to comprehend what she'd just heard. "He's supposed to be at Brenda's this week!"

"I know, but he came in ten minutes ago," Zeke said. "I'm sorry. Since he's my boss, I didn't think I had the authority to prevent him from entering."

"Buzz me in," Mimi demanded.

Zeke pushed the button that opened the security door. Mimi slammed her first against it, then stormed into the office. Max was sitting in his usual chair, as if he'd never left. Mimi should have been suspicious when she didn't hear from him for three hours.

"Dad!" Mimi marched to his desk. "What are you doing here?"

"What do you think I'm doing?" Max said. "Working! This is my office. I have the right to be here. If you won't take my phone calls, I'm coming in."

"You should be at Brenda's house, relaxing, like the doctor said."

"So I came in a little early."

"Dad, you're supposed to stay home all week. You were gone for less than a day! You are disobeying your doctor's orders."

"So the doctor's a dictator now?" Max said. "What's he going to do—arrest me?"

Mimi eyed her father. He was definitely moving slower than usual. His hands trembled slightly. So did his upper lip.

"Does Brenda know about this?" Mimi asked.

Max visibly recoiled. "No, thank God. She's running errands all day. She thinks I'm this frail *alter kaker*, too senile to find my way into Manhattan from her house. Luckily, I've stayed there often enough that I know the bus schedule." He smiled, clearly proud of himself.

"So you just left her house, without notifying her?"

"I wasn't aware I needed her permission. You may have forgotten. I'm Brenda's parent. It's not the other way around."

"Call Brenda," Mimi said firmly.

"That's the last thing I need, your sister screaming at me. Listen, I know you two mean well, but I had to come in. The industry's gone nuts. If I don't unload my inventory now, I'll be stuck. I can't just sit in her basement, while the business melts down."

"Dad, the industry's always in some kind of crisis."

"Yeah, and all those other crises were house parties compared to this. I don't know if the business has a future anymore."

"You've said that for years."

"Yeah, and I should have listened. With everything going on, I'll probably have to shut this place. At least your sister will be happy."

"Dad. You're exaggerating. The industry's definitely had a shock, but you won't have to close."

"Oh yeah. Look at this." He handed Mimi a piece of paper. "The main diamond price list just sent out an 'emergency edition.' Where the numbers are bold, that means prices have dropped. What do you see?"

"A lot of bold."

"All bold! They should have just printed the entire list that way. All those prices going down are like knives to my heart. The guy who runs the list, I think he enjoys making us all suffer."

"This is crazy," Mimi said. "Diamond Superior only announced the Chrysalis diamonds yesterday. There's a lot we don't know about them. Why is everyone panicking?"

Max clicked his tongue. "Because we see where this is headed. If there's no way to tell the difference between these synthetics and regular stones, the price of regular stones will fall to where synthetics are, and the synthetics will lose what little value they had, because they'll be competing with every other stone on the market. It'll be a complete downward spiral. Dealers are selling their entire inventories at ridiculous prices. They're taking enormous losses. They've totally lost their minds."

"And you haven't?"

"What are you kidding? I'm dumping everything in sight. I'm as scared as everyone else. I need to unload my entire inventory while there's still some semblance of a market. When they release those Chrysalis stones a few weeks from now, I'll get nothing."

"I'm sure you'll get *something*," Mimi said.

"You don't understand. I have all the wrong stock. I've sold most of my old inventory. I used to think that was a good thing. But now, any diamond with a report less than a year old is considered suspect. Nobody knows how long those diamonds have been in the market. There's rumors someone tried to pass them off as naturals in India a few months ago. The only desirable merchandise right now is old inventory with old reports. And the only stone I have like that is 'The Yellow.'"

"Yeah," Mimi said. "But you're not going to sell *that*."

Max always said his office wasn't a museum, but that didn't account for his enduring affection for "The Yellow," a two-carat pear-shape the color of apple juice. It wasn't the nicest diamond in the world, but it was nice enough, and Mimi's mom sometimes wore it as a broach. That probably explained Max's reluctance to part with it, and why it sat in his safe year after year. Sometimes,

Mimi would catch him staring at it, or sinking his eyes to its level and spinning it like a top.

"I have no choice," Max said. "It's one of the few items I have that will move."

"I thought The Yellow was—" Mimi hesitated. "Special."

"Of course it's special," Max said. "Your mother used to wear it. It reminds me of her, how beautiful she was." He took a second to compose himself. "Unfortunately, it's one of my few salable items, and I need to sell it now, before the market collapses completely. I was just talking to someone who might buy it. He made me a lousy offer, but I'll probably take it. It's better than nothing, which is what my stock will be worth soon." He shook his head. "I used to think I owned good inventory. Now, I realize, my inventory owned me."

Mimi rubbed the back of her neck. "Dad, don't assume every-thing's hopeless. I know something about the scientist who invented the Chrysalis formula. He's told people there's a way to detect those stones."

"Where'd you hear that?" Max looked skeptical. "If there was a way to spot them, Vanderklef would have announced it already. You think they want this panic to continue? Their stock price is getting hammered." Max reached into his pocket and pulled out a piece of paper. "You think they're not worried? Someone put this flier under our door."

It was a notice of a seminar—titled "Should We Panic?"—taking place at eight p.m. that night at the Metropolitan Diamond Bourse.

"Look who's going to be there. John Charles Harrington. He's *the* top guy at Vanderklef. A high-level guy like that never talks to us *pishers* on Forty-Seventh Street. That's how badly they want to calm the market.

"Not that it's going to help, mind you. The only thing that might soothe the industry is several bottles of these." He held up his new-ly-prescribed Valium.

Mimi fingered the flier. "Are you going to this meeting?"

"No," Max said. "Every industry meeting has maybe fifteen good minutes before it dissolves into chaos. Besides, that *schmuck*

Garstein will be there. And I don't want to see his face. This week's been bad enough."

David Garstein was the head of the Metropolitan Diamond Bourse, whose oversized ego bore little relation to his actual accomplishments. Max always called him "that *schmuck* Garstein," and after tangling with him a few years back, Mimi could think of even worse things to call him.

"I'd like to go," Mimi said.

"Be my guest," Max said. "You know who else will be speaking? Paul Michelson. Everyone's furious at him because his lab missed those Chrysalis diamonds. I guess he enjoys being yelled at."

Mimi had been friends with Paul Michelson when they were kids. Back then, his face was dotted with pimples and kids called him Pizzaface Paul. When he and Mimi reconnected a few years back, he'd dropped the zits, but had gained much more. They went out on one date, but they weren't involved long enough to call it a relationship. Mimi just dubbed it a "thing."

It would be nice to see him again. One Pizzaface Paul would make up for one *schmuck* Garstein.

CHAPTER EIGHT

THE LAST TIME MIMI VISITED THE Metropolitan Diamond Bourse, its trading floor was empty. On the night of the Chrysalis seminar, it was packed. Dozens of dealers sat on metal chairs with their arms folded, anxious to hear if their world was ending. Mimi was angling for a seat when someone called her name.

It was Paul. He had a laptop bag slung over his shoulder and his hair had a few more gray streaks than the last time she'd seen him, but she had to admit, he looked good.

"I'm surprised to see you here," he said. "I thought you'd be out of the industry by now."

Mimi wasn't sure if that was a knock or a compliment, and Paul apparently sensed her confusion. "I mean," he said, "I'd have thought you'd have reinvented yourself as a famous investigative reporter."

"No, I'm still working for my father, doing my thing," she said, then worried that sounded stupid. Who else's "thing" would she be doing?

"Let's talk later," Paul said. "I'm speaking tonight. I don't want to miss my chance to be screamed at."

He walked to the dais, and sat next to a white-haired, ruddy-faced, portly man in a three-piece suit. According to his nameplate, that was John Charles Harrington, the CEO of Vanderklef.

David Garstein, the bourse president, was the night's master of ceremonies. "Please, be quiet!" he yelled at the crowd, in his thick Israeli accent. "We have a lot to discuss and when we finish, we have nice refreshments."

The first time Mimi met Garstein, he dressed in flashy suits and was touted as the industry's fresh young hope. This night, he wore standard business attire, and looked as worn-out as everyone else.

"This is a very important seminar," he said, as the buzz tapered off but didn't quite dissipate. "Yesterday, when I heard about this Chrysalis situation, my administration sprang into action. Because the last thing the industry should do is panic. We need to stay calm."

Max was right; saying "don't panic" doesn't stop people from doing it.

"Let me tell you what we've done," Garstein declared, holding up his finger like a sword. "This afternoon, I called Eugene Thorble, the head of Diamond Superior, and told him if he releases these Chrysalis diamonds, it'll sink him and his company. The entire trade will never buy from them again.

"We also reached out to Vanderklef. As you know, they usually don't appear at events like this. But the company's CEO, John Charles Harrington, was flying in from London to speak at this week's Jewelry Expo, and I said to him, before you do that, share your perspective with my members. And he told me, 'if you, David Garstein, who has done so much for our industry, believe that's important, then I'll do it.' We are lucky to have such an important person speak to us tonight—especially on such short notice."

He went on, mixing over-the-top praise for Harrington with an equal amount for himself.

Finally, Harrington stepped up to the microphone, and declared, "thank you for that generous introduction, David," with a thinly-disguised smirk.

"The question posed tonight is, 'should we panic?'" Harrington began. "Let me respond with a simple answer: no. Panic is never helpful, nor is it conducive to sound decision-making.

"I have always been amused at the industry hysteria over synthetics. At Vanderklef, we are firm believers in what we call the 'diamond dream,' which has been the basis of our business for one hundred years. We sell unique precious objects, which were formed billions of years ago, and are uniquely qualified to symbolize that special moment when two people commit to each other. That means more than that cheap publicity stunt yesterday from Diamond Superior, who sell a mass-produced item created in a factory.

"To address the elephant in the room: yes, it is possible that a few synthetics were not detected by the lab run by our friend Paul Michelson."

Paul turned his face to the floor. His embarrassment was palpable.

"However, we expect there will be an announcement at this week's Jewelry Expo which will end this crisis once and for all. Unfortunately, I can't reveal any more about that at the moment. Until then, I urge everyone to stay calm and not panic. This should be over soon."

Harrington said all this in a manner that reeked of confidence—and no small amount of condescension. And it worked as well as Max predicted.

"Can you please make this announcement now?" a man called out. "My life savings are on the line."

A hush fell over the crowd. In the diamond business, confronting Vanderklef was like confronting God.

Harrington offered a pinched smile. "I'm afraid I've said all I'm able to at present."

This only increased the mumbling. Even Paul appeared mystified.

"In addition," Harrington raised his voice to drown out the naysayers, "to make sure this episode doesn't recur, we have an exciting announcement. Vanderklef is creating a blockchain that will track our diamonds from the mine to the retail counter, and will provide incontrovertible proof of a diamond's natural origin."

"Will that work with the inventory we have?" a man in back called out.

Harrington scanned the crowd for the person who dared interrupt him. "As designed, our system will only track new goods coming out of our mines. It won't provide guarantees for existing stock. Regrettably."

"Thanks," said the guy in back. "You'll have this great technology and we'll all be out of business."

"I appreciate your feedback," Harrington said. "I assure you we do everything with the industry's best interest in mind. And with that, I thank you for your attention."

Harrington received only scant applause as he sat down.

Garstein popped up from his chair. "Interrupting a distinguished guest like Mr. Harrington is very rude," he said, shaking his finger at the crowd. "I hope people will be more polite to our next speaker—Paul Michelson, head of Michelson Gemological Associates."

Paul looked like he didn't expect to be called so soon. He reached inside his bag and fumbled for his laptop, then speed-walked to the podium.

Paul began by apologizing that his lab missed the Diamond Superior synthetics. "We've been trying to figure out what went wrong," he said. "As many of you know, we have extensive experience studying lab-grown diamonds, and are confident in our ability to spot them."

It only took a minute for order to break down again. "Then why'd you screw up?" a man called out.

This so startled Paul, he didn't even wince at the words "screw up." "We made a serious error," he said, "for which we take full responsibility." That last part felt forced and obligatory, like he'd said it so many times it had lost its meaning.

"Diamond Superior has developed a new type of synthetic that managed to fool our equipment," Paul continued. "That is something we only found about yesterday, with the rest of you. We believe it's only a matter of time before we can distinguish those diamonds, just as we're able to detect all the others. In fact, we hope to solve this problem using artificial intelligence."

The words "artificial intelligence" sparked an approving round of murmurs. But then a man in the back yelled, "How long will that take?"

"I can't give you a timetable," Paul said.

"So, a week?" The man virtually levitated from his chair. "A year? The industry's just about dead, if you haven't noticed. Thanks to you."

Paul nervously fiddled with his glasses. "We are working very hard on this. Until then, please remember, it's unlawful to sell lab-grown diamonds without clearly communicating their non-natural origin. So we'll be okay as long as everyone follows the law."

"Yeah, good luck with that," a dealer shouted, causing a flurry of laughter and side conversations.

"I'm never using your lab again!" screamed a second man.

"Don't worry about it!" said another man one row away. "None of us will ever use any lab again. We'll all be out of business soon." His comrades roared and talked amongst themselves.

"I understand why you're upset." Paul strained to be heard above the din. "My lab messed up. Badly. I feel terrible about that. But I want you all to know, I care about this industry. I care about the people in this room. I've known some of you my whole life. You've stood by me many times and I appreciate that."

That was an apparent reference to the diamond grading scandal Paul got caught up in a few years back. Since then, his reputation had recovered, but that cloud still hung over him.

"I know I've let you down," he said, eyes pleading behind his glasses. "I will do my best to regain your trust."

The crowd was unmoved. Paul returned to sit next to the equally glum Harrington. Their vague assurances hadn't assuaged the audience, which had stopped listening, and was now venting.

Garstein returned to the podium. "Be quiet!" he cried. "If everyone doesn't stop talking, we will end the meeting early and not serve any refreshments."

When that didn't work, Garstein angrily declared the session over—not that anyone listened or cared. Mimi looked at her watch. Her father was right. It only took fifteen minutes for that meeting to collapse into chaos.

Mimi watched Paul trudge off the stage. Her heart went out to him. She sent him a quick text. "Would you like to grab a drink?"

Seconds later, the response came. "Yes!"

CHAPTER NINE

"THANKS FOR INVITING ME OUT, MIMI," Paul said, blowing the foam off a glass of beer. "I can sure use a drink after getting yelled at for ten minutes."

They were sitting in Connolly's, a gold-plated Irish bar near the Diamond District that served as the trade's unofficial after-work haunt. Paul had ordered a Guinness; Mimi, white wine. When Mimi and Paul had their thing, they'd gotten into a nasty fight at this bar which ended their relationship. Mimi remembered that. She wondered if Paul did.

"I think the last time I was in here was a few months ago with my boyfriend," Mimi said.

In truth, Mimi had never been to Connolly's with Michael, but she wanted Paul to know she had a boyfriend, in case he considered this friendly drink anything more. She had no reason to think he did, except for how excited he was when she invited him out. In her younger days, her friends called that an "obligatory boyfriend reference," or OBR. It had been a long time since Mimi dropped one.

Mimi turned away from Paul after she said that, then glanced back at him. He didn't react, one way or another.

"So how are you doing?" She wanted to grab his hand for moral support, but didn't—just in case.

"Let's just say my talks usually get a better reception," Paul said. "But you know the diamond business. If someone's hysterical about something, that means it's Tuesday."

Mimi chuckled. Paul could always make her laugh.

"Though honestly," he said, "I don't blame those people for being mad. We did screw up. We checked in the system, and found the three stones Diamond Superior submitted—using a fake name, of course, with a virtual address. They were all D Flawless—the best quality a diamond can be, and they were all one carat. It was like they were spit out by a machine." He paused. "Which, come to think of it, they were.

"That should have set off alarm bells. But Diamond Superior was clever. They used our expedited service, which means the stones didn't get a thorough check. Still, we should have flagged them. That's on us.

"In any case, getting roasted back there wasn't close to the worst part of my day. This afternoon, I laid off my entire staff. That's sixty people! Some of them had been with me since the beginning. But I had no choice. Diamond Superior's little stunt killed our business."

He finished his beer with an uncomfortably long, showy gulp, then leaned back in his chair, completely spent. Mimi thought Paul had looked good at the bourse, but now that she was getting a closer look at him, she could see the crescents etched below his eyes, the worry lines snaking across his face.

"Though, honestly," he continued, "the lab may have been doomed regardless. If the diamond industry collapses, we'll go down with it. It's hard to see how the business survives if you can't tell a natural diamond from a lab-grown."

"But we don't know for sure you can't tell those diamonds apart," Mimi said. "I've learned some things about the scientist who invented this formula. He believes there's a way to detect it."

Paul's eyebrows came together. "Did he say what it was?"

"No. And now he's missing, along with his notes. He worked for a company based out of India. They've hired my detective agency to find him."

"That's right." Paul emitted a small chuckle. "You're a part-time investigator."

Yes, Mimi thought. *Which you never liked. That was one reason we stopped seeing each other.* She wondered if Paul remembered that, too.

"Why was John Charles Harrington so confident we'll get out of this?" Mimi said.

"Beats me," Paul said. "I asked him afterward, and he told me the same thing he said on stage. 'We'll announce it when we're ready.' There's something weird going on, because I talk to their scientists, and they're just as clueless as I am, and just as pessimistic we'll find a solution in time."

"Why is detecting these diamonds so hard?"

"Well, first off, we only found out about this yesterday, and Diamond Superior says they're releasing these diamonds in a few weeks. That gives us a pretty tight deadline. We also don't have any specimens to examine. I've contacted Diamond Superior for samples, but lovely people that they are, they never called back." He bounced on his chair as he spoke, like he was receiving electric shocks.

"Wait a minute," Mimi said. "I have some diamonds this scientist grew. They were in his hotel room."

"In *where?*"

"It's a long story," Mimi said. "But I can send them to you."

"Yes, please. That would definitely help."

"Don't you plan to use artificial intelligence to solve this?"

Paul's mouth broke into something resembling a smile. "Yeah. When I said that, that was the only time the audience didn't want to lynch me. You may have noticed that I said that I *hope* to use AI to solve this. The key word is *hope*. I don't know the first thing about AI. I have a little money left, so I want to hire an AI expert. God knows where I'll find one."

"Paul!" Mimi said excitedly. "I know a guy. Zeke. He works at our office. He knows AI and is brilliant. And he's looking for work. I'm sure he could help you."

Paul shrugged. "I'll gladly speak to him. But please let him know, I can't pay much. I have sixty people to pay severance to."

"Don't worry. Zeke works for my father. He's used to low pay."

Paul produced a wan smile. He wasn't in a laughing mood. "Have him call me tomorrow. Though I'll be out part of the day. Diamond Superior is giving a presentation tomorrow at the Jewelry Expo, to show off their brilliance."

Mimi took out her notebook, and wrote, "Diamond Superior educational session, tomorrow, at Jewelry Expo." She should go to that.

Once their professional chatter was exhausted, Paul and Mimi asked about each other's families. Paul happily shared pictures of his children. "They're so grown-up now, it's crazy. They're great kids. Sometimes, when I talk to them, they even look up from their phones."

Then, Paul grew serious, and told Mimi his father had died, which saddened her. And Paul was upset to hear about Max's heart issues.

That was it, as far as personal stuff went. Paul didn't mention a girlfriend—though he did say his "life has been all work, for the last few years," which was a strong sign he didn't have one.

"Speaking of which," he said, checking his watch, "I should get back to the lab. I'll probably be there all night, trying to find an answer to this thing." He shook his head. "When I first started my business, I was at the lab day and night, getting it off the ground. And now, I'm doing that again, trying to save it."

Mimi and Paul exited the bar into the New York night. The streets were alive and full of people. The air was soft and warm. Mimi felt relaxed; the wine had taken the edge off.

The first time Paul and Mimi reconnected, he'd said goodbye to her with a surprisingly confident kiss on her cheek, which lit up her whole body. There was a moment—as their eyes met and locked and Paul's Adam's apple bobbed—when Mimi thought that might happen again.

But it didn't. Instead, Paul just flung his arms around her. He was so tightly wound, Mimi felt like she was being hugged by a wall. She was okay with that, and apparently, Paul was, too. He had a lot on his mind.

CHAPTER TEN

T HE NEXT MORNING, MIMI WAS AT her father's office, gathering the D Flawlesses she found in Dr. Shranka's hotel room, to send to Paul.

When Max saw his daughter putting together a package of perfect-looking diamonds—not a common occurrence at the Max Rosen Diamond Company—he asked, "where'd you get those?"

"They're synthetic," Mimi said. "They're the Chrysalis diamonds. You want to take a look?"

Mimi handed him the parcel. He carried it to his desk, holding it away from his chest, like it was diseased. He sat down and examined the diamonds one by one with his loupe, grumbling the entire time.

"Do you think they're D Flawless?" Mimi asked.

"Either that, or close. I'm not seeing any flaws, or body color."

"Can you tell the difference between them and regular diamonds?" Mimi asked.

"I'm not a scientist, more a loupe-and-tweezers guy." Max exhaled noisily. "But no. I can't." It clearly pained him to admit that. He scowled, and pushed the parcel toward Mimi. "Take them away. It makes me sick to look at them."

Mimi scooped them up, then handed them to Channah to send to Paul's lab.

"Make sure you keep those fake diamonds away from my real ones!" Max hollered to Channah. "I don't want them getting mixed up! You could cause big problems that way." He fell back in his chair. "Though who knows if that even matters anymore?" He waved his hand, like he just wanted to make those diamonds—and this whole crazy situation—go away.

A LITTLE LATER, MIMI ARRIVED AT THE Omnichannel Hotel, to attend the educational sessions before the Jewelry Expo. Walking through the lobby, Mimi remembered Michael's theory: someone besides Shranka could have attacked Andy Mehta, then snatched Shranka from the hotel room. She should find out who else was staying at the hotel.

She approached the concierge, an older man with slicked-back hair and a nose like a hawk. "I'm a guest at the hotel," she told him, flashing Andy's key. "Can you call Eugene Thorble's room? I'm supposed to meet him in the lobby."

The concierge's chin rose. Surely, having to "call up" to a guest's room was an outdated practice in this age of cell phones. Mimi hadn't done it in years.

Even so, the concierge dutifully typed into his computer, nodded, then picked up the phone. He stood with his ear to the receiver, as the dial tone trilled on the other end, looking like he'd rather be doing anything else. "He's not in his room, madam," he said, hanging up. "If you want, I can leave him a message."

Thorble was staying at the hotel. Bingo. Mimi decided to see who else was there.

"How about John Charles Harrington from Vanderklef? He might be joining our group. Can you call his room?"

The concierge typed again, then made another call.

Wow, Mimi thought. *Harrington's staying at the hotel, too?*

"He's not in his room, either," he said.

Mimi felt she'd learned something significant: Harrington and Thorble were staying at the hotel where Shranka disappeared. If he was kidnapped, they'd be prime suspects.

"Can I help you with anything else?" the concierge asked.

"Are a lot of people staying at the hotel for the Jewelry Expo?"

"Several hundred," he responded, stone-faced.

Mimi thanked him and slinked away. Her discovery no longer felt that significant.

THE EDUCATIONAL SESSIONS WERE HELD ON the hotel's second floor, in small conference rooms with the air conditioning cranked. Dr. Raj Shranka was listed as a presenter on the program, but his session, "New Frontiers in Synthetic Diamond Production," was—not surprisingly—canceled. In its place was "How the Chrysalis Formula Will Rock the Industry," presented by Diamond Superior CEO Eugene Thorble. That session was set for five o'clock, the end of the day.

Mimi spent the afternoon going to different Expo education sessions. Max kept texting her she should be in the office. Mimi kept responding that Max should be at home.

She Googled the prior night's guest of honor, John Charles Harrington, CEO of Vanderklef. Articles inevitably described Harrington as a member of Vanderklef's "old guard," a lifer who'd gradually ascended the ranks at its London headquarters. Many believed Harrington would eventually hand the reins to forty-five-year-old Conrad Vanderklef, grandson of the company founder. The press had dubbed Conrad "the prince of diamonds," while his father was "the king," and his grandfather, "the emperor."

Harrington was said to be dead-set against Conrad heading the company, and reporters were riveted by their rivalry.

One article quoted "a source familiar with Harrington's thinking"—which, Mimi knew from her journalism days, was probably Harrington—dismissing Conrad as a callow playboy, who'd spent years skiing and dating supermodels before finally settling down and joining the family business. "Elevating him runs contrary to every tenet of modern corporate governance," this source said. "Conrad Vanderklef's qualifications begin and end with his last name."

On the other hand, a "source close to Conrad Vanderklef"—most likely the Prince of Diamonds himself—slammed Harrington as "well past his sell-by date," and argued "Conrad will infuse the company with new energy and fresh ideas."

The article concluded: "It appears that the diamond giant is caught in a classic corporate battle, between someone who's clawed his way to the top, and a rival who was born there."

DIAMOND SUPERIOR'S SESSION WAS THE DAY'S last, and it generated huge buzz—and a large enough crowd that it was held in the hotel's main auditorium. Mimi spotted Paul in the lobby prior to the session, and considered saying hi, but he was engaged in hushed conversations, and looked too intense and focused for a friendly chat.

When the doors opened, thumping electronica was playing overhead, and the words "Diamond Superior" were displayed on a giant screen. A large group of reporters and TV cameras were clustered along the side wall.

After a five-minute wait, the lights came down, and the crowd grew quiet. An announcer declared, "ladies and gentlemen, the CEO of Diamond Superior, Eugene Thorble."

Thorble appeared, wearing a black jacket, white-soled sneakers, an untamed beard, and a mop of prematurely gray hair. He looked like the epitome of a Silicon Valley CEO—or someone trying to look like the epitome of a Silicon Valley CEO. The smirk Mimi had seen on the video was still there; it appeared permanently etched on his face.

"My name is Eugene Thorble," he announced, mic clipped to his collar. "And I am proud to be CEO of Diamond Superior. We plan to make an exciting announcement this afternoon, which I guarantee will make your jaws drop. But first let me tell you about Diamond Superior. We are backed by Newford Ventures, the investment fund supported by the world's most socially conscious billionaires. They recognize that Diamond Superior is more than a company. It is a mission. Our dream is to democratize diamonds, so that one day, marginalized women will no longer have to suffer the trauma of ring-shaming.

"In addition, as the most efficient diamond producer in the world, we have set a new standard for eco-friendliness," Thorble declared. "Every time you buy a ring from Diamond Superior, you become a superhero, because you are literally saving the planet."

Mimi's father often said that Vanderklef created the diamond business by promoting its products as the best way to say, "I love you." Now, a new generation was billing its diamonds as the best way to say, "I love the Earth." Same pitch, just updated.

"Two days ago, we announced our plan to introduce Chrysalis diamonds to the market," Thorble said. "These beautiful gem-stones are so perfect, they cannot be differentiated from mined diamonds, even by the most sophisticated equipment. To show you how advanced our technology is, I'd like to give you a glimpse of our new Chrysalis factory—through the magic of virtual reality."

A team of twenty-somethings handed out sleek white VR head-sets to the crowd. Mimi put hers on. She spent a few minutes wait-ing in the dark. Then, almost at once, she was transported to a factory with endless rows of growing machines. The suddenness of the transition was jarring; Mimi felt like she'd been woken from a dream, or fallen into one. She initially heard traces of the audito-rium outside, but the more time she spent in the virtual world, the more the real one faded away.

Diamond Superior's factory had the clean uncluttered look of an Apple store. "This is our production facility," Thorble—or his avatar—said, as he stood in front of the machines. Behind him, people worked silently, without acknowledging him or the audi-ence. Which made sense; they weren't actually in the same room.

"While other companies take weeks to create their diamonds," Thorble said, "we produce ours in a little over two hours, then cut and polish them in a half hour using 3D printing."

That was almost exactly what Raj Shranka said in his video. They were clearly using his technology.

Thorble flipped a switch on a big gray machine. A metallic tube began spitting out sparkly gems, one after another, like a faucet that dripped diamonds. They landed on a huge mountain of stones with an audible "plink" that sent the others leaping into the air. Thorble plunged his arms into the pile, until his hands were filled with stones. Then he let them fall to the floor, his eyes shining as bright as the gems.

"Each of these diamonds," he pronounced, "is a D Flawless."

If those were natural D Flawlesses, that pile of diamonds would be worth millions. But now that Diamond Superior could churn out indistinguishable gems like they were widgets, who knew what a real D Flawless was worth? Thousands? Hundreds? Nothing?

Thorble wiped the gems from his hands. "As amazing as all this is, we aren't close to done. The money we make from the diamond business will help us produce other minerals, including lab-grown tin, copper, and cobalt, at prices far less than their mined equivalents. We call it 'synthesis as a service.'"

Mimi sighed. Reverend Kamora's co-op in the African Democratic Republic had hoped to invest some of its diamond proceeds into an ethically-sourced cobalt business. Guess that dream would have to die, too.

"These minerals are necessary for everyday life," Thorble added. "Without them, you wouldn't have electronics, or medical care, and you can't prepare food. Whoever controls these minerals, controls the world. We will build a supply chain so vast and all-encompassing the entire planet will line up to buy from us."

Mimi couldn't get over how this guy, who resembled the geeky dudes she used to date, was speaking like a comic book villain.

"And so today," he said, "we are rebranding ourselves. Our new name will no longer be 'Diamond Superior,' but 'Superior.'"

At this, the word "Diamond" disappeared from the back wall, and the word "Superior" grew, until it filled the entire space.

"And now," Thorble said, "please remove your helmets, so we can show you one more jaw-dropper." The factory disappeared and the sounds of the auditorium returned.

When Mimi removed her headset, Thorble was back on stage, wearing an impish grin. The screen behind him now said, "SuperiorCo, Inc."

"As I mentioned," he said, "we have another incredible announcement that will shake the traditional diamond industry to its core. Many of you know the name Vanderklef. They are one of the most famous and feared companies in the industry. Well, now, they're running scared, and you're about to see why.

"Going forward, I will be chairman and CEO of SuperiorCo. The new CEO of our Diamond Superior division will be a man whose name you know. He used to be a director of Vanderklef, but since Monday, he's been CEO of Diamond Superior. Please give a warm welcome to the 'Prince of Diamonds,' Conrad Vanderklef."

The crowd collectively inhaled as Conrad Vanderklef emerged, a huge smile on his face. Half the audience cheered; the other was too stunned to do anything but gape.

Conrad strode confidently to center stage, filling the spotlight in a way Eugene Thorble never could. It helped that he was six-feet tall and handsome, with a rock-like jaw, lush black hair, and super-high cheekbones. It was easy to see why he'd been dubbed "the Prince"—he looked like a CGI version of one.

In his newspaper portraits, Conrad always wore a dark suit—no doubt to escape his past image as a playboy. Today, he sported a black jacket, sneakers, slacks, and a five-o'clock shadow, as if he was trying to be Eugene Thorble Jr.

"Thank you," Conrad declared in his South African accent. "I don't want to talk too long, as I don't want to take attention from all the amazing things that Eugene just showed you. As most of you know, my father and grandfather built Vanderklef. Unfortunately, Vanderklef is no longer the same company they built. Instead, it's a rotting dinosaur sadly mired in the past. That is why I have decided to join Diamond Superior, to create the diamond business of the future."

He pumped his fist, and was greeted by scattered applause.

"The new Chrysalis diamonds are just one of many exciting innovations we have planned at Diamond Superior. We are also introducing Delphine V, a revolutionary new jewelry collection created by the most talented jewelry artisan in the industry today." He paused and smiled. "My daughter Delphine."

On the screen above Conrad, the camera briefly cut to Delphine, who was sitting in the front row. She was young, slim, and pretty, with long brown hair. She laughed and shielded her face when she appeared on screen. The auditorium responded with dutiful applause.

"As you can see, Delphine is a beautiful young woman. She also creates beautiful jewelry. Everyone, feast your eyes on the most exciting new jewelry collection in the world—Delphine V." Conrad turned and stretched his arms to the overhead screen.

But the "Superior" logo stayed on screen. Conrad stood, waiting for it to change. The audience began to murmur. Conrad swerved back. He moved the clip-on mic away from his face, and screamed at the off-stage technicians to show his daughter's jewelry.

Thorble returned to the stage. "I am sorry, Conrad," he said, with a smile that made it clear he was not, in any way, sorry. "We've decided not to show Delphine's things today. We've had such an incredible presentation, we don't want the crowd to get overloaded with excitement. Everyone, please give a huge hand for Conrad Vanderklef."

Thorble put his hand on Conrad's shoulder and gave him a small but perceptible shove to the left, so Thorble was back center stage. It felt like Thorble was sending his new partner a message— *you might be the prince, Conrad, but I'm the king.* Conrad at first looked puzzled; he clearly wasn't used to being shunted aside. He tried to act okay with it, but it wasn't hard to see the anger and humiliation building up under his frozen smile.

"With so much media here," Thorble said, "we wanted time for questions." Reporters raised their hands and vied for Thorble's attention.

The first question came from a man stationed in front of the pack. "Mr. Thorble," he asked, "are you worried about your life being in danger, given that you're taking on established interests?"

That sounded like a planted question to Mimi, and judging by Thorble's satisfied reaction, it probably was.

"Of course we are, going against the fearsome mined diamond cartel," Thorble said. "Fortunately, I am protected. Our company has produced special body armor, studded with Diamond Superior polycrystalline gems. Not many things can stop a bullet, except for diamond—the hardest material known to man. And no diamonds are harder than those produced by Diamond Superior.

"Let me demonstrate how protected I am—with the help of Newford Ventures portfolio company, I-Zipper." He tapped his smartwatch and his shirt flew open, revealing diamond-studded armor, which gleamed under the lights. It was quite a visual, which made cameras snap and reporters scribble. Thorble was living out every geeky kid's fantasy; he was wearing a Superman cape.

By this point, it must have hit Conrad that Thorble had basically used him as a prop, and he was now being upstaged by a better one. Even so, Conrad stood behind Thorble, nodding frequently, though in unguarded moments he looked ready to melt into the floor.

The reporters kept tossing softballs at Thorble, including several variations of "how likely is it you'll be killed?" Mimi maneuvered her way to the press area, hoping to ask a question that would "smoke out" Dr. Shranka. She thrust her hand up over and over, trying her best to out-scream the other reporters, until she could no longer be ignored. When she was finally called on, she delivered her question loudly and clearly. "Mr. Thorble, is it true that the Chrysalis formula was invented not by Diamond Superior but by an Indian scientist named Raj Shranka?"

Thorble's expression clouded. Mimi had broken up the lovefest. "Of course not," he snapped, punctuating his answer with an anxious laugh. "We are the technological leaders in this field. Every one of our engineers went to Stanford.

"Unfortunately, when you take on established interests, people attack you with fake news. Perhaps I need another diamond-coated vest to protect myself from the lies uttered by people like you."

The reporters laughed and rushed to talk with Thorble. Mimi wanted to talk to him, too, but he soon disappeared backstage, and she gave up and left.

MIMI WAS WALKING BACK TO HER father's office when she received a call from a California number she didn't recognize. She picked up.

"Miss Rosen," declared an angry voice. "Eugene Thorble."

"My number is unlisted. How did you get it?"

"Newford Ventures has access to an extensive data service that includes a phone directory. We use it to develop customer insights. We would never abuse it."

"You're abusing it now," Mimi said.

"Never mind," Thorble said. "I was disturbed by that question you asked. Our presentation was extremely well-received, and you nearly ruined it by insinuating that Diamond Superior didn't develop our proprietary technology. We found your insinuation highly offensive and possibly defamatory. We are discussing the matter with our attorneys."

Mimi was way-too-familiar with legal threats from her time at the newspaper, and knew he was completely full of it.

"What I said was true," Mimi said. "And you know it. The Chrysalis formula was developed by Dr. Raj Shranka."

"Did Dr. Shranka prompt you to say that?"

"No," Mimi said, "I've never met Dr. Shranka. I've been hired to locate him."

There was a pause. "What do you mean?"

"Dr. Shranka has been missing since Thursday night. I'm wondering if you've heard from him."

"Who is paying you to find him?" Thorble asked.

"I can't disclose that," Mimi said. "Have you heard from him?"

"Answer my question first."

"I guess we both have questions for each other," Mimi said. "How about we get together and talk?"

There was a brief pause. "I have to meet someone at eight-thirty, so we can meet at eight. Are you a member of TogetherCo?"

TogetherCo was the invitation-only "real world social networking platform" aimed at affluent professionals. For seven-hundred dollars a year, members got to "participate in a community of intellectually curious and socially aware people" who hung out in "T-Pods," big white buildings located in cities around the world. Celebrities frequently posted "T-Selfies" on Instagram. Mimi couldn't afford the annual fee, even if she was invited to join, which she wasn't.

"We can meet in front of the T-Pod at Fifty-Fourth Street and Madison Avenue at eight o'clock," Thorble said. "I'll get you in. I'll text you a link to make an appointment on my online calendar."

Mimi wanted to comment on the absurdity of setting up an online appointment for a meeting that was two hours away, but let it go. She may not have smoked out Raj Shranka, but she had gotten the attention of Eugene Thorble.

CHAPTER ELEVEN

WITH AN HOUR TO KILL BEFORE she met Eugene Thorble, Mimi returned to her father's office. As she walked down Forty-Seventh Street, she heard constant chatter about Conrad Vanderklef joining Diamond Superior. While the "Prince of Diamonds" joining the enemy was a mostly symbolic blow, the diamond business was built on symbols, so his defection hit extra-hard.

In the elevator in her father's building, one dealer blurted, "it looks like this is the end." The rest of the car solemnly nodded.

Even the Max Rosen Diamond Company—usually a vital and alive place—was suffused with gloom. Mimi used to think its run-down wood paneling gave the place character. Now it seemed to symbolize its decline.

When Mimi got back to her desk, her father asked about the Diamond Superior event, but when she started to tell him what happened, he cut her off. "You know what? Spare me. I'll end up on the floor again." He held up a piece of rough. "I have this headache to deal with. I just got it from the co-op. It's the largest stone they've ever found."

It was a three-carat piece of rough, slightly larger than a blueberry—and it was accompanied by a picture of the co-op's director, Reverend Kamora, smiling and holding it up to the camera.

"I've been examining it for hours," Max said. "I can't make it into anything."

Determining the best—meaning, most profitable—way to turn a rough stone into a sparkling piece of polished was the central art of the diamond trade. It was all about balance: removing an inclusion might improve a stone's clarity grade, but then it could lose carat weight. Max likened it to a "puzzle," one he enjoyed solving. When Mimi was a girl, she'd find stray notepads around the house, covered with scribbled numbers and shapes. In the old days, Max was considered such a skilled planner, other dealers would come to him, seeking his advice on how to best slice and dice a troublesome stone.

Today, machines could do those calculations—and come up with more options than Max ever could. He never used them, convinced his fifty years of experience mattered more.

"It's a decent size," he said. "But it's got a yellow tinge and pepper spots. Maybe I could sell it in a normal market. In this one, I won't get a cent for it. I don't know what to tell the Reverend."

"Dad, I've heard some miners are using blockchain to track their production, so they can prove it's real."

Max's eyebrows rose. "I've heard of blockchain. What is it, exactly?"

Mimi had read dozens of articles about blockchain, but only now realized she had no idea of what it was or how it worked. "It's a chain," she sputtered. "You block things on it."

Max smirked. "I'll get Zeke."

Zeke was visibly excited to talk about blockchain. "I'll explain it to you, quick and simple," he said—before launching into an explanation that was neither quick nor simple. Max popped a Valium a few sentences in.

Finally, Max cut him off. "Look, Zeke, *tachlis*, can this help us track diamonds from this co-op?"

"Sure," Zeke said. "That's the point of blockchain. It's an immutable ledger."

Max picked up Kamora's diamond. "How about this stone? Could we use blockchain to prove it came from the co-op?"

"Probably not," Zeke said. "It's already been mined. You need to start tracking when it comes out of the ground."

"Eh," Max grumbled. He dropped the diamond on his desk.

"But if you want," Zeke said, "I can draft a proposal on how the co-op can use blockchain for their future production."

"Yeah. Do that," Max said, even though he'd probably never read or understand it. "How long do you think it would take to set up one of these chains over there?"

"It's hard to say," Zeke said. "There would likely be logistical challenges. They'd need Internet access at the mine. It would probably take six months to a year."

Max grimaced. "Okay. Thanks."

"By the way, Mr. Rosen, I have some bad news," Zeke said, awkwardly moving his feet. "You probably wondered where I was this afternoon."

"Oh yeah," Max said. "I think so."

"I was meeting with Paul Michelson of Michelson Gem Lab. He's asked me to write an AI program that will help distinguish these new lab-grown diamonds from naturals. After thinking it over, I've decided that, as much as I enjoy working here, it would be better for my career if I accept his offer. I am extremely sorry."

Max brightened. "You have nothing to be sorry about, Zeke. That's terrific. If anyone can get the industry out of this mess, you can."

"Thanks," Zeke said. "I've told Mr. Michelson that initially, I will only work nights, so I can fulfill my obligations here."

"You mean the blockchain thing?" Max said. "Don't worry about that. If you solve this detection problem, we won't need it. You should start there right away."

Zeke appeared confused. "No, I mean my other projects. I've installed several new plug-ins on your website. I'm still fine-tuning them."

"Honestly, Zeke," said Max, "I am not sure what's happening with my business right now. Whatever you were up to, forget it. I never understood that *mishigas* anyway."

Mimi saw Zeke's face fall.

"What my father means, Zeke," she said, "is that the work you will do with Paul Michelson is so important, you should start on it right away. And then, at some point, you can come back and work on the plug-ins."

"Okay," Zeke said, smiling. "I'll tell him I can start tomorrow."

"And we really appreciate and thank you for all the work you've done for us," Mimi said. "Right, Dad?"

"Sure," Max said. "Thanks."

"And thank you, Mr. Rosen, for being so generous," Zeke said. "You giving me a chance to work here with my beautiful wife was such an incredible *mitzvah*." Zeke pumped Max's hand vigorously.

"No problem," Max said. "It's been great having you. Thanks for all the plug-ins."

"My pleasure!" Zeke enthused, walking away. "*Zei gezunt!*"

After Zeke left, Max turned to Mimi and whispered, "What's a plug-in?"

A LITTLE LATER, MAX WHATSAPPED REVEREND KAMORA in the African Democratic Republic to talk about the diamond. It was almost midnight in the ADR, but the Reverend didn't want to go to bed without hearing what Max thought of the new discovery.

"Max, how lovely to hear from you," the Reverend said. "I hope you are well."

"I hope you're good, too, Reverend. It's nice to speak with you." Max paused for a second. "Everything's fine. I mean, I had a little health issue, but I'm fine now."

"Oh no," Reverend Kamora said. "I am extremely sorry to hear that. I will say a prayer for you."

"Thanks." Max squirmed in his seat. "Maybe I should stop beating around the bush and discuss this diamond that you sent me."

"How much will we get for it?" Reverend Kamora asked expectantly. "When we found it, the village went wild. People were cheering and celebrating that we'd received this wonderful gift from God."

Max made a sour face. "That's what I want to talk to you about, Reverend. This diamond has flaws in it."

"Well, sure," said Reverend Kamora. "But look how big it is! We measured it. Three carats! It's the biggest we've found. It's like a miracle."

"Unfortunately," Max said, "the market's just had a major shock. You won't get much for this stone right now."

"Oh." Reverend Kamora's face grew long. "Maybe we should wait until the market bounces back."

"Honestly, Reverend," Max said, "I don't know if the business will bounce back. We're in a situation where you can't tell a real diamond from a fake one. You might have to use this thing, chainblock—"

"Blockchain," Mimi corrected.

"Yeah, that," Max said. "Apparently, it can prove your diamonds came from a mine. Because right now, no one's sure which diamonds are real and which are fake."

"Of course, our diamonds are real!" Kamora protested. "I saw them come out of the ground myself. How would this blockchain work?"

"I'm not sure," Max said. "It was just explained to me, but I didn't understand it. Tell him, Mimi."

Mimi hadn't followed Zeke's lecture, either. "It's a chain. You block things on it. You would need Internet access at the mine."

"But we don't have that!" Kamora said, his voice jumping an octave. "We're a poor village. I'm one of the few people who has any kind of service, and it's very expensive and unreliable. Can we work together to set this up?"

Max bit his lip. "Probably not, I'm sorry to say. This synthetics thing has turned the industry upside down and I don't know how much longer I'll stay in business."

Kamora's mouth became a circle. "Max! You're not serious! You always told me you would never retire. You have done so much for our village. Because of you, we have a new well."

"I know. We've been happy to help. I wish I had better news.

Believe me, this synthetics thing is killing me. If you want, I can send you the diamond back to you and maybe you can get a better price from someone else."

"No, that's okay, Max," said Kamora. "I trust you."

Max blinked rapidly. After a few seconds of silence, he perked up. "You know what? I just got a text from a guy who's interested in this stone. I'll give you five thousand dollars for it."

"Five thousand!" Kamora was beaming. "That is more than we expected. It will do a substantial amount for our community. *Mazal!*" The Reverend had uttered the magic word that seals deals in the diamond industry.

"Glad to hear it," Max said. "Unfortunately, this might be the last payment you get from us."

"That is very sad to hear, Max," said the Reverend. "Our plan was to keep mining for years."

"I wish things were different. The industry's in big trouble right now. I'm just happy I could give you something for that stone."

"Max, tell me the truth," said Reverend Kamora, looking straight at the phone. "Did someone really offer you money for that diamond? We are not looking for charity. We just want to be paid fairly for our goods. If that diamond isn't worth five thousand dollars, we don't want it."

Max's voice broke. "Let me get back to you, Reverend. This is very difficult for me to discuss right now."

Reverend Kamora's eyes grew soft. "Okay, my friend. Let's talk some other time."

After Reverend Kamora had hung up, Mimi sprang out of her seat. "You're giving him five thousand dollars for that stone? You said it was worth nothing."

"Nothing is generous. During good times, I couldn't get five thousand dollars for that thing. Today, I'll have to pay people to take it."

"Can you really afford to pay him five thousand dollars?"

"Not really." Max lowered his head. "I mean, I can afford some of it. Yesterday, I sold 'The Yellow' for three-and-a-half thousand.

That'll cover most of it. Look, maybe I shouldn't have given him that much, but this will probably be the last money I ever give those people. And they have nothing over there."

"But don't you need that money?"

"Of course I do," Max said. "But they need it more. And when he said that he trusted me, that really—" He sucked in a breath. "When we started this project, everyone on the street said it wouldn't work. I remember a dealer who regularly bought from African dealers telling me, 'you can't trust those people.' And I thought to myself, those African dealers probably go home, and say the same thing.

"But there's never been anything like that with me and the Reverend. We're from different places but we've always trusted each other one hundred percent. This was the only time I came close to shading the truth with him. And he saw right through it. I just didn't want to let him down."

Mimi smiled. "Okay, Dad. I get it. That was very nice of you. You always said 'The Yellow' reminded you of Mom. I'm sure she's looking down, very proud."

"Actually, she probably thinks I'm an idiot. And God knows what your sister Brenda will say."

Mimi laughed. "I can't imagine."

Max fingered the piece of rough. "Anyway, you got me into this whole co-op thing, so you can have this as a souvenir. I won't bother to get it cut. You can use it as a five-thousand-dollar paperweight."

Mimi took the uncut diamond back to her desk. Her father was right: it wasn't that nice a stone. It certainly wasn't as nice as those perfect diamonds churned out by Diamond Superior. Yet when she thought about the Reverend's smile in that photo, and how much this find meant to the people in his village, she couldn't imagine a diamond being any more beautiful.

CHAPTER TWELVE

A

T SEVEN-THIRTY, MIMI VENTURED TO THE Fifty-Fourth Street T-Pod to meet Eugene Thorble.

T-Pod locations were unmarked, but it was hard to miss the large all-white square structure that took up most of the block. Its obfuscated appearance seemed designed to draw attention to itself.

"If you've never been inside a T-Pod, you're in for a treat," Thorble said. "TogetherCo is a Newford Ventures portfolio company. I believe that within five years, T-Pods will wipe out the conventional restaurant and bar business."

He placed his phone against a well-concealed reader on the left side of the building. A beam of light moved up and down Thorble's face.

"It's scanning my features," he said admiringly.

He was greeted by a mechanical female voice. "Hello, Eugene Thorble, T-Member number two-forty-two. You are a high-status member with seven thousand T-Points. There are ten T-Members inside who might want to meet you, including four with the same status ranking. Would you like to meet them?"

"No," Thorble replied curtly.

"One of your T-Contacts is inside this T-Pod." A woman's picture appeared on a screen above the scanner. "Shall we notify her that you're here?"

Thorble repeated "no," then added, "so annoying." Mimi bit back a laugh. Those were probably the most frequently uttered words in the computer age.

"Welcome," said the voice. A door slid open and they both went inside.

Mimi had read enough about T-Pods that she was genuinely excited to enter one. The interior was as cleanly designed as Diamond Superior's factory. The floor, ceiling, and walls were smooth, spotless, and white, like they were made out of earbuds. There were a few homey touches, like the roaring fireplace in the corner—though when Mimi examined it, she saw the flames were virtual.

They walked to a white plastic table—pre-reserved by app—surrounded by white plastic chairs. Thorble pressed a button on his phone, and a hologram-menu materialized in front of them. "Please order when you're ready," said the female voice. "All T-Pod selections are prepared by robot chefs—which ensures that all our food is hygienic, eco-friendly, and certified hypoallergenic. If you don't know what to order, simply answer our taste questionnaire, and our algorithms will prepare a customized T-Meal for you."

"For a drink, I'll have the usual," Thorble declared.

"Sure, Eugene," replied the voice. "The tech CEO special—vodka and Red Bull."

Thorble checked to see if Mimi was suitably impressed. "Get whatever you like," he told her. "It's all on my account. And by the way, you can change the voice talking to you. You can make it male, or give it a different accent. It's like going to a restaurant and being able to create your own waiter."

Mimi almost said, "why would I want to create my own waiter? That's the stupidest thing I ever heard." But she held her tongue, figuring that, by night's end, she'd hear something stupider. She paged through the hologram-menu, but was so overwhelmed by the choices, she just ordered water. Even that was complicated; the voice asked if she wanted it "fortified with brain-boosting chemicals."

"Isn't this incredible?" Thorble asked, without waiting for an answer. "The food preparation is all mechanized. The ordering is all done virtually. There's no security or bouncers, as customer behavior is all enforced by self-regulation. If you act badly, members downvote you, and you lose status points.

"So all they have to do is keep building these T-Pods, and after the initial capital expense, it's all profit. It's a beautiful business model." He clearly liked nothing more than a beautiful business model.

"So basically," Mimi said, "they are country clubs that have fired their employees."

Thorble scowled. "That's an incredibly cynical view of one of America's most innovative companies. I can assure you that TogetherCo's aspirations go beyond these structures. Their ultimate plan is to build T-Villages in space. That will become more important as our planet becomes uninhabitable. Think of all the issues we'll solve, if people can eat and socialize in beautiful places like this on Mars."

That was too much for Mimi's brain to handle. Fortunately, their conversation was interrupted by a beep. The center of their table opened, and up popped a tray carrying their drinks.

As Mimi sipped her water, she found herself staring at a jumbo screen on the wall. It featured a rapidly-changing montage of people all over the world enjoying T-Pods, and posting pictures with the hashtag #T-Selfie. She had to force herself to stop staring at it.

When she turned back to Thorble, he was no longer paying attention to her. He had taken out his phone and was playing a video game. Mimi considered asking him to put it away, but knew that was pointless. The Silicon Valley credo was "it's better to ask forgiveness than to ask permission." The problem was, people like Thorble never asked for either.

"So, let's talk," he said, as his robot avatar blew away aliens. "What did you mean when you said that Shranka was missing?"

"Just that. Nobody can find him."

"And your detective agency is looking for him?" Thorble said. "The one you started with your boyfriend, Michael Matthews. I know he retired from the force last year. I was surprised to see he's working at a jazz club. Is the detective agency not doing well?"

"How do you know all that?" Mimi couldn't believe how much information he had on her. She felt violated, like when she was a kid, and her sister read her diary.

"As I mentioned, we have access to excellent data streams."

"Creepy."

"It's just data," said Thorble. "Nothing creepy about it."

Actually, Mimi thought, *I meant you.*

"Do you deny Raj Shranka invented the Chrysalis formula, and sold it to you?" Mimi asked.

"I don't concede that at all," Thorble said. "We've worked very hard to develop our proprietary technology. You could never prove that contention."

Mimi found that phrasing telling. "Have you spoken with Dr. Shranka in the last four days?"

"I barely know him, and have never met him," said Thorble. Again, interesting wording.

Mimi was finding this interview challenging. She always tried to connect with the people she questioned. But how could she connect with someone who was killing aliens while they talked, who never looked her in the eye?

"All this talk about Shranka is rumors spread by Vanderklef and their toadies," Thorble continued. "This industry's full of out-of-touch people and obsolete businesses that need to be put out of their misery."

Nice, Mimi thought. *You just insulted my dad.*

"Look, I know that the diamond business has issues," Mimi said. "But I don't understand why you're so anxious to destroy it. A lot of people in developing countries depend on diamond revenue. Your formula could wreck entire economies."

Thorble gave a shrug so indifferent, it barely counted as one. "Ah, yes. That's me. 'Death. Destroyer of worlds.' Like it or not, that's how business works. The new drives out the old. Disruption is now a permanent part of the economic landscape. And that's good. It's healthy. It's how the planet advances."

"But it's not sustainable!" Mimi protested. "The reason I started working in diamonds was because my old industry, journalism, had been disrupted. And now my new business is being disrupted, too. How can people plan their lives if everything's getting disrupted all the time? There's no stability."

"Oh please," Thorble said, glued to his game. "The only reason people like yourself are suddenly worried about disruption is because artificial intelligence might put you and your friends out of work. You've spent decades taking advantage of new innovative technology, and now all of a sudden you worry about jobs being lost. Maybe you'd look less like hypocrites if you cared when it happened to others." He glanced up from his phone. "How do you book plane trips?"

Mimi wasn't sure what he was asking. "I use a website."

"You don't care that puts travel agents out of work?"

"I didn't do that personally."

He returned to his game, with a satisfied look. "You didn't help. You can still use a travel agent if you like. There may be a dozen or so left. Tell me, when you want a phone number, do you call information?"

"No, I—"

"And how many telephone operators have you put out of work? There used to be two-hundred thousand of them in this country.

"People love disruption, when someone else is disrupted. Then they complain when it happens to them. But that's how it goes. Things continually change in business. You either sink or swim. Ride the wave, or go under. It may not be pretty in the short run. But long-term, we're creating a better world."

Mimi sensed an opening. "I can tell you care about the planet," she lied. She plucked photos of the mining village from her purse. "This is a truly ethical diamond project. We're sourcing diamonds from a mine in the African Democratic Republic. It adheres to the highest environment and labor standards. A year ago, this village had a hard time getting water. Now they've built a new well."

"With what technology?"

"No technology," she said. "It's a well. Built out of bricks. It provides water to a village. And if you introduce your Chrysalis formula, this village will be left with nothing."

"I'm sorry to hear that. But to make an omelet, sometimes you have to break a few eggs."

"This is about people, not eggs!" Mimi thrust the photos at his face. "Seriously, look at these pictures."

Thorble didn't even pretend to glance at them, which only made her madder.

"You need to pay attention to what I'm saying!" she said.

When he again didn't react, she smacked the phone out of his hands.

Thorble looked stricken as his device fell to the floor. "What the—" he shouted. "That was extremely rude! I was in the middle of a mission!"

Mimi sat back. "I know. And I disrupted you! Disruption is good, right?"

Their raised voices caused other patrons to stop and stare, particularly a young woman at a nearby table—the "connection" Thorble had been shown earlier.

"Hey, Thorble!" the woman called out. "I see you're still pissing people off! Mad respect to that woman."

"Be quiet, Lydia!" Thorble barked.

"You be quiet, Thorble!" Lydia shot back. "Or I'll tell everyone about your deal with Vanderklef."

Thorble stomped over to her, in such a rage he left his phone on the floor. From what Mimi could hear, Thorble was threatening to sue.

As they bickered, Mimi picked up Thorble's phone. She pressed the home button. The front screen showed a calendar notification: "meeting with Raj S., 8:15 p.m." That had to be Raj Shranka, the person Thorble had just insisted he'd never met.

When Thorble was done lecturing Lydia, he walked back to Mimi.

"Who was that?" she asked.

"A nobody," Thorble said. "A girl we just fired. When I'm done with her, her status points will be zero."

Mimi handed him his phone, along with the photos of the village. Thorble clutched his phone but appeared puzzled by the pictures. "What are these?"

"They show the African village I was talking about."

"Oh yes. Those poor people. I'll send them money." He stuffed the pictures in his jacket pocket. "I have an appointment I must attend. Feel free to stay at the T-Pod as long as you like; everything's on my account. Just make sure you place any silverware and glasses in the cleaning bin. If you don't, they'll dock me status points." He gave her a dead-fish handshake and sped out the door.

Mimi left the table, making sure not to clear the silverware. She walked to the frosted one-way window up front, which let T-Pod patrons look out to the street, while those on the outside couldn't see in. Mimi positioned herself to peer over Thorble's shoulder. He was ordering an Uber to take him to the Chelsea Piers T-Pod. She felt weird snooping—though in his words, she was just collecting data.

As Thorble tapped his foot waiting for his car, he removed the photos of Reverend Kamora's village from his jacket pocket. He glanced at them for a second, then ripped the photos into pieces and tossed them into the air, watching as they were swept away by the wind. His ride came and he jumped inside.

Mimi went outside and hailed a taxi—the old-fashioned way, by raising her hand and shouting. She told the cabbie to take her to the Chelsea Piers T-Pod.

CHAPTER THIRTEEN

Mimi worried that Thorble might suspect she was on his trail, but by the time the cab dropped her off in front of the Chelsea Piers T-Pod, he was nowhere to be seen, and had presumably gone inside.

The Chelsea Piers T-Pod was, like the uptown version, an unmarked, oversized white box, which was connected to the Hudson River promenade by a five-foot-long bridge. It was surrounded on all four sides by water, making it look like a ghostly floating cube.

Mimi knew she couldn't get into the T-Pod as a non-member. She walked across the bridge to the entrance and considered knocking on the door, but she couldn't find one amidst the T-Pod's frosted exterior. She decided she'd wait outside until Shranka or Thorble came out.

Just then, she heard noise coming from atop the building. She glanced up and saw a roof deck, presumably for T-Pod members to relax and gaze at the water on a nice night like this. Except the people on the roof didn't sound relaxed. They were screaming.

Mimi moved back, to get a better look at the two quarreling outlines. One was Thorble; she could tell from his distinct nasal voice. The other person sounded like he had an Indian accent, and was probably Dr. Shranka, though Mimi couldn't be sure. He sported a baseball cap, sunglasses, and a bushy beard in an obvious attempt to disguise his appearance.

Mimi could only catch vague snippets of their conversation. Shranka mentioned "Vanderklef" and was apparently demanding money, which Thorble kept insisting he didn't have. Their voices grew louder and angrier, and they soon added a generous amount of profanity to the mix. Then Thorble started laughing, loudly and theatrically—which enraged Shranka, who took a swing at him. Thorble swung back. They were now engaged in a full-fledged fistfight. Neither appeared to be landing any blows, and their wild flailing would be comical if they weren't so obviously intent on hurting each other. Mimi decided to speak up before things got out of control.

"Dr. Shranka!" she called out.

There was no response.

Mimi cupped her hands around her mouth and hollered at the top of her lungs: "Eugene Thorble! Raj Shranka!"

They stopped tussling and turned to see who was calling them. Thorble walked to the edge of the rooftop, visibly panting, while Shranka stayed in the shadows.

Thorble peered over the railing, which, in keeping with the T-Pod aesthetic, was smooth and white. When he saw Mimi, his eyes popped. "Miss Rosen, what are you doing here?"

"I'm trying to find Dr. Shranka!"

Thorble gave a showy, dramatic laugh. "He's not here. He's—"

Thorble never finished that sentence. Shranka snuck up behind him and shoved him against the railing, trapping him there. Thorble waged a spirited fight to break loose, but Shranka had the advantage. He crouched down and grabbed Thorble's legs, then lifted him halfway over the railing. Mimi was petrified that Thorble was about to be tossed off the roof. So was Thorble. "Let me go!" he screamed. "You wouldn't dare throw me over."

He was wrong about that. Shranka gave Thorble one final push, which catapulted him over the edge. Mimi watched in horror as Thorble flew through the air, arms flailing, and splashed into the river below.

Mimi ran to the concrete barrier which separated the sidewalk from the river. She searched the water for Thorble. After an agonizing second, his head popped up. Mimi called 911—for the second time that week—and told them someone had just fallen in the Hudson River, and needed help—quick. The operator told her to not hang up, someone would be there soon.

Mimi glanced at the roof deck to see if Shranka was still there, but he'd vanished into the darkness.

"I've called 911," Mimi yelled to Thorble. "Are you okay? Can you swim?"

"Of course, I can swim!" Thorble screamed, expelling water from his mouth. His face was beet-red, and his hair and beard were soaked. He appeared to be wrestling with something. "I need to get out of this gem vest. Diamond has a high density. It doesn't float!"

"Can't you take it off?"

"No! It has an I-Zipper, which can only be opened with an app. The app's on my smartwatch, which isn't working!" He held up his watch, then looked at it, disgusted. "I'm trapped in this thing!" He thrashed around frantically, trying to escape his high-tech straitjacket.

"Can I help?" Mimi asked.

"Yes!" Thorble screamed. "Get the I-Zipper app."

"Okay!" Hands trembling, Mimi searched for I-Zipper on her phone. She found and downloaded the app, but was greeted with a log-in screen. "What's your username and password?" she called out.

"It's EugeneT at—" He groaned. "Never mind! It requires two-factor authentication!"

"I'll get T-Pod security!" Mimi shouted.

"T-Pods don't have security!" Thorble screamed, his voice increasingly shrill. "They don't have employees!"

"Are you still there, ma'am?" asked the 911 operator. "The police are on the way. Don't hang up."

"Help is coming!" Mimi told Thorble. "Hold on, please!"

"I can't!" he screamed, struggling to speak. "I'm drowning!"

Mimi was aghast. *Would she have to jump in?* The river was a long way down from the promenade.

"I can't jump in the water," she cried.

"You have to!" Thorble screamed. He then let out a piercing wail that was so childlike, so scared, so *human*, that Mimi's blood froze.

"Okay," she called to Thorble. "I'm coming in!"

The 911 operator must have heard her, because she warned Mimi not to do anything rash. "The police should be there any second," the operator said.

Mimi tossed the phone on the floor, and removed her shoes. She put one leg over the top of the guardrail, then the other. She grabbed hold of the concrete barrier, and kept a tight grip on it as she lowered herself to the narrow stone ledge that loomed over the river. She gazed down, horrified. To jump in, she'd have to fall ten feet, and risk crashing into the sharp rocks by the river's edge. Yet, she had no other choice. If she didn't act now, Thorble would drown. She steeled herself and got ready to take the plunge.

Before she could, she heard sirens. A squadron of police cars had arrived. An officer screamed at Mimi, through a bullhorn, to hop back over the barrier "immediately." She happily complied. She ran to the officers, and led them to the water.

The officers shone their flashlights on the black river, but they could only see a gold circle surrounded by a white plastic strap. It was Thorble's smartwatch, the only thing he'd been able to remove. It bobbed to the surface, but he didn't.

CHAPTER FOURTEEN

THE POLICE RESCUE TEAM CLEARED THE area, and two members dove into the water, hunting for Thorble's body. Mimi provided the other officers with a quick, dazed description of what happened. A second group broke into the T-Pod in search of Shranka, but they emerged empty-handed.

Mimi knew Thorble was probably dead. Even so, when the rescue team pulled his corpse—gray and dripping wet—out of the water, she knew that horrible image would stay with her forever. While she wanted to turn away, she couldn't help but stare, half-hypnotized, as the EMTs pronounced Thorble dead, and zipped him into a body bag, which they lifted wordlessly into an ambulance.

Mimi sat down on a nearby bench, unable to speak. When she finally decided it was time to talk, she called Michael.

"Jesus," he said, sounding slightly annoyed. "How come every time you get involved in a case, somebody gets killed?"

"It's not like I ask for this to happen," Mimi said, near tears. "This has really affected me. I'm not jaded, like you."

"What do you mean 'jaded, like me'?"

"I just watched somebody die. I tried to help him, and I couldn't. In all the time I've been doing this, I've never seen that. I don't think I'll ever get over it. I called you, hoping you might comfort me, and you're just giving me crap!"

She started to cry, then moved the phone from her mouth so Michael wouldn't hear. She didn't want to give him any more evidence she wasn't cut out for this type of work.

Michael didn't respond right away. When he spoke again, his voice was quieter, his words more deliberate. "I'm sorry. I shouldn't have said that. I was in the middle of something, and wasn't expecting a call like this. For the record, I *have* seen someone die. And it's horrible. It's something you never forget."

"Yeah," Mimi said, trying to compose herself. "But you're used to it."

"I am not! I never got used to that. Maybe some people did but I didn't. I'm not a machine. That kind of thing takes a toll on you. It did to a lot of guys I worked with. I can only repeat what my captain told me the first time I saw it happen: 'it stinks, and you never get over it.'"

"That was his wisdom?"

"There's nothing else to say."

Mimi leaned back on the park bench, and began to cry, and she let Michael hear her this time.

"I'm sorry about what you saw," said Michael. "I will get involved in this investigation. It's obviously become a lot more serious. Why don't you catch a cab to my place? I'm sure you don't want to stay alone tonight."

"I don't," Mimi whispered.

"Okay," Michael said. "I'll get someone to cover for me and leave the club in a bit."

Mimi wanted to tell Michael that she loved him but before she could, he hung up.

Just then, a fleet of police cars roared to the pier, their sirens loud enough to shatter a few eardrums. Mimi knew the officers would want to speak with her, but she was surprised to see Detective Rita Brill—Michael's old comrade from the NYPD detective squad—emerge from the front car. Detective Brill was a short, thin African-American woman, who always sported slim bifocals and a stern look. Her hair was slightly more silver than Mimi remembered, close to the color of a dime. Yet, from the minute Detective Brill marched out of the car, Mimi knew there was still lots of power in that tiny frame.

Detective Brill had handled the last case Mimi was involved in, and she and Mimi had bonded a bit during one of Michael's going away parties. Mimi greeted her with a friendly, "hi, Rita!" but Brill just muttered "hello" before taking out her notebook and getting down to business. The cool reception made clear that Brill was a detective, and Mimi was a witness, and they would stay in those roles until this investigation was over.

Brill led Mimi into the now-empty T-Pod. Shorn of its high-tech bells and whistles—the rotating T-Selfies, the fake fireplace, and the hologram menus—it felt like they were sitting in a big plastic box.

Before Brill asked a question, Mimi said, "Rita—I mean Detective—can I ask you something, as a friend?"

Brill stared at her quizzically, as if to say, "in this context, I'm not your friend." But she said, "Sure."

"I'd like to tell you the whole story behind what happened tonight. But I told my clients I'd keep certain things confidential, and I don't want to go back on my word, without calling them first."

Detective Brill inhaled. "Mimi, you are a material witness to a murder. I don't want to scare you, but your life may be in danger. If we're going to catch the culprit, we'll need as much information as possible, as soon as possible. You can call Michael and ask his opinion, but I can't imagine him feeling any different about this."

That was what Mimi figured she'd say. She whispered, "okay." She wasn't up for arguing with Detective Brill, never mind Michael.

At first, Mimi edited out key details from the story—like the name of her client, KM Diamonds—but Brill zeroed in on the gaps, until Mimi had no choice but to spill it all. Mimi told her about Dr. Raj Shranka and the Chrysalis formula, which he'd stolen and sold to Diamond Superior—whose CEO, Eugene Thorble, she had just watched die.

Brill conducted the interview with characteristic thoroughness, repeating questions several times to make sure she had everything straight. But memory's a strange thing—sometimes Brill would ask Mimi a question, and Mimi would be sure of the answer, and then Brill would re-ask it, and the truth would feel fuzzier.

For the most part, Brill stayed professional. When Mimi collapsed into tears when she recounted seeing Thorble drown, Brill didn't react; she just sat silently until Mimi stopped crying. The second time that happened, the detective dropped her guard and looked at Mimi with concerned eyes, and stroked her shoulder.

When Mimi talked about Raj Shranka, Brill quickly Googled him, and found a photo which resembled the bespectacled, shy scientist Mimi had seen on the video.

"Is this him?" Brill asked.

"Yes," Mimi said. "I know he doesn't look like a killer."

Mimi expected her to say something like, "looks can be deceiving," but Brill just glanced at the image, nodded, then saved it to her phone.

"We'll keep an eye out for him," Brill said. "Are you going to keep investigating this case after the detective agency closes?"

This jolted Mimi. "What? The detective agency isn't closing."

Brill looked up from her notepad. "Michael told me it was."

"He told you that? He never said that to me."

Brill folded her arms. "Maybe I misheard or misremembered."

Mimi knew Detective Brill was a careful listener, not prone to mishearing or misremembering. Mimi was about to follow up, when another officer approached.

"There's no video of Eugene Thorble," the officer told Brill. "We just talked to TogetherCo headquarters. They have video cameras in the building, but Thorble had some kind of high status with the company, and he used what they call 'incognito mode.'"

"What's that?" Brill asked.

"From what I understand, it uses AI and facial recognition to ensure he couldn't be tracked. They said Thorble specifically chose that option when he visited this location."

Detective Brill's brow furrowed. "Does that mean there's no video of Thorble meeting the man who threw him off the building?"

"We haven't found any," the officer said.

Brill shook her head and shut her notebook.

By then, it was eleven p.m., and Brill and Mimi could barely stifle their yawns. They ducked out of the T-Pod, and were greeted by a flock of reporters. Word of what had happened had spread, probably by police radio.

The reporters formed a circle around Brill and fired questions at her. "Earlier today," one said, "Eugene Thorble suggested that Vanderklef might try to kill him. Are they responsible?"

"Our investigation is ongoing," Brill said. She told the reporters "off the record" that the police were pursuing a number of leads, and had no reason to suspect Vanderklef in particular. She then turned to Mimi, and asked her, "Do you need a ride home?"

"I'm going to Michael's," Mimi responded.

"Good," Brill said. "I'll call you a car. If you don't mind, I'd like to keep the rest of this briefing confidential."

Mimi wasn't sure what that meant—wasn't the briefing already "off the record"?—until she realized "confidential" meant without her. Brill led the group out of earshot, and continued her briefing. Mimi tried her best to eavesdrop, but when her car came, she had no choice but to get in.

WHEN MIMI MADE IT TO MICHAEL'S place, he unsurprisingly supported her decision to tell everything to Detective Brill.

"Rita's a pro," Mimi said. "I'm sure she'll understand what needs to be kept confidential."

The corner of Michael's mouth turned up. "She *is* a pro, but I don't know if everything will stay confidential. She needs to track down this Dr. Shranka. So I wouldn't be surprised if certain things, shall we say, leak out."

Before they went to bed, Mimi considered asking him about the future of the detective agency. But the day had been upsetting enough, and she didn't want to risk another argument. She was just grateful to have Michael next to her, so she could once again fall asleep in his arms.

THE NEXT MORNING, MIMI UNDERSTOOD WHAT Michael meant when he said news might "leak out." After she woke up, she went down to his kitchen, and checked the news on her phone.

"BLOOD DIAMONDS," blared one headline, over a picture of Thorble displaying his bullet-proof vest.

"Eugene Thorble, CEO of Diamond Superior, a leading manufacturer of lab-grown diamonds, was murdered Wednesday, just hours after he mused that he might be killed by business rival Vanderklef, the famed diamond miner," it said.

"Thorble made the eerie prediction at a news conference which delivered a humiliating blow to the gem giant, as company scion Conrad Vanderklef defected to Thorble's company."

The story noted that police are looking for an Indian scientist who they called a "person of interest."

"Police believe the diamond growing expert, Dr. Raj Shranka, worked for one of Vanderklef's biggest clients, KM Diamonds."

That was exactly the kind of press coverage Kabir Mehta wanted to avoid. Mimi could only imagine Kabir's reaction. A few minutes later, she didn't have to imagine, because he was on the phone, screaming.

CHAPTER FIFTEEN

Mimi knew Kabir Mehta wouldn't be happy about the newspaper stories, but she underestimated the depth of his fury. She could feel it through the phone.

"How could you do this to me?" he shouted at Mimi. "You have destroyed my business!"

Mimi was still processing what she saw the night before, and was in no mood to deal with a shrieking client. She remembered the advice her old newspaper editor, Lewis, once gave her when she received an angry email about a story. "A lot of times, you can defuse problems by meeting someone face to face," he said. "Sometimes it just helps to know you're dealing with another human being."

Mimi asked Kabir if they could talk in person.

"Come to my office at ten a.m.!" he bellowed.

By that point, Michael had puttered down to the kitchen, and was firing up the coffee machine. Mimi showed him the headlines, and told him she was leaving to meet Kabir Mehta.

"I'll go with you," he declared. "This case is now a murder investigation. I need to take charge of this."

This heartened Mimi. Perhaps Michael hadn't given up on the P.I. firm after all—and if Mimi was accompanied by a retired New York City police officer, maybe Kabir wouldn't be so hostile.

As Michael drove them to Forty-Seventh Street, he sounded newly engaged in the case, firing a long list of questions at Mimi. This so delighted her that she blurted, "I'm happy you want to be a part of the agency again." She knew that was pushing it, but she hadn't forgotten what Detective Brill had said the night before, and wanted reassurance. She didn't get it.

"I'm interested in this particular case because there was a murder," Michael said, "and a possible threat to your safety. But I can't do this full time. I'm still managing the club. It's crazy busy over there."

"Got it." She ended the conversation before it wandered into uncomfortable territory.

From then on, Michael's ambivalence returned with a vengeance. By the time they'd parked in a garage near Forty-Seventh Street, he was grumbling about how much he had to pay for parking and how this meeting would probably be a big waste of time.

Michael and Mimi were ushered into KM Diamonds' plush conference room—no small adjoining office this time. On the walls were pictures of Kabir Mehta next to such luminaries as the prime minister of India and John Charles Harrington, the CEO of Vanderklef. The receptionist popped her head in and said that Kabir and Andy would be there "soon."

The wait stretched to ten minutes, then to twenty. Michael grew angrier with each passing second. Finally, after a half hour, Kabir entered, followed by Andy. Kabir didn't apologize for the wait, or even mention it. Mimi introduced Kabir and his nephew to Michael, noting that Michael was a former New York City detective, who'd spent years solving cases on Forty-Seventh Street, and had won numerous awards for his work.

Kabir didn't care. He wasted little time before laying into them. "What a mess you've made!" he said, banging the table as he spoke. "You know who was just here? John Charles Harrington, the top person at Vanderklef. He saw our company mentioned in the newspaper. That is exactly what we are paying you to prevent!

"I can't tell you how disgusted I am," Kabir continued. "You gave me your word that you would keep our information confidential.

Instead, you told the police, and they told the newspapers. We hired your agency because we wanted discretion, which you have completely failed to provide. Between you and my idiot nephew, your incompetence is only matched by your dishonesty."

Mimi could hear Michael's breathing grow louder with every insult, and finally, he erupted.

"Listen, here, pal!" Michael shouted, red-faced. "Mimi did the one-hundred percent right thing last night. She had just witnessed a murder. If she didn't tell everything she knew, she'd be putting her life at risk. Maybe you should think about that, and not just your stupid company, you jackass!"

Mimi was aghast. *Why is Michael escalating this?* she wondered. *This could be the detective agency's biggest case. Does he want us to lose it?* Then it hit her. *Yes. He does.*

Mimi stood up. "Everyone calm down!" The entire room turned toward her. "In case you've forgotten, I saw someone die last night, and I'm still pretty messed up about it. I'm not asking for sympathy, but I shouldn't have to spend the next morning listening to a lot of dumb arguing."

Mimi shot dirty looks at everyone there. Michael ducked his head.

Mimi had the floor, and wasn't about to cede it. "I swear to you, Mr. Mehta, I didn't want the name of your company publicized. But I had to tell the police the truth. I'm sorry about those articles. But they're the police's fault. Not mine."

Michael angrily crossed his arms.

"I know you were worried that Vanderklef would blame you for this," Mimi said. "But maybe they'll understand. What did John Charles Harrington say to you?"

"Not much," said Kabir. "He asked what occurred, I told him, and he listened and said he understood that it's not my fault."

"That's good!" Mimi brightened.

"No, it isn't, it's terrible!" Kabir shouted. "That is the worst thing you can hear from those British people. If he got angry, it would be fine. He'd yell at me, and it would be over. I'd know where I stood.

But when they don't say anything, that means the knife's coming at your back."

"You don't know that," Mimi said.

"Yes, I do," said Kabir. "Vanderklef can be extremely vindictive." He sat down. "Years ago, when they were the only game in town, your business lived or died depending on your relationship with Vanderklef. Every time they gave you a box of diamonds, you had to take it, no questions asked. It didn't matter whether the goods were right for you, or if their prices made sense. Their philosophy was 'take it or leave it,' and if you left it, they'd find another customer.

"Vanderklef particularly hated when clients sold boxes to each other, because that meant the extra money was going in your pocket, not theirs. We'd go to their headquarters in London, and every inch was covered in cameras, and everything we said was taped. They said that was for security, but they were also keeping an eye on us.

"The only place that cameras weren't allowed was the bathrooms, because that was illegal. So that's where clients would trade boxes. The third-floor men's room was a particular hotspot, because the Vanderklef people never used it. They had their own private washroom on the executive floor.

"They must have realized something was happening, because they'd see clients head into the bathroom and spend a lot of time there. So, one time, an executive walked into the third-floor bathroom, and saw me and another client doing a deal. He didn't say anything, just smiled and nodded. I knew right then, my goose was cooked.

"For years after that, they gave me terrible boxes, at prices where they knew I'd lose money. And I had no choice but to take them. That one mistake cost me a fortune. It took me years to get back in their good graces. After this, I'll be lucky if they keep me as a client. Actually, when those Chrysalis stones come on the market, we'll be lucky if we still have an industry. What a nightmare."

"Mr. Mehta," Mimi said, "I have an idea. You originally told me you didn't want to sue Diamond Superior for stealing your IP because Vanderklef might find out. That doesn't matter anymore. You're free to sue."

"I have already spoken with my attorneys," Kabir said. "They will send Diamond Superior a letter. But since we didn't patent our process, we have to submit proof. That means either getting Dr. Shranka's papers, or forcing him to testify. But his papers are missing, and so is he. That was why we hired you! To find him!" He was getting worked up again.

"I understand," Mimi said, speaking calmly to avoid another outburst. "But you only hired us two days ago. Do you want us to keep looking?"

Kabir didn't reply. He was considering this.

"Uncle, I don't think we need their agency anymore," Andy said. "The police are looking for Raj."

"Don't be an idiot, Hrundi," Kabir said. "I do not trust the police. They are the ones who put our names in the newspaper. Do we want every part of this investigation broadcast to the world?"

"Your nephew's right," Michael interjected. "We're just a small P.I. firm. The NYPD is probably doing a massive manhunt for this guy. And if he has any brains, he'll be miles away from here. There's not much we can do."

Great, Mimi thought. *Michael is now actively trying to drive our clients away.*

"There's things we can do," Mimi declared.

"Like what?" Michael said in disbelief.

Everyone's heads again turned toward Mimi. She needed to come up with something—fast. She searched her mind. "I could attend Thorble's funeral," she said, so hesitantly it came out like a question.

"Why would you do that?" asked Kabir.

"Many homicide detectives go to victims' funerals," Mimi said, with greater confidence. "Sometimes the killer shows up. They like to see their handiwork. It's like a sick compulsion they have."

"Where'd you hear that?" Michael asked.

Mimi's face grew warm. "On a podcast."

Michael audibly groaned.

"An FBI agent said it!" she added.

Kabir turned to Michael. "Is that true?" It was the first time he'd acknowledged Michael's law enforcement expertise.

"Sometimes," Michael mumbled.

"So I'll go," Mimi said. She didn't know what she'd accomplish at Thorble's funeral, or if one was even planned. But Kabir was mulling it over, and Mimi sensed she'd bought herself time.

"Do what you have to do," Kabir declared. He rose from his seat and headed for the door. "This is your last chance!" he screamed on his way out. "No more screw-ups!"

Mimi, Michael, and Andy sat quietly after he left, digesting what just happened.

Michael finally broke the silence. "I probably shouldn't have lost my temper before," he said to Andy, though Mimi sensed that was aimed at her, too. "I didn't like your uncle talking to you that way. I don't know how you put up with it."

Andy shrugged. "I just tune it out. My uncle's under a lot of pressure, so he takes it out on me. Besides, like he said, it's better when people get mad to your face, than behind your back. My uncle just stabbed you in the front. But you're still working for him, right?"

"Yeah," Michael groused, "but there's no excuse for some things. Growing up, my dad used to speak to me that way. At one point, I let him know I wasn't going to take it anymore. We didn't talk for three years. But eventually, he got the message."

Mimi looked at Michael, puzzled. He had never told her that.

CHAPTER SIXTEEN

After they left the Mehtas, Mimi hoped to have coffee with Michael, so she could pin down how he felt about the detective agency (and maybe a few other things). She wasn't surprised when he nixed the idea, saying he was needed at the jazz club.

"You have no idea how busy I am," he said.

Mimi almost said, "of course I have an idea, because you always tell me." Instead, she followed him to the garage, while he scrolled through work texts, and she searched online for information about Thorble's funeral. She discovered it was taking place the next day, but every obit listed its location as "confidential."

When they reached his parking spot, he gave her a quick kiss and hopped in his car. She saw scattered coffee cups on its floor—a clear product of working so many late nights. When Michael was a cop, he kept his car neat and orderly. Now that he was part of the music scene, he was more willing to let things go.

She knocked on his front window. He lowered it.

"I want to attend Thorble's funeral," she said. "It's being held tomorrow."

"I got that," Michael said. "I know I can't stop you. Just be careful."

"I will. And, honestly, I probably won't make it. Everything I find says it's being held tomorrow but the location's confidential."

"Makes sense. The guy was murdered. That brings up all sorts of security concerns."

"So how can I go to his funeral if I don't know where it is?"

"Guess you'll have to be a detective," Michael said, and drove away.

MIMI RETURNED TO HER FATHER'S OFFICE, and scoured the Internet for info on Thorble's funeral, but she kept running into roadblocks.

She wondered who would know where the funeral was being held. Diamond Superior's employees might, and while she found plenty of employee profiles on LinkedIn, she couldn't imagine how she'd approach them: "Nice to meet you. Can you tell me where Eugene Thorble's funeral is?"

Mimi *did* cross paths with one ex-employee, but while their encounter was brief, it was memorable. At the T-Pod, a woman named Lydia had threatened to "spill the beans" about Thorble's "deal with Vanderklef." Thorble dismissed her as "a nobody," but she clearly possessed information he didn't want the world to know.

But how to find her? Lydia struck Mimi as a young creative type who worked in marketing or graphic design. She plugged "Lydia" into Google, then added, "Williamsburg, Brooklyn," because if Lydia was a young creative type who worked at a tech company, chances are she lived in Williamsburg.

Which she did. Within seconds, Mimi found Lydia's TikTok page, and from there, her LinkedIn profile. A few searches later, Mimi had located Lydia's email, phone number, and address. Mimi felt both proud of herself and completely creeped out.

Just because Mimi had located Lydia, didn't mean Lydia would talk. Generally, reporters win over sources by being friendly and building trust. That takes time, which Mimi didn't have.

She resorted to the other method reporters sometimes use, particularly when they're on deadline: being a pest. Mimi had found that if you're persistent enough, people will respond. Sure, their response might be full of threats and obscenities. But at least you've broken the ice. You can always mend fences later.

Mimi first reached out to Lydia with a friendly email. "Hi, Lydia. I don't know if you remember, but last night, I was having a drink with Eugene Thorble at the Fifty-Fourth Street T-Pod, and you got into an argument with him. I am a journalist—" Mimi wasn't really acting as a journalist here, but figured that was better than saying she was a private investigator. "—writing about Diamond Superior, and I was wondering if you wanted to meet sometime. I will keep everything confidential. Thanks."

Lydia didn't respond. Mimi didn't expect her to. She left Lydia a voicemail a few hours later, then sent her a Facebook message. Still, no reply. She had one final option: go full stalker, and show up at Lydia's house.

At four p.m., Mimi arrived at Williamsburg's main drag, Bedford Avenue. Williamsburg was a former industrial section of Brooklyn which had morphed into a playground for post-college hipsters in the early 2000s (though its residents used the term "hipster" ironically). Two decades later, the neighborhood had become so cool that many of its coolest residents could no longer afford to live there, which added another layer of irony, though not a particularly funny one. When Mimi got out of the subway and spotted young moms with strollers and older men in suits, she knew Williamsburg's days as an indie paradise were over. Still, it remained a magnet for young people like Lydia, who piled into apartments the size of closets, often with parental subsidies. Its side streets still harkened back to its hipster heyday, with telephone poles swaddled in leaflets for every conceivable cause, and so many brunch places, Mimi wondered if people there ever ate dinner.

Lydia's apartment was located on one of those side streets. When Mimi rang her buzzer, her roommate said she wasn't home. Mimi decided to wait for her at the coffee shop two doors down. She sat in its front window for two hours, keeping a close watch on Lydia's apartment and munching an oatmeal raisin cookie. At six p.m., Mimi spotted the woman she'd spent the day chasing.

Lydia kept her hair in a Beatlesque bob, with black bangs covering her forehead. She had brown eyes, hooded by long eyelashes, and a sharp nose which pointed downward. She wore a pronounced frown, as if the act of walking home was extremely annoying to her. She looked like a typical college graduate, navigating that tough period when expectations crash into the brick wall of reality.

Lydia was entering her apartment when Mimi approached her.

"I'm Mimi Rosen. I am interested in talking with you. I saw you the other night at the T-Pod."

"My God," Lydia exclaimed. "You're so weird. You've been harassing me all day. Leave me alone."

Mimi wasn't surprised by that reaction, but tried to stay calm.

"I just want to talk," she said. "Remember, in the T-Pod, you said you had mad respect for me. That's—" Mimi groped for words. "A lot of respect."

Lydia appeared unmoved.

"You said you wanted to spill the beans about Thorble's deal with Vanderklef. So—" Mimi smiled, in a way she hoped was disarming. "Feel free to spill!"

"Yeah, I know," scoffed Lydia. "You already told me that in the five messages you left. Listen, lady. I'm not stupid. You want me to believe that we were both in that stupid pod-place, and you magically discovered where I live?"

"Yes!" Mimi said. "It wasn't hard to find you. All I had to do is Google 'Lydia' and 'Williamsburg,' because I figured you live in Williamsburg—no offense, but you seemed like the kind of person who would live in Williamsburg—and then I found you on TikTok and LinkedIn—"

Lydia stood wide-eyed as Mimi laid out how easy she was to track down. "You know what?" Lydia cut Mimi off. "I don't need to know this. I understand no one has any privacy anymore. I don't know who you're working for, lady, but people like you disgust me."

This comment stung. "You want to know who I work for?" Mimi yelled. "Let me show you who I work for." She grabbed the remaining co-op photos from her purse and thrust them at Lydia. "I'm not just a journalist. I run a project where we source diamonds from a village in the African Democratic Republic, and then the money's invested in the local community." She held up a shot of the villagers, gathered around their makeshift mine. "*This* is who I work for. And the Chrysalis formula, which your old company helped introduce, will destroy their chance at a better life."

Lydia tried to act indifferent, but the ferocity of Mimi's rebuttal stopped her in her tracks. She craned her neck to glance at Mimi's photos. Mimi had shown them to dozens of people, and they generally reacted in the same way. At first, they were skeptical. That soon morphed into curiosity, and once Mimi explained the goals of the project, their faces radiated surprise and even joy. Mimi's co-op represented a real chance to do good in the world, which was something so many people longed to do, but few knew how.

"Wasn't there something about this in one of the trade publications?" Lydia asked.

"Yes!" Mimi said. "That was our project!"

"I always thought if I worked in the regular diamond business, I'd do something like that."

"Me, too!" Mimi clutched the pictures excitedly. "And for the last year, I've been doing it. We've helped the village build a new well. I'll tell you about it. I mean, I also want to talk about other stuff, but we can discuss that, too."

Lydia chuckled. "You know, when I first got your emails and messages, I was sure you were a spy hired by Diamond Superior or Newford. There's no way they'd hire someone so awkward and goofy."

Mimi was momentarily stunned, but said, "You know what? I'll take that. Can we talk somewhere? Please? Let's go for a drink."

Lydia lowered her chin, then her eyes floated up to Mimi's. "I have to be careful. You saw how Thorble threatened me in the T-Pod. Diamond Superior is owned by Newford, and Newford is owned by billionaires, who can afford to file all sorts of lawsuits to make my life miserable. I've been too scared to say anything. And it's frustrating, because my time at Diamond Superior was—" She looked haunted, like a cascade of ugly memories had come flooding back. "Bad. Really bad."

Mimi let that thought linger. "I understand," she said softly. "But that's why you *should* talk. Because if you don't, they'll treat other people the same way they treated you."

Lydia was quiet for a moment, then nodded yes.

MIMI AND LYDIA DECAMPED TO A local dive down the street. The bar was shrouded in darkness, even though it was light outside. Nineties rock blared overhead. The air smelled like beer and cigarettes, despite smoking being banned in New York bars for decades. Its black-and-white tiled floor appeared to have never been mopped. Mimi couldn't imagine what the bathroom looked like, and didn't want to.

When Mimi worked at the newspaper, she and her fellow reporters loved neighborhood joints like this. There was an unpretentiousness about them, a lack of judgment, which felt welcoming.

Mimi ordered a white wine, while Lydia ordered a locally brewed "craft" beer, one of five on tap. This place might be old school, but it knew its audience.

"I know this isn't glamorous," Lydia said. "But it's better than a T-Pod."

Mimi laughed.

"I hate those places!" Lydia said. "Newford, which owns Diamond Superior, also owns TogetherCo, so they made us join. That's why I was there that night. I wanted to get my money's worth."

"Hold it," Mimi said. "They *made* you join?"

"Yeah. You know how certain websites use bots to goose their numbers? That's the function we filled at T-Pods. We were human bots."

Mimi laughed at the absurdity of that, and of so much of this new world.

"It's cool you're a journalist," Lydia declared. "That's what I wanted to be in college. I thought I'd be doing something good for the world. But you know how screwed up that industry is, so

I became a copywriter. When I heard about Diamond Superior, I was so excited to work there, I took a pay cut. Even when Thorble acted like a jerk, I put up with it, because I thought I was part of this noble mission, taking on Vanderklef and other big companies. I can't believe how gullible I was."

She hung her head, like she was scolding herself for her naivete. "All the eco-friendliness they talked about, who knows how true that is? We never saw our factory. They said that would jeopardize trade secrets."

"But hold it," Mimi said. "They gave that presentation, and showed it to us."

"All fake," Lydia scowled. "Remember, the presentation was virtual reality, as in: not real. I helped put that together. Think about it: Diamond Superior just announced the Chrysalis formula a few days ago. They couldn't produce that many new machines that quickly. We were worried the media would question that during the presentation. But they were so enthralled by our narrative, nobody did.

"Just like all that stuff about how we were going to produce other lab-grown minerals. The Chrysalis announcement pissed off the entire diamond industry and basically killed that business. So to placate investors, Thorble announced we'd be making other minerals. It was just smoke and mirrors."

This was all very interesting, and if Mimi was still a reporter, she'd be diligently taking it down. But Mimi wanted to learn about what Lydia mentioned at the T-Pod.

"It must have been surprising when they hired Conrad Vanderklef," Mimi said.

"Oh yeah," Lydia said. "Especially since we were supposedly at war with his old company."

Mimi pressed some more. "And I remember, at the T-Pod, you mentioned spilling the beans on the deal with Vanderklef."

"Yeah," Lydia stared at the table. "That's one thing I'm still not sure I should talk about. Diamond Superior are not nice people."

"You're already told me plenty of dirt."

"Yeah, but—" Lydia nervously scanned the bar. "This is big. Really big. It's what got me fired."

"Okay," Mimi said.

Lydia took a breath, then a drink. "I might as well tell you. Even if they sue me, I have no assets. That's one of the benefits of being poor." Lydia laughed. "So on Tuesday, I was working late, finishing Thorble's presentation for the Jewelry Expo. I was going out to get some fresh air, when I saw Thorble and John Charles Harrington, waiting by the elevators."

Mimi jumped in. "So hold it. The Vanderklef you were talking about was—"

"The company. Not Conrad. When they hired Conrad, that was annoying, but nothing compared to what I learned afterward.

"When I saw Harrington and Thorble together in the hallway, they were acting very chummy. The minute Thorble saw me, he clammed up, which Harrington found amusing. When I got back to my desk, I looked around on the server. Thorble was going to sell the Chrysalis formula to Vanderklef for thirty million dollars. Then Diamond Superior would say it ran into 'production problems,' and the company would pivot to other minerals. Vanderklef would announce they'd found a way to detect the diamonds, and the crisis would be over. But they both wanted to keep the arrangement secret. Neither Vanderklef nor Diamond Superior wanted it known they'd made a deal with the other."

"Wow," said Mimi.

"Yeah. I couldn't believe it. And coming so soon after the Conrad thing, it was another betrayal of the company's supposed values. I was so mad, I fired off a text to Conrad, who, of course, had no idea about any of this. And he was head of the diamond division! He went ballistic."

She nervously sipped her drink. "In retrospect, that was not my best move. Because the next day, Thorble sent me an email announcing they were eliminating my position. No one else in my department got fired. He probably figured it was me who told Conrad about his meeting with Harrington. And he was right. I did."

Lydia's features sank into a pout. "I feel like I was part of a cult. I totally believed in the company. In the end, all we were doing was selling cheaper diamonds. Worse, we were selling a lie. And I believed it. It makes you wonder: why even bother trying to do good?"

Mimi touched her hand. "Lydia, I've been a journalist for a while, and I've always tried to make a difference. It's not easy."

"Yeah," Lydia said, nursing her drink.

"That doesn't mean you shouldn't try. I've done some good things. I'm proud of what we're doing with this co-op.

"You seem like a good person," Mimi continued. "Unfortunately, you worked for not-great people. It may not feel that way now, but you're lucky Thorble fired you. When I was younger, I worked for some bad bosses. And I never quit, because I thought that would reflect badly on me, make me look weak. In retrospect, that was the absolute wrong thing to do."

"And you don't work for a bad boss now?" Lydia asked.

Mimi chuckled to herself. "It's complicated. The person I work for now, he's very stuck in his ways. But he tries his best. We don't always agree, but he has a good heart. And that makes a difference."

They both sat and sipped their drinks, lost in their thoughts. Finally, Lydia said she needed to go home to walk her dog and Mimi remembered why she'd sought out Lydia in the first place: she wanted the details for Thorble's funeral.

Lydia searched her email, discovered the funeral notice, then forwarded it. "The invites were sent out by this online funeral organizing service, which is also owned by Newford. It's supposed to disrupt the traditional mortuary business, and be 'death-positive' or something like that." She rolled her eyes. "The funeral is happening tomorrow. As you can imagine, I'm not going." She got a mischievous glint in her eye. "Unless there's a dance floor."

Lydia let out a long, celebratory laugh. Mimi didn't laugh with her; she still had memories of watching Thorble drown.

Lydia picked up on Mimi's reaction. She suddenly turned somber. "Maybe I shouldn't have said that. It's just annoying to hear all these people praise Thorble, when I know what kind of person he was. Maybe dealing with someone so devoid of humanity, has robbed me of some of my own. And that's on me."

"It's okay," Mimi said. "You have mixed emotions. That's normal." She lifted her wine. "I hope you work for better people in the future." They clinked glasses. "So what's your next move?"

Lydia threw up her hands. "I'm looking for a job. Let me know if you hear anything. Unless all the copywriting jobs get taken by AI."

Mimi touched her arm. "Just talking to you I can tell you're smart enough to kick the crap out of any AI."

"So what should I do?" Lydia looked at her expectantly, and Mimi realized—to her surprise—Lydia was asking for advice. After all, Mimi had presented herself as a journalist—a job Lydia aspired to—with a cool side hustle running a diamond co-op in Africa. Lydia probably thought Mimi had it all together—when, in reality, Mimi was about to join her on the unemployment line, and cringed having to lay out ten bucks for Lydia's beer.

Mimi tried to whip up some instant wisdom. "I'll keep an ear out if I hear anything. And I would keep trying to—" Mimi stopped. "You know what? You don't need my advice. You'll be fine. Really. I admire you. You were worried about speaking to me, yet you did it anyway. That's brave."

"My father's a lawyer. He'll probably say I was stupid."

Mimi laughed. "Brave and stupid are pretty similar. I've been called both."

After that, they left the bar, hugged, and promised to stay in touch.

MIMI WAS NOW ABLE TO PUT some of the pieces together. Vanderklef's deal with Diamond Superior was undoubtedly the crisis-ending "announcement" Harrington mentioned at the Metropolitan Diamond Bourse. Based on what Mimi overheard at the T-Pod, Shranka found out about the deal, and wanted in on the action. But how did Shranka discover such a closely-guarded secret? She filed that question away for later, because she had another thought: if Vanderklef and Diamond Superior were about to make a deal for the Chrysalis formula, the industry was no longer in danger. Her father had collapsed on the floor for nothing. She phoned him instantly.

"Remember, you told me to call you if I heard anything about this formula. Well, I did. Vanderklef is making a deal to buy the Chrysalis formula from Diamond Superior. If that happens, the market will go back to normal."

"Really?" Max responded. "Then why hasn't Vanderklef said something?"

"I don't know. That's what I heard."

"I just spent hours uploading my inventory to the clearance section of the industry's biggest trading site. I'm offering the most ridiculous *mitziahs* in history. I'll be taking huge losses. Obviously, I'd prefer not to do that. Should I take them down?"

Mimi hitched her breath. "Probably."

"Okay, let me explain something," Max said. "This business is all about timing. My sense is the market has only a few weeks left before it totally tanks. If I sell my inventory now, that could mean the difference between getting a small nest egg and getting goose egg. This is my retirement we're talking about. Are you one-hundred percent sure this thing will be solved?"

Mimi grew uneasy. "Not one-hundred percent. Maybe ninety. Or seventy-five." She stopped walking. "You should probably take it down. But that's up to you. Obviously." She pinched the bridge of her nose. "What are you going to do?"

There was a long silence.

"Take a Valium."

CHAPTER SEVENTEEN

Thorble's funeral took place Friday morning at a T-Pod near Lincoln Center. Mimi wore a dark suit, but she didn't have to; almost everyone there was dressed in a sports jacket, a collared shirt, jeans, and sneakers—the Silicon Valley uniform-of-choice.

Prior to the service, the attendees mingled, talked shop, and swapped e-cards by knocking their phones together, as if they were kissing. It felt more like a networking event than a funeral.

Detective Brill was there, surveying the room with alert, practiced eyes. So was Conrad Vanderklef. Conrad's former colleague—John Charles Harrington—was there, too, and Mimi wondered how he discovered where the funeral was, considering how difficult it was for her to find that information. She remembered that Andy Mehta said Vanderklef had "spies everywhere." Another question she'd file away for later.

No one else came from the diamond business, despite Diamond Superior being a major player in the synthetic space. Its recent actions appeared to have alienated everyone, in a way even death couldn't forgive.

Mimi considered approaching Conrad Vanderklef, but he was encircled by a group hanging on his every word, laughing loudly at his jokes. Harrington, meanwhile, stood in back, scanning the crowd, trying not to attract attention, though that's not easy when you're the only person in the room dressed in a three-piece suit. Mimi walked up and introduced herself.

"Miss Rosen," Harrington beamed, extending his hand. "Lovely to see you again."

"We've never met," Mimi said flatly.

"Ah, yes." Harrington adjusted his vest. "I wasn't sure and didn't want to look stupid. Regrettably, I made the wrong choice." He extended his hand again. "Nice to meet you."

Harrington had just defused an embarrassing *faux pas* with artful self-deprecation. Mimi admired someone who could pull that off.

"I'm surprised to see you here," Mimi said.

"I came to pay my respects to Eugene Thorble," Harrington said. "Obviously, we didn't see eye-to-eye on everything, but I admired his passion and keen intellect, and feel terrible about his tragic loss."

That was a lie, and Harrington didn't even try to pretend it wasn't.

"I remember," Mimi said, "at the diamond bourse, you said that Vanderklef had a solution to the Chrysalis issue."

Harrington nodded. "That is true. And when the time comes, we will announce it. Sadly, I can't say more at the moment."

"You don't have to," Mimi said. "I know that you're buying the Chrysalis formula from Diamond Superior for thirty million dollars."

"How did you hear that?" said Harrington, his mouth agape. "That's confidential information."

Mimi gave a winking smile. "Let's just say I have good sources."

Harrington's eyes zeroed in on Mimi. "I'm sorry. Who are you again?"

"Mimi Rosen. I work in my father's diamond business, and I also run a detective agency that investigates crimes on Forty-Seventh Street. I'm helping Kabir Mehta find the scientist who developed the Chrysalis formula."

Harrington's eyebrows flicked upward. "The man implicated in the murder?"

"Yes. Raj Shranka. Would you like to have coffee after the funeral?"

Harrington audibly sighed. "Given all you know, I don't suppose I have a choice."

ORGAN MUSIC PLAYED ON THE OVERHEAD speakers, a signal the service was about to begin. The T-Pod had replaced its white plastic tables with white plastic benches. Even its funerals had a clean uncluttered look.

The minister, a small, sober man with a soft voice, stood at a pulpit in front of two virtual urns. "Eugene's associates have told me that everyone should feel free to look at their phones during the service. He would have wanted it that way.

"Eugene Nicholas Thorble was a man who lived to create. Just look at his accomplishments during his way-too-brief time on Earth." He then listed all the companies Thorble founded, as well as their valuations, in what came across as a combination eulogy and LinkedIn profile.

"And now," he intoned, "to say a few words, I call upon one of Eugene Thorble's closest business associates at Diamond Superior, Conrad Vanderklef."

Conrad strolled to the podium. Like the rest of the crowd, he was not dressed in standard funeral garb, though both his sports jacket and sneakers were black. "Thank you," he said, glancing at the crowd. "I will admit that I didn't work with Eugene that long. But I did want to say something on the company's behalf.

"I remember the first time I met Eugene. I've crossed paths with many prominent people in my life. But I found Eugene intimidating. The man was a threat-level genius. An idea machine. Someone with incredible passion and dedication. And in the end, I believe that dedication cost him his life."

Murmurs rippled through the crowd.

"When Eugene founded Diamond Superior, he was taking on powerful interests—including Vanderklef, the company I once worked for. I will not comment on Eugene's murder, as there's an ongoing investigation. But I do know, from firsthand experience, that Vanderklef was determined to stop Diamond Superior from releasing the indistinguishable diamonds it developed. We've all read that the main suspect in Eugene's murder worked for one of Vanderklef's biggest clients. I don't believe that's a coincidence."

Mimi glanced at Detective Brill, who cocked an eyebrow at this comment.

"At an emergency meeting last night," Conrad continued, "Diamond Superior's board of directors voted to continue the company, with me as chairman and CEO. We all felt that shutting down the business would be an affront to Eugene's memory. I want to warn my former colleagues at Vanderklef, and I see at least one here today, that if they believe Eugene's murder will weaken our resolve, they've made a grave miscalculation. This is now a war, one where we will prevail."

His face turned grim. "Eugene had considered holding the Chrysalis diamonds off the market and selling the formula to Vanderklef. That is no longer an option. We will not make a deal with the devil.

"Beginning next week, Diamond Superior will flood the market with undetectable Chrysalis diamonds. That will destroy Vanderklef and the rest of the traditional diamond industry.

"Sadly, Eugene is no longer with us. Yet, we still have the innovative work he did, and we shall use that to avenge his memory." Conrad strode from the pulpit with his chest puffed out.

The minister returned, a little dazed. "Thank you, Conrad, for those impassioned words. Would anyone else like to offer thoughts about Eugene?"

No one volunteered. Because who could top that?

Mimi turned around to look at Harrington, one of the few people in the audience whose eyes weren't glued to a device. He was staring ahead, his face white.

AFTER THE SERVICE, MIMI APPROACHED HARRINGTON, who

was engaged in some frenzied texting. When he saw Mimi, he tucked his phone in his vest pocket, like the polite English gentleman he was.

"What do you think about Conrad's speech?" she asked him.

"Let's just say I've heard better eulogies. We had absolutely nothing to do with Mr. Thorble's untimely demise, and to suggest otherwise is an appalling slander."

"I believe you," Mimi said. "I was there when Thorble got killed at the T-Pod."

"You were?" Harrington eyed Mimi with a mix of curiosity and suspicion. "We should definitely talk. You are an interesting character, to put it mildly."

"You said we could grab a cup of coffee."

Harrington took out a card and handed it to Mimi. "Meet me at the European Club in a half hour. It's about eight blocks from here. As you may imagine, I have a few phone calls to make."

As MIMI WALKED TO THE EUROPEAN Club, her father called.

"I may regret this, but I've taken your advice. I removed all my goods from the clearance section. It took me all morning but I did it. Hopefully, you're right and I haven't jeopardized my retirement."

Mimi almost gagged. "Actually—"

"Oh no. Don't give me an 'actually.'"

"Put them back up."

"You told me yesterday to take them down!"

"I'm sorry!" Mimi was near tears. "The war's back on."

CHAPTER EIGHTEEN

Whilе Mimi didn't need a business suit for Thorble's funeral, they were required at the European Club. One of the oldest social clubs in Manhattan, it was located in an unmarked three-story building on Fifty-Ninth Street and Fifth Avenue, across from Central Park. Mimi had to meet John Charles Harrington outside and be escorted in.

The foyer was one of the most ornate rooms Mimi had ever seen. It looked like something out of the 19th century—which made sense, since John Charles Harrington seemed like he came from then, too. Its windows were stained glass and its walls bathed in gold. Its ceiling was a pastiche of famous paintings—and nice enough to be an artwork itself. Mimi felt like she was in a museum, or maybe a church, though she wasn't sure what was being worshiped.

An elderly man sat at the front desk, unphased by the pageantry around him. He removed "Mr. Harrington's" coat with a practiced smile, then ushered him and Mimi to the European Club's dining room—another sight to behold. Its front window had a panoramic view of Central Park. The walls were dotted with portraits of prestigious former members—all white-haired white men. If Mimi wasn't working, she'd stand and gawk. Hell, she *was* working, and still wanted to stand and gawk.

Harrington was led to a private area. He parked his stocky frame into a giant leather chair. Mimi sat across from him in a smaller chair, which was made of leather so buttery, she felt she might melt into it. Harrington asked the waiter for "the usual"—an Old Fashioned. Mimi again asked for water.

Harrington's starched white cuffs were monogrammed with "JCH" and held together with diamond stick-pins. He lit up a cigar, then asked, "you don't mind if I smoke, do you? They have excellent ventilation here, so it shouldn't disturb you." Mimi preferred he not smoke—and wasn't that impressed with the ventilation—but she didn't object, as he was already puffing away. Smoking was barred in most New York City establishments, but apparently the rules didn't apply here.

"So you claim to have witnessed the murder of Eugene Thorble," he asked. "Can you tell me exactly what you saw?"

Mimi had relayed the story of Thorble's death so many times it had lost some of its sting, but the sight of his dripping corpse emerging from the river still turned her stomach. Even so, she shared her memories with Harrington, who listened attentively, sucking on his cigar.

"It was horrible," Mimi said, her voice shaking. "I don't think I'll ever get over it."

"Sounds ghastly," Harrington said. "Can I get you a pastry? Their blueberry scones are rather good."

"I'm fine," Mimi said, as she caught her breath.

"Nothing you've said is in any way surprising," Harrington said. "Conard's insinuation that my company killed Mr. Thorble was absurd and offensive. I'm always amused when people accuse us of all sorts of nefarious activities. We're not that competent." Harrington smiled. "That was a joke."

He leaned back in his chair. "Seriously, what motive would we have to murder Eugene Thorble? As you are well aware, we had a deal to acquire the Chrysalis formula from Diamond Superior. On a purely mercenary level, if our sole intent was keeping the formula off the market, it wouldn't make sense for us to kill Thorble. Not that we would have done so regardless. Our company doesn't kill people." He blew out a large stream of smoke. "At least we haven't lately. I can't speak to everything that happened in the past. Times change, you know.

"I agree with Conrad on one point: Vanderklef is a very different company than the one run by his father and grandfather. They were complete sociopaths. Brilliant businessmen, of course, and quite charming on a personal level. But they did have that character flaw."

"So hold it," Mimi said. "If you had a deal with Thorble to buy his formula, how can Conrad cancel it?"

"It was still in the handshake phase. Our lawyers were in the process of drafting formal language. Unfortunately, a handshake agreement means little when the person you've shaken hands with is dead."

Harrington traded his cigar among his stubby fingers. "Mind you, I'm still shocked they want to cancel the deal. Thorble basically came crawling on his knees to us to make it. Diamond Superior's plan to sell undetectable synthetics was one of the stupidest moves I've seen a company make—and being in the diamond industry, I've seen some doozies. He destroyed his customers' liquidity. They all swore they'd never do business with Diamond Superior again. I'm not saying we didn't have problems following their announcement, but from what Thorble told me, theirs were worse. We were willing to pay them a sizable amount for that formula, which would have made them profitable for the first time in their sorry existence."

"So essentially," Mimi said, "you were going to bribe them to keep the new diamonds off the market."

"That's a rather cynical and reductive way to look at it. It also happens to be accurate." Harrington winked. "Basically, Thorble wanted us to clean up the mess he'd made with that Chrysalis announcement. I've always said that lab-growns are parasites to the natural business. The worst thing a parasite can do is kill its host."

"Shouldn't Conrad have warned him?" Mimi asked.

"Warn him? Conrad set the whole thing up. We've found emails that Shranka sent to Conrad, while Conrad was still working for us, trying to get us to buy the formula. Instead, Conrad took the formula to Diamond Superior, and used that to get himself named CEO."

"So hold it," Mimi said. "Conrad got the formula from Shranka? Why would he want to hurt his family company?"

Harrington shook his head, making his jowls jiggle. "Conrad has no loyalty to his family or to Vanderklef, only to his own ego and entitlement. He believed it was his birthright to become Vanderklef CEO. Once his family sold their holdings, we no longer had to pretend he was competent. He spent most of his time trying to convince us to market his daughter's dreadful jewelry line."

"You mean Delphine V?"

"Yes. Internally, we used to say the V stood for 'vomitous.'" He ashed his cigar. "Needless to say, most of us were quite happy when Conrad packed his bags. That was before we knew about the Chrysalis formula, of course. It appears that Conrad was cleverer than he came across." He lifted his drink. "I guess he'd have to be."

Harrington drained the rest of his Old Fashioned. A waiter quickly appeared with another.

"When Thorble approached us," he continued, "we insisted any negotiations be conducted without Conrad's knowledge, since we knew he'd try to use this situation to become CEO of Vanderklef. Thorble readily agreed.

"I'll be frank: over the last few days, I've had quite a few low moments. But when I picture Conrad's face when he discovered that Thorble was negotiating behind his back, it's an instant pick-me-up." He grinned. "Of course, I didn't say that." But, of course, he did.

This helped Mimi fill in more of the puzzle. If Conrad was in touch with Shranka, he may have tipped off Shranka that Diamond Superior was making a deal with Vanderklef. That, in turn, led to the fight on top of the T-Pod, Thorble drowning, and Conrad being named head of Diamond Superior. Conrad had come out of everything ahead, whether or not he planned it that way.

"So if the deal's cancelled, what are you going to do?" Mimi asked.

"This is a chess game, and it's our move. If Conrad wants war, that's what he'll get. Over the last few days, we've developed what we call the nuclear option. It's no secret that we have a big stash of diamonds in our vaults, which we save for a rainy day. It's currently a thunderstorm. Before Diamond Superior gets a chance to release its product, we will flood the market with both regular and synthetic diamonds, at bargain basement prices. Right now, the market is nearly dead. By the middle of next week, it will be moribund. Diamond Superior will get zero for their products. Unless, of course, they use jewelry designed by Conrad's daughter. Then they'll get less."

Harrington grabbed a fistful of pretzels, and chewed on them as he spoke. "We've run the numbers. There is no way for them to produce these diamonds affordably in a depressed market, never mind a dead one. They will likely return to the table in short order, assuming Conrad and company get their heads out of their rears." He winked again. "Apologies for the salty language."

"But Conrad just said he'd never negotiate with you."

"I take that as seriously as I take everything else he's said. We've gamed out every possible scenario. Vanderklef is a real business. We have financial reserves to sustain us through hard times. Diamond Superior is only kept afloat by the largesse of its investors. At some point, their patience will run out. So they either negotiate with us, or they'll go bankrupt, in which case we'll buy the formula during the court proceedings.

"Of course, there's a slight chance that Conrad will continue to prop up Diamond Superior, using the family money he's spent his life not earning. Then, we'll simply set up our blockchain system, which will certify all our diamonds as natural. Those goods will fetch a considerable premium, while Diamond Superior's will get nothing. And *that* will be checkmate."

Mimi was stunned; Vanderklef's plan to combat the current chaos was unleashing more upheaval. "When will you do this?"

"We're preparing it this weekend. We plan to release the announcement Monday morning, London time."

Mimi's stomach lurched. "Monday? Isn't that a little soon? Think of what will happen. So many companies in this industry rely on bank financing. The minute your announcement appears, every bank will pull their lines. Half the companies on Forty-Seventh Street will close. It'll be a bloodbath."

"Correct," Harrington said. "That's the plan. I thought I explained that part."

Mimi couldn't decide what was more disturbing: the havoc Harrington's "nuclear option" would cause, or that none of it seemed to bother him. Mimi felt like the club's gilded walls were closing in on her.

"Do you have to do it so soon?" she asked. "My father wants to sell his inventory next week."

"He better do it over the weekend. Otherwise, he'll be out of luck."

"He can't sell his inventory that fast."

"I'm sure your father's a lovely man, but we can't postpone our strategy just for him."

"It's not just my father," Mimi said. "You'll wipe out all the dealers you spoke to at the diamond club. The ones you said you always think about. We source from this small village in the African Democratic Republic, which is totally reliant on diamond revenue." She searched her purse for pictures, but she'd given them all to Thorble and Lydia.

"There might be a bit of mayhem, sadly," Harrington said, though the "sadly" was definitely an afterthought. "But as Conrad said, this is war. And war hurts innocents." He gazed up, and for a moment, Mimi glimpsed the ruthless businessman underneath the polished veneer.

"Is there any way to stop this?" Mimi asked.

"Not unless someone comes up with a way to detect these diamonds before Monday. I think we both agree that's extremely unlikely. At this point, we're not sure if detecting those stones is even possible.

"Our preference was to buy the formula. That would have been a far more pleasant outcome. This strategy poses a significant amount of risk for us, at least in the short term. In the long run, we're hopeful our business will make a strong recovery."

Harrington let his cigar burn. "On the bright side, we've long felt there's too many people in the industry. There's a whole layer of dealers who just trade stones back and forth without adding any value. We need to be a modern business. We see this crisis as an opportunity, a way to clear some of the debris in this industry, for lack of a better word."

Did he just call my father garbage? Mimi wished he'd used a better word.

Harrington put his cigar out in the ashtray. "In any case, you can't blame us for this. It was Diamond Superior and Conrad that caused this mess. They're the bad guys here."

Mimi hoisted her purse on her arm. "I don't see this as a situation where there are good guys and bad guys." She got up from her seat. "I think you all suck."

CHAPTER NINETEEN

MIMI WALKED BACK TO HER FATHER'S office in shock. Yesterday, she'd told Max to take down his goods from the clearance area. This morning, she told him to put them back up. If Harrington carried out his plan, it wouldn't matter what her father did with his diamonds. The market would be dead, and he wouldn't get anything for them either way.

As Mimi approached Max's building, she received a call from her sister Brenda. Against her better judgment, she picked up. Brenda barely said hello before launching into her tirade.

"I just heard Dad's paying five thousand dollars for this diamond from Africa," she said. "What is this nonsense? Why is Dad still buying diamonds, when he's closing down his business? And why is he paying so much for something that he basically admitted is worthless? I asked him, 'what kind of a businessman does that?' You know what he said? 'A stupid one.'"

Mimi fought the urge to hang up. "Okay, Brenda," she said, when her sister took a breath. "Buying that diamond may not be the best idea, business-wise, but think of it as *tzedakah*. That's a good thing, right?"

"Not in this case!" Brenda said. "If you haven't noticed, our father isn't a billionaire. He's barely a thousand-aire. The only thing he owns now is his home, and a safe full of inventory he says is worth zero.

"And you know, charity begins at home. Dad will be moving into my basement soon, and it would be nice if he had a little money to tide him over before he sells his house, instead of acting like he's Mr. UNICEF.

"And Mimi—" Brenda shifted to older-sister voice. "You're supposed to be his office manager. God forbid, you tell him it's not the smartest thing in the world to throw away the company's final bit of cash. I feel like I'm the only person in this family with any sense."

"Stop!" Mimi snapped—and to her surprise, Brenda did.

"Dad wants to do something good for people who need it," Mimi continued. "That's not your business. It's his. Literally. He can run it how he wants."

Brenda tried to talk over Mimi, but Mimi raised her voice loud enough to drown out her sister—no mean feat.

"He's a grown man," Mimi continued. "And it's not our place to tell him what to do. You are being quite disrespectful to him and that's not the way I want our father to be treated."

Before Brenda could respond, Mimi hung up. Brenda phoned back immediately. Mimi let the call go to voicemail. That felt like a victory.

MIMI RETURNED TO THE OFFICE TO find Max on the phone. Judging by the creases on his forehead, it wasn't a pleasant call. When Max saw her, he immediately lowered his voice. It reminded her of how, when she was younger, her parents would mouth words like "cancer," as if saying them aloud gave them power.

After he hung up, she asked him how he was doing.

"Not good," Max said. "The industry's still a mess. I was just at the diamond club. There was a guy sitting in the middle of the floor, crying. Nobody asked why he was upset. We all knew."

The weight of what was happening again hit Mimi. "I'm sorry, Dad."

He gave a hapless shrug. "That's the way it goes. One day you're chugging along, like everything's normal, and the next, the world goes haywire. I was just talking to the landlord, telling him we'll probably move out at the end of the month."

"What did he say?"

"Nothing. What could he say? The whole building's probably telling him the same thing. He'll be fine. He'll sell this place and they'll make it into a hotel, like they're building across the street. And the Diamond District will be like every other Midtown block, and that'll be the end of it.

"It's a shame. I've worked on Forty-Seventh Street over fifty years. It was a nice place to work. Not perfect, by any means. But nice. It's a real community—a little *shtetl*, in the heart of Manhattan. And now—" He waved the rest of the sentence away. It was too depressing to talk about. "You know, Mimi. It's been great working with you."

"Please—" Mimi cut in, a lump forming in her throat. "Let's not do this now. We're not there yet."

"We're close," Max said. "What are you going to do when the office closes?"

Mimi felt a sudden chill. That was a good question. For the past three years, this job had been her anchor. Now, she was being set adrift.

"I don't know," Mimi said.

"You'll be able to find a new job, right?"

"I'll have to," Mimi said, releasing a feeble laugh. "What will you do?"

"I've been talking to Brenda. She keeps *hocking* me to sell my house and move in with them. And she's right, that house is probably too big for me. But you know what? I like it there. I can go into the city whenever I want. I don't want to live with your sister in the suburbs. It's boring there."

"So you're not going to sell it?"

Max turned his head down. "No, I'll probably have to. I'll need something to live on, now that my nest egg is going down the tubes. I can't just live on Social Security."

"So when will you sell it?"

"I don't know. It has to get fixed up, which will take a couple of months. So while that's going on, I'll stay in Brenda's basement. And we'll see if I like living there. It'll be nice spending time with the *enikels.*"

"Is that what you want?"

"It'll be fine." He began fiddling with papers. He didn't want to talk about this.

"Dad, you shouldn't move in with Brenda if you don't want to," Mimi said.

"It doesn't matter what I want. It's my best option."

"Okay, but don't let Brenda boss you around. I just had a big argument with her—"

"Are you girls still fighting?" Max shook his head disapprovingly. "It's like when you were kids. I hoped at some point you would get along."

"This has nothing to do with when we were kids. We're mature adults."

"If you say so."

"Dad, I'm serious. I don't like how she talks to you. It's completely disrespectful. She just gave me this whole lecture about you giving the five thousand dollars to Reverend Kamora's co-op."

"Yeah. I talked to her about that this morning."

"I told her she has no right telling you what to do with your money."

"Mimi, stop." Max held his palms up. "You don't know everything."

"What don't I know? I know the co-op needs the money. I know what you did was extremely generous. I know I'm proud of you for doing it."

"Yes, but it's—" Max evaded his daughter's eyes. "It's complicated. The money I'm giving them, it's not really mine. It's hers."

Mimi stood frozen as the shock washed over her. "What?"

"For the last year, ever since lab-grown started hurting my business, Brenda's been lending me money. She doesn't always do it with the biggest smile on her face, but she does it. And when I say 'lend,' we both know I'll never pay her back. It was originally supposed to be a one-time thing, but unfortunately, it's become more than that. After a while, it adds up.

"Her husband works in tech. Don't ask me what he does; he keeps telling me, and I never understand it. I only know he makes good money. And thank God, they've been able to help me when I needed it."

Mimi took a seat, so she was now sitting eye-to-eye with her father. "I had no idea."

"Brenda didn't want me to tell you. She thought it would make me look bad. But I don't care. How do you think I was able to hire Zeke, and let him sit around here and do whatever it was he did? Because of your sister. Remember that springtime lull? During that time, your paychecks still came, right? You can thank Brenda for that."

He leaned over the desk. "I know your sister can be opinionated. But you've been known to have an opinion or two yourself. Brenda's a good kid. She's more like you than you realize.

"I understand why she's not thrilled about me giving that money to the co-op. She doesn't know Reverend Kamora, or any of the people there. When I move into her basement, it'll be a huge expense for her. And, unfortunately, I won't have that much to help her out. She's probably right about me buying that diamond. It would be nice if I paid the Reverend that money, but I'm not in a position to do nice things. I'm canceling the sale."

Mimi gulped. "You are?"

"I have to. Theoretically, Reverend Kamora can take me to arbitration for breaking the deal. But he won't. He's too nice a guy."

"Dad, are you sure you want to do this?"

"Of course I don't want to do it. I've never gone back on a deal before in fifty-two years in this business. This isn't how I want to end my career. But Brenda was right. I shouldn't have agreed to pay him all that money without telling her. Anyway, I'll send the stone back to the Reverend. Who knows? Maybe he'll get more for it."

"You know he won't get more than five thousand dollars for

that stone. He won't get a fraction of that." Mimi stood up. "What if I pay him the money?"

Max looked appalled. "Oh please. Where will you get five thousand dollars? You keep telling me how poor you are. You gonna rob a bank?"

Mimi did some quick mental math. "No, but if you don't pay me this week, and don't give me any severance, that should cover most of it. I'll scrape together the rest."

Max was incredulous. "That's crazy. How are you going to afford food? And your rent? You have to eat."

"I'll think of something." Mimi stood straighter. "If I pay for that diamond, that means it's mine, right? I'll sell it."

"To who? A blind person? The stone is ugly, and the market's dead."

"I'll think of something. Maybe I'll set up a GoFundMe. My friends will contribute."

"You keep telling me how poor your friends are! Come on, Mimi. Don't be crazy. You always jump into things without thinking them through. One of these days, it'll catch up with you."

Mimi knew her father had a point. But she couldn't let him know that. "Dad, I feel strongly about this. Until you give Reverend Kamora the money you promised him, I forbid you from paying my salary."

"Come on!"

Mimi raised her finger. "Seriously. If you insist on paying me, I'll call the bank, and tell them to stop payment. Any check you give me, I'll tear up. And, in case you forgot, I currently have the diamond, and I'm not giving it back. So you can't return it to Reverend Kamora.

"Face it. You're stuck. You can't cancel that deal. Understand? That's final!" Mimi stomped away.

Max sank his head in his hands. "God. Why couldn't I have normal daughters?"

CHAPTER TWENTY

O**N HER TRIP HOME TO NEW** Jersey, Mimi marveled how she'd just agreed—more than that, she'd *demanded*—to work the rest of the month for free, and she'd gain nothing but a clear conscience and cloudy diamond.

She would now have to spend the weekend reviewing her finances, but she didn't expect to learn anything besides "they're bad." She'd recently made progress winnowing down her debt. Somehow, she'd just added five thousand dollars to the pile.

She also needed to write a new resume, and brief Andy Metha on the latest developments. This was not looking like a relaxing weekend.

S**UNDAY MORNING, MIMI SPOKE TO ANDY** Mehta over Zoom. He was sitting in front of a Batman background.

"There's no good news," she told him. "Diamond Superior had a deal to sell the Chrysalis formula to Vanderklef, but now Conrad's canceled it, because he blames Vanderklef for Eugene Thorble's death.

"So Vanderklef plans to dump inventory on the market starting tomorrow, because they think that will bankrupt Diamond Superior. Of course, that will also wipe out my father and probably your uncle. It's basically become a fight between two gods, with us mortals down below hoping to avoid becoming collateral damage."

They were both silent for a second.

"Wow," Andy said. "Is this definite?"

"I asked Harrington if there was any way to prevent it. He said, 'not unless someone comes up with a detection method before Monday.' I know people who are working on that, but I doubt they'll find something by tomorrow." Mimi took a breath. Just talking about this was exhausting.

"That's crazy," said Andy. "My uncle's gonna go ballistic when I tell him. He'll probably blame me for it."

"Andy," Mimi said, "I've been thinking. I was just talking to someone who worked for a bad boss. It made me think about all the bad bosses I've worked for, and how I probably worked for them longer than I should have. You shouldn't let your uncle belittle you like he does. Some of his rants border on abusive."

Andy shrugged. "They don't bother me."

"Come on, Andy. They have to."

"You have no idea what you're talking about," he snapped, sounding surprisingly like his uncle. "Do I wish that my uncle had more respect for me? Of course I do. But I'm grateful he lets me work at his company. As he says: respect isn't granted. It's earned."

"I disagree," Mimi said. "Every person deserves to be treated with respect. Are you saying his yelling and insults never bother you? Ever?"

Andy was quiet for a second. "Of course, they do!" he said with surprising emotion. "And you haven't seen the worst of it. Sometimes he'll berate me for hours. And I can't do anything but take it." He hung his head, like a sad little boy.

Mimi felt she'd made a breakthrough, and was finally seeing the real Andy.

"My uncle's in his sixties," Andy said, lifting his head. "He's not going to change. He has many good qualities. I just have to live with the bad ones."

"No, you don't!" Mimi said. "You can go out on your own. You're very bright and motivated."

"It's not that easy." Andy looked pained. "My whole career has been in diamonds, and you know what's happening to that industry. I have money saved up, but I don't want to jeopardize it by starting my own business. It's taken a lot of work just to get where I am.

"My whole life, my uncle was the only person I knew who had money. My father was a decent man, but he never amounted to much. So I had no real choice but to work for my uncle. Is it easy? No. But when my uncle started out, he worked twelve hours a day behind a polishing wheel. I shouldn't get a free pass. I'm determined to make something of myself. I don't expect you to understand where I'm coming from. Your life has been very privileged."

That comment felt like a slap in the face. Mimi tried to regroup. "It hasn't been all smooth sailing for me. I never planned to work for my father. I just did it because I had no other options. I understand what it's like to feel trapped. The difference is, my father isn't abusive."

"But what if he was?" Andy jumped in. "You'd have to work for him anyway, right?"

"Maybe. But I'd look for other options." Mimi was now on the defensive, and wasn't sure how she got there. "Like, for instance, I don't just work for my father. I have a detective agency on the side."

"Right," Andy interrupted again. "But doesn't your boyfriend own that?"

"Yes, technically. But that's different. He isn't abusive or bossy. Just the opposite. I never listen to a word he says.

"And we set up the agency that way because he has the P.I. license. After I've worked for him for two years, I can get my own license, and set up my own agency."

Mimi had been playing with that idea for some time, but that was the first time she'd spoken it aloud, and she was surprised when that fell out of her mouth.

"The point is," she concluded. "I'm exploring my options, and you should, too."

Andy scowled. "It's not that easy. I wish it was, but it isn't. I don't want to talk about this anymore. Have a good day." He abruptly hung up.

Mimi stared at the screen, surprised the call had turned so contentious. Maybe she shouldn't have said anything, but she felt for Andy. She wanted to help him. She didn't expect him to throw everything back at her.

Yet, a few hours later, she realized: Andy wasn't wrong. She *had* spent too long working for other people—other male people in particular. Maybe she also needed to go out on her own.

LATER THAT SUNDAY, MIMI WAS TYPING up her notes from the case, when she heard a noise outside her apartment. She looked out the window to see a large package on her front stoop. When she opened the door to examine it, she saw a delivery drone hovering above her. The drone was the size of a skateboard and consisted of a big glass circle, bracketed by four skinny arms with whirling propellers for hands. It didn't look in any way human, more like an oversized insect, though the glass circle appeared to be staring at her. It lingered for a moment, then flew away. She watched as it grew smaller and smaller, soaring over the trees into the late afternoon sky.

Mimi took the package inside her apartment and opened it. On top was a box, which held a loupe and a huge diamond, which was probably about ten carats. Mimi figured it was synthetic, since she couldn't imagine anyone delivering a ten-carat natural to her door.

Mimi examined it with the loupe. Inside was a hologram of Dr. Shranka, speaking. She moved the diamond closer to hear him.

"Hello," he said. "This is Dr. Raj Shranka. We need to talk. Put on the headset inside this package. It works by satellite, so go outside for better reception."

Underneath the diamond was a bigger box, which contained a headset—just like the one from Diamond Superior's presentation. Mimi brought it outside to her stoop. Before she put it on, she sent Zeke a text: "Dr. Shranka wants to speak to me over a virtual reality headset. He said the signals are transmitted via satellite. Can I trace where he's calling from?'

Zeke wrote back instantly. "I believe so. When you're done, bring me the headset, and I'll crack it open and examine the hardware."

Okay, good. Mimi sat down and donned the helmet. She initially saw only darkness, but one second later she was back in Diamond Superior's virtual factory. Except this time, the person standing in front of the machines wasn't Eugene Thorble, but Raj Shranka—the man she had spent the last week looking for. She had finally smoked him out.

CHAPTER TWENTY-ONE

D R. RAJ SHRANKA GAVE MIMI A knowing smile, like they were two acquaintances who had just bumped into each other, rather than a fugitive and the detective who'd been hired to find him.

"Miss Rosen," he said. "It's nice to virtually meet you. I trust you understand why we can't meet face-to-face."

Shranka didn't look much different from the video he'd recorded at the hotel; he stood ramrod straight, in his white lab coat, his hands interlaced in front of him. Yet, there was a harshness to his manner that wasn't there before.

"I have been looking for you, too," she said. "And so are lots of other people. Including the police."

"They can look," Shranka said dismissively. "They will not find me. Just like you haven't been able to."

Mimi considered this an insult to her investigative skills. "You may remember, I *did* find you. On the roof of a T-Pod."

"Ah yes." Shranka wrenched his mouth into a smile. "Unfortunately, I didn't have a chance to say hello. There's a whole backstory to what happened that night, which you may not be aware of. I had sold the Chrysalis formula to Diamond Superior. All these machines in this factory that you see behind me, they're my creations. They were stolen from me.

"Diamond Superior agreed to pay me twenty million dollars—ten million upfront, and a second ten million, which was due last week. Thorble didn't want that expense on their books, because he wanted his investors to believe his team created the formula. So he paid me with cryptocurrency, from an offshore shell company."

"Is that legal?" Mimi asked.

"He was quite anxious nobody find out about it, so my guess is no. But that's Diamond Superior's problem. Here's mine. They never paid me the second ten million."

"Is that why you killed Thorble?" Mimi asked.

"Absolutely not. I simply warned him that if he didn't remit what I'm owed—plus a percentage of what he received from Vanderklef—I would tell the authorities about the offshore entity he used to transmit money. That message was, needless to say, poorly received. In fact, Thorble pulled a knife on me, using one of the diamonds on his vest. When you called his name, he walked to the edge of the roof, which allowed me to get the jump on him. I have to thank you for that, Miss Rosen. You saved my life."

"Don't blame me for what you did," Mimi said. "That's on you."

"Actually, it's on him. I acted in self-defense."

Mimi thought it odd that Shranka was basically admitting to murder. He sounded weirdly proud of beating his enemy in a fight, like he'd won some real-life video game.

"I think you're better off explaining all this to the police," Mimi said. "If it's simple self-defense, they'll let you off."

"I will not do that," Shranka said flatly.

"Why not? You need to clear your name. Do you want to spend the rest of your life running away?"

"No. I plan to spend the rest of my life enjoying the money I've earned. I didn't contact you for advice. I want a favor."

"I don't do favors for killers," Mimi said.

"You may want to consider this one. I know you've been talking with John Charles Harrington of Vanderklef. Please let him know that I can provide his company with a way to detect the Chrysalis diamonds. I can also give them evidence of Diamond Superior's offshore payments, which they can deliver to law enforcement. That will solve every one of Vanderklef's problems, all for the low price of fifteen million dollars. If they're interested, they should write the word *Mazal* on their Instagram.

"If they do," Shranka continued, "I'll send their account a message where to send the money. Make sure you tell them there's no negotiating here. That's why they must write *Mazal*. It's my terms, or nothing."

"Why don't you contact them yourself?"

"Vanderklef is a big company. They might have software that can trace where I'm calling from. I only want to communicate with them on specific VPNs, set up by me."

"Sorry," Mimi said. "You'll have to find someone else for that. I won't be your stooge."

"Then you'll have to live with what happens as a result. Vanderklef is planning to crash the market. And many people will be hurt, including your father."

Mimi considered this. That was hard to argue with.

"I hope you'll pass my message along," he said. "And one other thing. The Chrysalis formula is my invention, and so is its method of detection. Anyone who tries to devise a detection technique will be taking their life in their hands."

Mimi felt a chill. The mild-mannered scientist had morphed into a cold-blooded killer.

"Give me a break. You're going to kill someone for practicing science?"

"I have been through way too much not to get what I deserve. I've demonstrated I will take serious measures to protect my interests. Please deliver that message to anyone who might need to hear it."

"Come on. You won't be able to do anything. The police are out looking for you. You're probably miles away from here."

Shranka grinned, in a way Mimi found unsettling. "I could be. I might also be very close."

"Maybe," Mimi said. "But we can also trace where you're calling from. So, your best course of action is to give yourself up now."

Shranka smiled. In an instant, both he and the factory disappeared, leaving Mimi in the dark.

Mimi was so startled by this that at first, she didn't hear the footsteps. But they soon became close enough and loud enough that she moved to take off the headset. Before she could, she felt a hard whack on the side of her head, which was followed by pain, and then, more darkness.

CHAPTER TWENTY-TWO

A FEW MINUTES LATER, MIMI BLINKED HERSELF awake. She was lying on her stoop, confused and dizzy, her vision a blur. She lay still, as she waited for the world to come into focus and stop swaying. She strained to recall what happened. One minute she'd been talking to Dr. Shranka, the next she wasn't.

Her neighbor, Patti, was kneeling over her, shaking her shoulder. Patti was a middle-aged administrative assistant, who Mimi occasionally said hi to and not much else.

"Are you okay?" Patti asked.

Mimi muttered that she was.

"What happened?" said Patti.

"Someone hit me." Mimi said, her brain filled with fuzz. "Did you see who it was?"

"No," Patti said. "Where did they come from?"

"I don't know. I didn't see them because I was wearing a—" Mimi patted her hair. The helmet was gone. She saw scattered remnants of it on a nearby patch of grass. "I was wearing this headset, but somebody took it."

Mimi had little chance of tracking Dr. Shranka now. But she didn't need to; he'd been nearby the whole time.

"Could that person still be in the neighborhood?" Patti asked, her eyes turning into circles.

"He's probably gone."

"Did he just attack you out of the blue?"

"I think he planned it ahead of time. It's someone I know. It's nothing you have to worry about."

Patti stood up, her eyes still wide. "You should call the police."

"I will." Mimi grabbed the stoop's railing to hoist herself up. Patti cupped Mimi's elbow to help.

Mimi and Patti had lived next door to each other for two years and, aside from sporadic gripe sessions about their landlord, this was the longest conversation they'd ever had. It wasn't that Patti was unfriendly—she was perfectly pleasant, and Mimi was always nice back. They just didn't hang out, because that wasn't a thing neighbors did anymore.

Mimi considered asking Patti for a drink, but this wasn't the moment to forge a friendship. Patti was already backing away from Mimi's stoop toward her own. She probably thought that Mimi was mixed up with dangerous people—which, to be fair, she was. Mimi hollered "thank you" as Patti popped back into her unit, locking her door so loud Mimi heard it.

Mimi entered her apartment, and staggered to her bathroom, steadying herself by clutching her furniture. She felt calm, oddly so; she knew from past experience that was the adrenaline surging through her body, fending off the waves of fear that were sure to come. She looked in her bathroom mirror, and noticed a small red mark—likely, a scrape from the stoop. She dabbed it with Neosporin. Then, she dropped into her favorite recliner, picked up her phone, and called Detective Brill.

Even though it was a weekend, Brill said she'd come over. Mimi always got annoyed when Michael would cut short weekend plans for a case. This time, Mimi felt grateful.

While she waited for Brill to arrive, Mimi called Michael to tell him what happened. He predictably flipped out. "You need to take immediate precautions," he barked into the phone like it was a bullhorn. "If you see anyone suspicious, call 911 immediately. Keep your phone with you at all times."

"I don't think Shranka will attack me again," she said. "If he wanted to hurt me, he could have. He needs me to deliver his message. I don't think I have to worry about him."

"What are you talking about?" Michael shouted. "Of course you have to worry about him. He just gave you a conk on the head, like he did to that kid. I wouldn't count on this guy being harmless. He strikes me as a pretty sick individual. I'm coming over to your place. I just have to get someone to cover for me tonight. That could take a while. I've already needed coverage twice this week."

"You don't have to come over."

"What do you mean?" Michael sputtered, like her comment appalled him. "I can't ignore a guy assaulting you. This guy is obviously bad news, and I'm gonna hunt him down."

"Are you sure? You said you didn't have time to get involved in this case."

"I don't. But I'm getting involved anyway."

"Okay, but—" Mimi appreciated that Michael wasn't delivering his standard lecture that she shouldn't investigate on her own. Yet, he was essentially offering to "ride to her rescue again." It was the same message, delivered more subtly.

Mimi would love for Michael to take an active role in this case—but only if he really wanted to. If he was just going to grumble and pick fights—like he did with the Mehtas—she was better off without him.

Mimi was about to tell him this, when she heard a car drive up to her place. The sound set her nerves on edge, until she peered out the window and saw Detective Rita Brill at the wheel, with another officer in the passenger seat. Mimi told Michael she'd call him back.

Detective Brill was once again in professional mode. She marched into Mimi's apartment, notebook in hand, barely offering a greeting before starting her questioning. Even though Mimi was only describing a short conversation, Detective Brill was so thorough that recounting it took a half hour.

When Mimi was done, something occurred to her. "Shranka

knew a lot about me," she said. "He knew my father was in the business, he knew where I lived. Maybe he learned some things online, but how did he know that Vanderklef plans to dump its goods? Or that I was home to receive his package?"

"Fair questions," Brill said. "I strongly recommend downloading an antivirus program, to make sure Shranka's not spying on your computer. And be careful what you write or text. Check under your car to see if he's installed any kind of GPS device. And stay aware of your surroundings. Do you have anyone you can stay with tonight?"

"Michael's coming over."

"Good." Brill smiled. "Once a cop, always a cop."

Mimi gave a small shrug. "I don't know about that."

"What do you mean?" Brill's head inclined a few degrees.

"Remember, last time we spoke, you told me that Michael wanted to close the detective agency."

"I said you needed to speak to him about that," Brill said, a touch of ice in her voice.

"Well, he just said he wants to get involved with this case. But I don't want him to if he's not interested. He's very caught up in his new job."

Brill's bifocals slid down her nose. "Maybe you two should discuss this. You guys *do* talk, don't you?"

"Sure." Mimi felt like she was being interrogated, which made her tighten up. "It's just a sensitive subject, because Michael can be—you know…"

Brill smiled. "I know." She placed a maternal hand on Mimi's arm. "You two are both smart; I'm sure you'll work it out." She shut her notebook. "Anything else?"

"Yes. What should I do about Shranka's request? Should I talk to Vanderklef?"

"Another good question." Brill tapped her pen on her palm. "Do you feel comfortable delivering his message?"

Mimi nodded. "I do."

"Then go ahead. Just keep us apprised of what's happening. The more contact people have with Dr. Shranka, the easier it will be to track him."

"Okay," Mimi said. "Can you reach out to John Charles Harrington, the CEO of Vanderklef, and tell him I'll be getting in touch?"

"I thought you knew Mr. Harrington," Brill said. "I saw the two of you talking at Mr. Thorble's funeral."

Wow, Mimi thought. *She is observant.* "I've met him, but the last time we spoke, I told him he sucked."

Brill laughed. "I'll give him a call."

That sparked another thought. "When you talk to Mr. Harrington, tell him Shranka won't do this deal if Vanderklef announces it's dumping its goods tomorrow."

"He told you that?"

Mimi's mouth grew dry. Shranka hadn't actually said that. But Mimi wanted to delay Vanderklef's "nuclear option," and this was a good way to do it.

"Yes," Mimi said with a gulp. "He made that explicit."

Brill flipped open her notebook to jot this down. "You didn't tell me that before. I thought we went over your whole conversation."

"He implied it, strongly."

Brill looked up. "Did he imply it, or make it explicit?"

Mimi froze. "Both."

"Okay." Brill appeared skeptical, but to Mimi's relief, didn't press the point.

After Brill left, Mimi checked all the things that Brill recommended, but couldn't find any sign Shranka was tracking her. She also searched outside for objects he may have dropped or left behind, but didn't find anything.

Once Mimi returned to her apartment, she weighed telling Michael not to come. She needed time to herself, to sort things out. So many things in this case didn't make sense. Dr. Shranka was a murder suspect. He should be far away. Yet, he was apparently close enough to whack her on the head. Why? Clearly, there was more going on with this case than appeared on the surface.

She was just about to tell Michael to stay put, when she decided there was more going on with him as well. When he talked about hunting down Dr. Shranka, there was a forcefulness in his voice that reminded her of the old Michael—Detective Matthews, the committed cop. Maybe he relished the chance to once again play knight-in-shining-armor. How many films had they watched where the old hero is reluctantly dragged out of retirement, for one last mission?

Mimi would let him have this.

WHEN MICHAEL ARRIVED AT MIMI'S APARTMENT, he was sweaty and discombobulated, and he continually called the club. When he became convinced things were running smoothly without him, he relaxed, and once again turned into the interesting and sympathetic companion Mimi had dated for the past two years.

It was only when Mimi brought up the future of the detective agency, that his expression turned sour. "I'm too tired to discuss that right now," he said. When she raised the subject again later, he snapped: "I'm helping you with this case, despite being super-busy. Isn't that enough?"

She told him it was.

Just before Mimi went to sleep, she received a text from John Charles Harrington.

"After speaking with Detective Brill, Vanderklef's board of directors has agreed to postpone tomorrow's announcement until after we meet. I propose we get together at the European Club tomorrow at one p.m."

A few seconds later, Harrington sent a follow-up.

"I warn you, there's no guarantee we will pursue any so-called offer that you present until we've determined it's legitimate."

"It's definitely legit," she wrote back—though she had no clue whether it was.

CHAPTER TWENTY-THREE

"**T**HIS IS ALL RATHER EXTRAORDINARY," JOHN Charles Harrington told Mimi the next day at the European Club, his left hand wrapped around his omnipresent cigar. It was one p.m., and the CEO of Vanderklef was knocking back Old Fashioneds. Mimi could smell the whiskey on his breath.

Harrington peered at his notes. "You're saying Raj Shranka, the man who invented these Chrysalis diamonds, told you that, for fifteen million dollars, he'll inform us how to detect them, and give us proof that Diamond Superior paid him illegally."

"Correct." Mimi fidgeted in her seat. Michael was sitting next to her, but he didn't say much; he just kept an eye on Harrington.

Mimi didn't relish acting as a messenger for someone possibly guilty of murder and assault. Yet if Vanderklef struck a deal with Shranka, that would save both her father's business and the co-op. Shranka knew that, which was why he chose her as his intermediary.

"If you're interested," Mimi said, "you must write the word '*Mazal*' on your Instagram feed, and he'll message you his bank account number. But you must accept his terms. No negotiating."

Harrington's mouth became a straight line. "This scientist friend of yours thinks like a diamond dealer, I'll give him that. But we have many issues to consider, including, frankly, your credibility."

"Why don't you find me credible?" Mimi asked, insulted, but also curious.

"This is quite an unusual circumstance. And you are an unusual person. If I'm not mistaken, the last time we spoke, you argued quite vociferously that we shouldn't proceed with our plan to sell our stockpile, because it would hurt your father's business. So how do I know this isn't just a ploy to stop us from doing that? And how do we know the money we wire him won't end up with you?"

"Detective Brill will keep an eye on that," Michael said. "Trust me. Mimi's legit. You can believe her."

Harrington shot Michael a look, which essentially said, "who are you, and why are you talking to me?"

"Honestly," Harrington said, "I'm beginning to think that this search for a detection technique may be a fool's errand. We might have to live with the unfortunate fact that these stones may not be distinguishable."

"But Dr. Shranka said that they were."

"So you've said," Harrington said. "And if we can't trust the word of a violent lunatic, who can we trust?"

Harrington picked up his pad and reviewed his notes, twisting his mouth in puzzlement. "Suffice it to say, we have a lot to consider here. This deal is a minefield from a compliance standpoint. Vanderklef has, I'm proud to say, a rather formidable corporate ethics department. I can't imagine they will look very kindly on us funneling money to suspected murderers. This will be subject to a thorough and prolonged review."

"Okay," Mimi said, "but remember that Shranka said that if you want a deal—"

"Yes," Harrington said. "We'll hold off the nuclear option, until we make our decision."

"How long will that be?"

Harrington lifted his shoulders. "I don't know."

That seemed the answer to everything lately.

"So what did you think?" Mimi asked Michael as they left.

"Another waste of time," Michael said. "Rita says she's working with the feds to trace Shranka's bank account. But if this guy's as tech savvy they say, he's probably put up all sorts of electronic barricades to hide his location. And the only thing I'm interested in is catching him."

"I believe everything's connected," Mimi said. "There's a bigger picture I'm not seeing."

"I'll give you the bigger picture," Michael said. "All these people are full of it." He looked at his watch. "I need to go to the club. But I'll try to come by later. And just—"

"Be careful, I know. I'll be fine. I'll keep my phone with me at all times and call 911 immediately if I see anything suspicious. Trust me, I know how to be paranoid. I've had plenty of experience."

Michael half-smiled. They hugged and went their separate ways.

CHAPTER TWENTY-FOUR

AFTER SHE SAID GOODBYE TO MICHAEL, Mimi went to her father's office, where it was another quiet day. Mimi sat at her desk, wondering how to convince Harrington to accept Shranka's deal. That represented the best hope for not only finding Shranka but saving the industry.

She was surprised Harrington said it might not be possible to detect the Chrysalis diamonds. Shranka had repeatedly insisted that it was—not just on the headset, but on the video he'd made in his hotel room. While Mimi was wary of headset-Shranka, the hotel room-version struck her as sincere. If only she could prove he was telling the truth.

She got an idea, and called Paul Michelson. "Can I come to the lab?" she asked him. "I have something to discuss."

"Sure," Paul said. "I'm just down the street. You can say hi to your friend Zeke."

"That's right. How's he been working out?"

"Well, just keep this between us, but so far—" Paul paused for effect. "He's been great! He's so enthusiastic and bursting with ideas. I wish we hired him months ago; we might not be in this mess. Though he can be a little, you know—"

"Verbose?"

"He definitely likes to talk. But not in a bad way. And when he starts going on about something, you can just pull out your phone and ignore him, and he doesn't mind. He keeps talking. It's like he's used to it." He paused. "I hope my saying that doesn't offend you."

"No. I'm well aware," Mimi laughed.

As MIMI LEFT FOR PAUL'S, SHE asked Channah if she wanted to come along and see Zeke. Channah's eyes flickered with excitement, then her face drooped.

"I don't think I should," she said. "At lunch, we had this really bad fight about, you know, the baby thing."

"Oh Channah. Is he giving you a hard time about that?"

"Not really. He just said that now that he has this new job, we might consider starting a family. Which wasn't such a bad thing to say, but I don't want him thinking this will continually be up for discussion. I got really mad at him, and I've decided I won't speak to him for the rest of the day."

Mimi grabbed Channah's hand. "I'm glad you're standing your ground."

"I'm not, though." Her lower lip curled. "I'm totally wavering. I would love to go with you and see Zeke. I miss him."

"But you just had lunch with him."

"Yes. But that was two hours ago! That might not sound like long, but we used to work together every day. My therapist says that he and I are—I'm trying to think of the phrase she used."

"Codependent?"

"No. That's not it." Channah stroked her forehead. "She said we're 'beyond adorable.'" She looked confused. "Codependent? Isn't that a bad thing?"

"I don't know, it's a term I heard once." Mimi dashed out the door before Channah Googled it.

MIMI REMEMBERED HOW IMPRESSED SHE WAS the first time she visited Michelson Gemological Associates. There were dozens of employees sitting before rows of microscopes, continually wrapping, unwrapping, and grading diamonds. A stream of packages came in and out. The phones rang constantly.

Today, the chairs and microscopes were there, but the people were gone. Mimi could hear the silence.

Paul beckoned Mimi into his office, one of the lab's few remaining islands of light. His desk looked like she remembered—a mess of devices and computers, with a picture of his kids on the side.

"I know it's a little desolate here," he said, leaning back on his chair. "It's funny. Six months ago, this guy told me he had a way to grade diamonds with artificial intelligence. He said I could eliminate most of my staff and be twice as efficient. I said, 'no way. I like my workers. I don't want to hang out with a bunch of machines all day. I prefer people.'

"And the irony is—" He brought his chair up to his desk. "In the end, it didn't matter. I had to lay off my whole staff anyway. I'd have done anything not to do that."

Zeke walked in from the next room. "Hey Mimi! I thought I heard your voice. Did Channah come with you?"

"No," Mimi said. "She couldn't make it. This is just a quick visit."

Zeke's eyes popped. "I would think she'd want to come and see me, even if it's just for a minute. We haven't seen each other for—" He checked his watch. "Two hours!" He grew more agitated. "Did she say why she didn't come? Was it related to what I said at lunch? Because I apologized for that! Repeatedly!"

"I don't know, Zeke," Mimi said, as flatly as possible.

Zeke started pacing. "I never should have opened my mouth to Channah. I'm the biggest idiot in the world." His hands turned into claws. "She must hate me right now. I don't think she'll ever forgive me."

"Of course she will," Mimi said.

Zeke stopped pacing. "Mr. Michelson, I know I told you I'd spend my afternoon refining the AI parameters. But I need a few minutes to call my wife. My marriage may depend on it. Is that okay?"

"Of course," Paul said.

Zeke called out "thank you!" and ran into the other room, slamming the door.

Paul shared a sly grin with Mimi. "Wow, he and his wife are kind of—"

"Adorable?" offered Mimi.

"I was going to say 'codependent,'" Paul said. "But 'adorable' works too."

A few seconds later, Zeke burst into Paul's office. "Update! I just heard from Channah. She's walking over here. She was going to surprise me. Can I take a break to go downstairs and beg her forgiveness?"

"Have fun," Paul said.

Zeke rushed out of the office, slamming the door behind him.

Paul chuckled. "The funny part is, Zeke's been working so hard, I wouldn't mind if he took ten breaks. He's really been amazing. I thought it would take him weeks to develop our AI program. He finished it in two days. It knows the details of every diamond we've seen."

"That's great."

"Yeah, but—" His eyes turned downcast. "It only has the data we provide it. So, it just proves that we're clueless, faster."

"No detection method yet?" Mimi asked.

"Nope." His mouth turned tight. "I've thoroughly examined the diamonds you sent from that hotel room, and can't find anything that identifies them as lab-grown. Yet, they're all perfect one-carat D Flawlesses. They have to be synthetic. We just can't prove that."

Paul turned toward a black device, which sat on the corner of his desk, and was about the size of a microwave oven. "This is the most advanced detector on the market. It sells for fifty thousand dollars." He opened a compartment on its top, and dropped a diamond inside, then pressed a button. A blue screen appeared, which said "natural." Paul frowned at it. "I've run that test so many times, and I'm always shocked by it."

Mimi inched up on her chair. "Let's say we could prove these diamonds were detectable, even if we didn't know the precise method. Would that be worth doing?"

"Sure," Paul said. "It would at least mean I'm not wasting my time. But I don't know how you'd do that."

"You said all these lab-growns are one-carat D Flawlesses. Do you have a natural one-carat D Flawless?"

"There's a reference stone in my safe."

"Okay. How about I gather all the synthetic stones together, and take them to Diamond Superior? I'll say I'm returning what they gave me. We'll put one natural in there. And we'll see if they can tell it apart. If they can, we'll at least know it's possible to detect them."

Paul laughed. "That's a devious little plan, I gotta admit."

"Can you help with it?"

"Sure. But there's one problem: unless you know someone at Diamond Superior, they won't talk to you. They've ignored all my calls and emails. You'll need a way to get through to them."

Mimi was already brainstorming how to do that.

MIMI SPENT THE NEXT FEW HOURS reaching out to Diamond Superior. She sent emails to its customer service address. She stopped by its building. But mostly, she phoned. That at least let her speak with a human being—though that person grew annoyed with constantly taking her messages.

And so, it was on to the next step: getting in touch with Conrad Vanderklef directly. She wondered who would have his contact info. Again, her mind went to Lydia, her disenchanted friend from Williamsburg.

Lydia sounded genuinely happy to hear from Mimi. "I had the craziest day," she said. "Conrad messaged me this morning. He was so angry. Diamond Superior knows I talked to you."

"Really? How'd he find out?"

"I don't know. It's probably that data service they use. It's scary stuff. He threatened to sue me."

Mimi felt like the wind had been knocked out of her. "Oh my God, Lydia. I'm so sorry."

"No, it's fine. My father's a lawyer. He told me they have no leg to stand on. They fired me so quickly, I never signed a nondisclosure agreement. When Conrad heard that, he quickly offered me a generous severance package to sign an NDA. Basically, they're giving me a huge pile of cash to keep quiet. I thought about not accepting it, but I need the money, so—"

"I understand," Mimi said.

"Conrad also said he'd get me a copywriting job at Newford Ventures' newest portfolio company. It's some kind of app that calculates your wellness with an algorithm, or as they call it, an 'algo.' It'll pay double my salary from Diamond Superior and they're offering me great stock options and benefits."

Mimi marveled at Lydia's reversal of fortune. "Wow. That's great."

"Yeah. But I turned him down. It'll probably be another Diamond Superior. The world doesn't need another wellness app. It certainly doesn't need another 'algo.'

"I've been thinking about how helpful it was talking with you. It felt so good getting things off my chest. I've decided I want to do that for other people. So I'm going to become a therapist. That was my favorite part of journalism class anyway—talking to people and hearing their stories. It'll mean I'll have to go back to school, and take on new loans, so I might have to work part time driving an Uber or something. I would definitely be better off financially working for Newford. But I think I've made the right choice."

"I think so too," Mimi said, a smile in her voice.

"Anyway, I don't know what you called about, but I can't say much, because of the NDA."

"Gotcha. I was just calling to see if you had Conrad's phone number, but if you can't give it out, fine."

"This NDA is really strict and—" She paused. "Hold it." Lydia began speaking slowly and precisely. "I can't give you that information. My NDA is very strict."

"I understand," Mimi said.

"Seriously, I'll forward you the NDA, so you can see how strict it is."

"You don't have to. I believe you."

"I'm texting it to you now."

The NDA arrived a moment later, accompanied by a text which declared, in all caps, "HERE'S WHY I CAN'T TALK!" Mimi immediately saw why Lydia sent it to her. The NDA had been sent from Conrad's cell phone, and included his phone number.

"Thanks," Mimi said, giggling.

"And thank you, Mimi. You may not realize it, but you helped me a lot."

"And you just helped me, too."

MIMI HAD CONRAD'S NUMBER, BUT STILL had to get his attention. He had proved quite adept at avoiding her—and apparently other people as well. She came up with an idea, but wasn't sure if it was brilliant or crazy.

She took out the jumbo diamond Dr. Shranka delivered to her door. She listened to the hologram inside. She recorded the first few sentences on her phone.

Then she called Conrad. When she reached his voice mail, she played the audio. "Hello," it said. "This is Dr. Raj Shranka. We need to talk." Then she hung up.

Mimi didn't know if Conrad would fall for that. But he did. Big time. He called back immediately.

Mimi answered with the recording of Dr. Shranka's voice saying "hello!"

"What the hell, Raj!" Conrad shouted. "I told you not to contact me on this phone, only by encrypted app."

Mimi moved the phone to her mouth. "Hi there, Conrad," she said. "You weren't actually speaking to Dr. Shranka just now. This is Mimi Rosen. The person who asked about Dr. Shranka at the event last week."

"Jesus!" Conrad shouted. "Is this a joke?"

"No," Mimi said. "But I do find it interesting that you've been speaking with an accused murderer."

"What is this?" Conrad demanded.

"I was hoping to stop by your office," she said. "I have something I need to return to you. Some diamonds you created."

"I'm not interested. We have plenty of diamonds."

"I would still like to speak with you. And just so you know, I've taped this conversation. Law enforcement might be very interested to learn you've been in contact with a missing fugitive. So you either meet with me, or I'll go to the police."

"Oh, I see!" Conrad said, his voice rising a register. "You want to blackmail me!"

"No. Of course not!"

"You better not be. Someone just tried to pull that on me and I fixed it so he'll regret it for the rest of his life."

"I simply have something I'd like to discuss."

"Fine," he barked. "Come to my office tomorrow at twelve."

AFTER HE HUNG UP, MIMI EXCITEDLY called Paul. "I'm meeting with Conrad tomorrow."

"Wow," Paul said. "How'd you swing that?"

"It's a long story. But I now have proof Conrad has been talking with Dr. Shranka. I said if he didn't meet with me, I'd tell law enforcement that he was speaking with an accused murderer."

"I gotta hand it to you, Mimi," Paul laughed. "You're something else."

"Yeah," Mimi said. "And now I'm thinking: if I have this much leverage over him, why should I stop at just dropping off the parcel? How about I go there tomorrow, and demand that Diamond Superior not release the Chrysalis diamonds, or I'll tell law enforcement he's been speaking with Shranka? He was so scared when I threatened him, he accused me of trying to blackmail him." She laughed. "Can you believe that?"

"Actually, now that I think about it, you did sort of blackmail him."

"Come on!" Mimi said, incredulous.

"Let's look up the definition of *blackmail*." Paul tapped a few keys. "'The criminal offense of demanding payment or benefit from someone in exchange for not revealing compromising or damaging information.' That's kind of what you did."

"Yeah, but come on. He asked if I was blackmailing him, and I said, 'no.' Would a real blackmailer say that?"

"Probably."

Mimi's mouth dropped.

"I'm just warning you to be careful," Paul said. "We are dealing with very rich, very powerful people. Make sure all you do tomorrow is return those diamonds. Don't threaten Conrad in any way."

"Okay," Mimi said. "Though obviously I would never blackmail anyone. If anything, it was misdemeanor blackmail. Is that a thing? It must be, right?"

"I can look it up," Paul said.

"Don't!" Mimi cried.

CHAPTER TWENTY-FIVE

T HE NEXT MORNING, MIMI WAS GETTING ready for work, trying to brush a troublesome knot out of her hair, when she received a call from John Charles Harrington.

"I was wondering if you have heard from our friend, the mad scientist," he said.

"No," Mimi said. "Why?"

"It's very strange. Yesterday afternoon, after running Shranka's proposal through our compliance department's express service, we decided to accept the deal and wrote 'Mazal' on our Instagram. Shranka immediately messaged us his bank account number. We sorted out the legal protocols and coordinated certain technical aspects with Detective Brill. But when we tried to transfer funds to his account, we learned it had been deactivated. We haven't heard from Shranka since."

Mimi stopped brushing her hair. "So he ghosted you?"

"It certainly appears that way. I'm rather surprised, as is Detective Brill. Perhaps Shranka found another source for the money. Or maybe he decided it was better to just disappear. In any case, it doesn't look like we'll take ownership of his supposed detection technique."

Mimi felt her stomach lurch. "So what happens now? I mean, with the nuclear option."

"We'll give the good doctor another day to get back to us. And if he doesn't, we'll start dumping goods tomorrow afternoon. I know you and others may not like that, but I'm afraid that's our best option at the moment."

Mimi had hoped that she'd put off—and maybe even cancelled—the diamond apocalypse. She'd only delayed it two days.

"But isn't your best option discovering a detection technique?" Mimi said.

"Of course it is!" Harrington said, sounding exasperated. "That's why we spent so much time on this Shranka folderol. But at some point, we may have to accept that it's not possible to detect these diamonds and move to Plan B."

"But I believe it *is* possible," Mimi said. "And I think I can prove it. Today, I'm going to Diamond Superior with a parcel of their synthetics, which has one natural in it, and I'll see if they notice."

"Clever."

"Thank you. And if my test works, will you hold off?"

"Possibly," Harrington said, and hung up.

WHEN MIMI WENT TO PAUL'S OFFICE to prep for her visit with Conrad, she found Paul getting a serious case of cold feet.

"So, hold it," he said, adjusting his glasses. "We're placing a valuable natural diamond in a parcel of synthetics, to see if Diamond Superior can spot it? And what if they don't? Will I get it back?"

"I don't know," Mimi said. "Probably not."

"Jeez," Paul said. "This is risky."

"I know," Mimi said. "But you agreed to it."

"I said I'd consider it if you were able to reach Diamond Superior. I didn't know you'd blackmail your way in."

"Hey!" Mimi said. "We both agreed what I did wasn't blackmail!" She forced herself to take a breath. "We have to do this. If we don't, Vanderklef will flood the market, and thousands of people will be out of work—including me and you."

Paul sighed wearily. He swiveled his chair to face the small safe behind his desk. He spun the dial, opened the door, and took out a small cardboard box and placed it on his desk. He grabbed a pair of tweezers from a desk drawer, and used them to pluck a diamond from the box. He held the diamond up to the light, and a flood of colors burst from it.

"This stone cost twenty thousand dollars—and that's with a steep discount," he said. "I don't know how much it's worth now, with all this craziness, and honestly, I don't care. Natural D Flawlesses are extremely rare, and even if machines can mass-produce them, I consider this a treasure of nature, and I'd rather not lose it. If nothing else, I find it beautiful, and enjoy looking at it."

Mimi found Paul's words unexpectedly touching; they sounded like something her father would say. Of course, Max had sacrificed his favorite diamond. Paul might have to as well.

"But you'll give it to me?" Mimi asked.

Paul stared at the stone. "Okay," he said finally. "But hold on." He removed a pen from a cup on his desk. "This is invisible ink." He marked the bottom of the diamond. "Now we can be absolutely sure it's mine." Then he dropped it into the parcel, next to its machine-made comrades.

Mimi had to admit, she couldn't tell Paul's diamond from the others. She turned away from Paul and shuffled the parcel. She swerved back and showed it to him. "Can you tell which diamond is yours?"

Paul stared at the diamonds for about twenty seconds. Then he picked one out. He reached into his desk drawer again, found a penlight, and flashed it on the stone. He smiled. "Yep. It's mine!"

"Wow," Mimi said. "How'd you do that?"

"It wasn't easy. Visually, they're identical. But I've spent a lot of time with this diamond, so I just kind of knew. This might be a weird analogy, but when my son was born, I remember him sleeping the first night in the hospital nursery. I looked at that big room full of babies, and they all kind of looked the same, and I thought there was no way I could pick out my boy. But the moment I saw him, I knew. Because he meant something to me. Like this diamond does.

"You know how they say certain diamonds speak to you. I've spent so much time with this stone, I guess I heard it talk."

He clicked the pen, and returned the stone to Mimi. "Anyway, the question is not whether I can tell this diamond apart. The question is whether Diamond Superior can."

"Yep." Mimi stuffed the parcel in her purse. "Look, Paul, I really appreciate you doing this. I know it's a gamble, but it's the right thing."

Paul closed his eyes. "It's okay, just—" He ended the sentence there.

As Mimi left with the parcel, Paul stared at it, like he was saying goodbye to an old friend.

CHAPTER TWENTY-SIX

M IMI HAD SEEN HER SHARE OF fancy offices, but Diamond
Superior's New York City office still struck her as over the
top. As she walked to Conrad's office, she noticed that all that venture capital money had gone to good use—if one defines as "good
use" an LED sign in the lobby flashing the word "Superior," a state-
of-the-art fitness center, and a room devoted to foosball.

Mimi wondered what it must be like to work at a place like
that. Her father's office didn't even have a coffee machine. Here,
one device produced macchiatos, and another made cold brew,
and that was just in the reception area. Still, she remembered what
a friend, who'd worked someplace similar, had told her. "It was nice
at first," she said. "Until you realize, they just do that to keep you
there day and night. It's nothing more than a big, beautiful, food-
stocked cage."

An electronic bulletin board in the hallway showed a picture
of Thorble, accompanied by the words, "we will never forget you!"
Underneath, there was an announcement of an upcoming virtual
town hall with Conrad Vanderklef. "Meet the new boss!" it said.

When Mimi reached Conrad's office, she was greeted by the
secretary who she'd spent the prior day harassing. She gave Mimi a
barely disguised look of disgust. Mimi didn't blame her.

The woman ushered Mimi into Conrad's office—which still

had Thorble's name on the door. A portrait of Conrad's father and grandfather—the two architects of Vanderklef—hung on the wall. There was a certain irony to this, since Conrad now headed a company devoted to tearing down what they'd built. Yet it was also fitting, since Vanderklef invented the modern diamond industry, and its shadow still lingered over every aspect of it, from lab-grown to natural. Diamond Superior was still selling Vanderklef's "diamond dream," with a high-tech twist.

Conrad sat on a large leather chair, upright, like it was a throne. His hands glided along the edge of his ornate mahogany desk, which was the size of a small car. His father and grandfather probably sat behind desks like that, and Conrad no doubt dreamt his whole life of sitting behind one, too.

He had hipped up his look, even more than he did for last week's presentation—he was sporting jeans and had wrapped the back of his hair in a ponytail. Still, from his posh South African accent to his regal bearing, his privileged background kept asserting itself—like a gold cufflink peeking out from under a leather jacket. And now that Mimi was viewing Conrad up close, she understood one secret to his picture-perfect good looks: he'd had work done.

"So who is Mimi Rosen," he asked, "and why is she in my office?" He stared at her with his piercing blue eyes—which, she was willing to bet, weren't that color naturally.

Mimi straightened her spine and got down to business. "Eugene Thorble gave me this parcel of diamonds to examine, and I wanted to return it." She placed the pack of synthetics—with the one surreptitious natural—on his desk.

Conrad let out an incredulous laugh. "This is crazy. You went through all that trouble to pretend Raj Shranka was calling, and all you want to do is return a bunch of lab-growns?" He stared at the parcel like she'd dumped a heap of trash on her desk.

"Your former CEO, Eugene Thorble, gave them to me," Mimi said, her voice so cool it surprised her. "I promised him I'd return them. I'm keeping my word. You know, the custom on Forty-Seventh Street: your word is your bond." She raised her hand. The irony wasn't lost on her that, as she said this, she was lying through her teeth.

"I give you credit for honesty, I guess," Conrad said, unaware he was being fed a crock of crap. "That's the problem with this trade—too many outdated traditions." He cast a skeptical glance at the parcel. "I didn't know Eugene gave out samples. That was unlike him." He picked up a loupe and brought one of the diamonds to his eye. "Looks like one of ours. A D Flawless."

Conrad hadn't noticed the natural, but Mimi didn't expect him to. As Paul said, the question was whether someone at his company would.

Conrad placed the stone on his palm, and closed his fist around it. "At my old company, when we discovered a D Flawless at a mine, it was huge news. We'd spend hours arguing which client would be lucky enough to get it. Soon, all those discussions, all those arguments, will be moot. We'll just crank out diamonds like this by the truckload."

He dropped the diamond back in the parcel. As much as he tried to act flip and dismissive, when he spoke about the old days, his face took on a faraway look, and he sounded almost wistful.

"Anyway, you can have this parcel," Mimi said.

"Okay. We'll probably just throw it in the garbage. You sure you don't want it? We'll soon have warehouses of these."

Mimi's gut tightened. Conrad was giving her one more chance to retrieve Paul's twenty-thousand-dollar diamond. Part of her wanted to grab it and leave. But she'd made it this far. She couldn't back out now.

"It's fine," she heard herself say. "So you're releasing the Chrysalis diamonds soon?"

"Our new plan is to start selling them this week."

"And you've cancelled the deal to sell the formula to Vanderklef?"

Conrad inhaled air through his nose. "We're releasing the diamonds this week."

"But why?" Mimi had done lots of pleading to corporate executives lately, to little effect, but figured one more time couldn't hurt.

"You must know that Vanderklef is planning to make your diamonds worthless. Your company can't survive that."

"I disagree," Conrad said. "Newford Ventures is funded by mission-driven billionaires. After Eugene died, they vowed to make Vanderklef pay. They're determined to ride this out."

"But aren't you worried that Raj Shranka might—" Mimi tread carefully here, trying to not accidentally commit a crime. "Say what he knows?"

"As I told you before," Conrad said, "someone tried to blackmail us recently, peddling bogus information about our business practices. That person ended up with egg on his face. I'm not worried about Raj Shranka releasing any so-called dirt. And Vanderklef better be careful. I know their dirty laundry, too. Don't forget whose family found the company."

He pointed to the picture of his father and grandfather. Neither of them were smiling in the portrait; it looked like they only posed for it because they thought it would boost their stock price.

"It's interesting you have that picture there," Mimi said, "Aren't you worried you're destroying their legacy?"

"To the contrary," Conrad said. "I *am* their legacy—me and my daughter, Delphine. My father said many times—in fact, he assured me—I would take over the business. Unfortunately, after members of my family sold their shares in the company, I became the victim of a vicious cabal which spread rumors I was unqualified to become CEO. The fact is, I've had to work twice as hard as everyone else, just to prove my worth. In many ways, my family background has been a handicap."

It took a lot of self-control for Mimi not to roll her eyes at that. Instead, she asked, "Do you feel the people at Vanderklef were fair to you?" Her old editor Lewis once advised her to couch questions in terms of fairness—because nobody in the world feels they've been treated fairly.

Conrad sure didn't. "Of course not. Mind you, I never expected everyone at the company to bow at my feet. However, there should have been some recognition that if not for my family, none of the people there would have jobs. And the things they said about my daughter's designs were abominable. Delphine is quite talented! She shouldn't be treated like a joke!" The more he spoke, the angrier he got, until he began to wave his fists, like a toddler. He must have noticed, because he stopped and took a breath.

"Fortunately, that's all in the past," he said with a sudden, disquieting calm. A wall had gone up. "In retrospect, I wasn't the right fit there. I'm a maverick. I wanted to make Vanderklef a modern company. The old guard didn't see it that way."

"I bet they do now," Mimi said, trying to lead him on.

"One would think, following the Chrysalis formula, they'd have learned not to underestimate me. But no. Yesterday, I had to teach them that lesson again."

Mimi was about to ask what that "lesson" was, but she didn't expect an honest answer, and she was already putting things together. Conrad had just told her that someone had tried to blackmail him, and ended up with "egg on his face." He'd also implied that person was from Vanderklef—probably John Charles Harrington—and that the blackmailing attempt happened "yesterday," which was when Harrington tried to make a deal with Raj Shranka. Harrington had also told Mimi that Shranka could have been paid off by someone else. She also knew that Shranka had been in touch with Conrad.

As Mimi untangled all the threads, Conrad looked on, mystified; at one point, his eyes turned into slits, and he asked, "are you okay?" She didn't respond. She was in the zone.

"Okay," she said finally. "I think I got it. Vanderklef didn't want to give money to a sketchy guy like Shranka. So once they made contact with him, they approached you, and said you either sell them the formula or they'd pay Shranka and get the information about Diamond Superior's offshore dealings. Basically, they tried to blackmail you. But instead, you contacted Shranka and sent him the money you owed him, in return for his silence. And that's why you don't have to worry about him anymore."

Conrad said nothing, but his jaw slackened.

"If I had to guess," Mimi went on, "I'd say Dr. Shranka wanted things to play out that way. Making a deal with you was far safer from his perspective than getting paid by Vanderklef.

"But since you were ignoring him, he had two choices: release the information or walk away. But once he released the information, it would be worthless. So he tried to make a deal with Vanderklef, using me as an intermediary. He probably knew Vanderklef would approach you first. I said I didn't want to be his stooge, but that's exactly what I was. This really is a chess game. Dr. Shranka is the only person thinking three moves ahead. I'm correct, aren't I?"

When Mimi finished, she was quite proud of herself; it had been a long time since she'd connected the dots like that. She wasn't sure what Conrad's reaction would be, but it wasn't the controlled fury that spilled out of him.

"I will not comment—" he said, with gaps between each word, "—on nonsensical allegations. There's a door over there, Miss Rosen. Please use it." He grabbed her parcel of diamonds. "And by the way, we're keeping these."

THAT WAS NOT HOW MIMI WANTED to leave Conrad's office. She might need his help later. She settled on a bench outside the office and compiled her impressions of him. "CV is arrogant," she wrote. "He has a HUGE chip on his shoulder. Yet, he was born a billionaire. He's the last person who should have one!"

She tried to put herself in his shoes. "He sits every day under a picture of his father and grandfather, knowing he'll never live up to their legacies. He clearly feels like he's been underestimated. Even Thorble treated him like trash.

"Overall, he seemed—" She waited for the words to come, and when they did, it surprised her. "Kind of lonely."

CHAPTER TWENTY-SEVEN

T HE MINUTE MIMI RETURNED TO MICHELSON Gemological Associates, Paul pelted her with questions.

"What did Conrad say when you gave him the parcel?" he asked. "Did he notice that one of the diamonds was different?"

"No," Mimi said, glancing down.

"Did he say what he'd do with the parcel?"

Mimi might as well tell him the truth. "He said they're keeping it. But he also said they'll soon have so many D Flawlesses, he might just throw it out."

"Great." Paul sank into his chair. "There goes my twenty-thousand-dollar diamond. I guess there are worse things to lose. Like my entire business. I've already lost that." He expelled a breath. "I can't complain. I let you take that diamond, knowing the risks."

Mimi put her hand on his back. "Let's wait. Maybe they'll call."

"And what should we do in the meantime?" Paul asked.

"We could grab lunch," Mimi said. "I already feel like I've had a full day."

AT A NEARBY DINER, PAUL AND Mimi hammered out the next stage of their plan.

"Diamond Superior must have some kind of testing procedure for items that have been outside their office," Paul said, while picking at his healthy green salad, which made Mimi feel guilty for ordering a cheeseburger. "Otherwise they might take in a cubic zirconia. But I don't know if they have a way to screen out natural diamonds. You'd think they'd want to know which diamonds are theirs."

They decided that if Diamond Superior didn't phone them by the time they finished lunch, Mimi would call them. They resolved to enjoy their meal and not worry about it—though Mimi couldn't resist sneaking glances at her phone to see if they'd called.

With work talk out of the way, Paul asked Mimi about her past investigations. This surprised her, since he wasn't a fan while she was doing them. Now, he apparently found them fascinating.

"You should write about them," Paul said. "You've certainly had an exciting life."

"Yes. Sometimes too exciting," Mimi said.

"I remember, even as a kid, you were adventurous. It drove your parents nuts."

"God," Mimi said. "Nothing's changed. My father still worries about me all the time."

Paul dabbed at his chin with his napkin. "I understand where he's coming from. I'm a neurotic mess with everything regarding my daughter."

"You also didn't like me investigating," Mimi said. She was possibly treading on taboo territory here, as that was why they ultimately stopped seeing each other.

"I didn't?" Paul said. "That sounds like me. I prefer to play it safe in life. The one time I tried to pull something—. Well, you know." That was another allusion to his grading scandal, and he became flustered after he said it, like he didn't understand why he'd brought that up. "The point is, I don't need any more anxieties. I have an impressive enough collection as it is."

Mimi laughed. "Me, too."

Paul put his elbows on the table. "Yet you investigate. I can't imagine anything scarier than tracking down a murderer. Doesn't it scare you?"

"Of course it does." Mimi speared a fry with her fork. "It can be terrifying. But when I hear about horrible things happening, I get so upset, I have to do something. And before I know it, I'm in so deep I can't get out."

"I admire that," Paul said. "I wish I had that kind of courage."

Mimi couldn't think of two more different men than Paul and Michael. Michael rarely revealed any weakness; Paul almost reveled in his. Paul wore his smarts on his sleeve; Michael hid his under layers of gruff.

They finished their food and Mimi checked her watch. "It's been an hour and a half, and Diamond Superior still hasn't called. I guess I'll have to call them."

FIVE MINUTES LATER, THEY WERE BACK at Paul's lab, shaking off their after-lunch fog. Before she called Conrad, Mimi reviewed her notes. He was obviously a person who wanted to be addressed in a certain way, and took umbrage when he wasn't.

Finally, she settled on her approach. "Him: 'Mr. Important.' Me: 'Damsel-in-distress.'" The idea made her queasy, but she figured it would work with Mr. With-the-Times Maverick.

The minute he picked up, she tried to sound upset. "Conrad, this is Mimi Rosen. I desperately need your help."

"Well, that's too bad," Conrad snorted. "Perhaps you should have thought of that before you made all sorts of wild charges in my office."

"I'm sorry about that," Mimi said. "I only said those things because I was so intimidated by you. Everyone told me how clever you were."

"Who is 'everyone'?" Conrad asked.

"Everyone!" Mimi said. "Even John Charles Harrington told me he'd underestimated you."

"He did?"

"Yes," Mimi said, knowing she had struck gold. "Though of course he'd never admit that to you."

"Of course not," Conrad said. "He has too big an ego."

"I think this Chrysalis thing has really humbled him," Mimi said. "He's made the wrong move at every turn, first by letting you leave the company, then by trying to blackmail you. He told me he's had a lot of low moments. And he's been drinking a lot."

"That's not surprising." Conrad was almost giddy. "That's part of that old-time Vanderklef culture. That's why they hated me. I wasn't part of their old boys club."

"I know that. You're more down to Earth. You're willing to help people. That's why I'm reaching out to you."

Conrad breathed out noisily, but didn't interrupt her.

"I really hate to bother you," she said. "You're CEO of a super-important company. I can't imagine how stressful that is and how busy you must be. I just need this small favor."

"Okay." Conrad gave an exasperated sigh. "What is it?"

"That parcel I gave you contained one natural diamond. Paul Michelson wanted to see if he could tell the difference between that and the others, and I accidentally included it in that parcel. And now he's beside himself and wants that diamond back. You can keep the other stones, but that one's really valuable. He paid twenty thousand dollars for it." She considered fake-sobbing, but didn't think she could pull that off.

"Well," Conrad cut in quickly, "he won't get twenty thousand for it now. Not in this market. And not next week when we flood the market with our product."

"I know that. And so does Paul. But it has sentimental value for him. He'd really like it back."

"I don't have that parcel anymore," Conrad said. "I gave it to my gemological department."

Interesting, Mimi thought. *He didn't throw the parcel out, like he said he would. He also understood why Paul would want that diamond back.*

"Can I talk to someone in that department? It would mean a lot."

"I'll have my guy there call you."

"That would be amazing. I can't thank you enough. You're the best!" Mimi worried she was laying it on thick, but Conrad was buying it.

"It's fine," said Conrad, exuding a fatherly calm. "I'll have them call you."

Conrad hadn't denied that it was possible to distinguish the natural diamond from the others. That was good.

AFTER ANOTHER EXCRUCIATING WAIT—ABOUT TWENTY MIN-UTES—MIMI received a call from the head of Diamond Superior's gemological department. "Miss Rosen," said a New York-accented voice that sounded like it had smoked too many cigarettes. "Sorry to say, we can't return your parcel. We added all the diamonds to our inventory. They're now mixed in with the others."

Mimi's heart sank.

"However, we spotted that mined diamond you were looking for. We were surprised to find it there. We don't see many of them around here, especially such a high-quality stone."

Mimi tried not to act too excited. "Thanks. That's a relief. I didn't know if we would get it back. I'd heard you couldn't tell the Chrysalis diamonds from naturals."

"It ain't easy, but we got a way. Our machine flagged it as 'old.' We'll messenger it over to you."

"Great, thank you so much." She asked the next question carefully. "What machine flagged it?"

"It's a standard—" His voice gained an edge. "Hey, lady. That's our intellectual property. I'm not allowed to talk about that."

"I was just wondering—"

"Wonder all you want. I ain't saying nothing. I'll send your diamond over later today." He hung up.

Mimi turned to Paul. "Good news. We're getting your diamond back. Diamond Superior flagged it as natural. That means they could tell them apart."

Paul shook his head, amazed. "Wow."

Mimi called John Charles Harrington, and put Paul and Zeke on speakerphone.

"Quite a caper you've pulled off there," Harrington said, a chuckle in his voice. "Though I'm afraid it doesn't get us any closer to being able to detect those diamonds."

"But we know that it's possible," Mimi said. "That should calm the trade down, don't you think?"

"Not really," Harrington said. "I'll just end up in the same situation I was in last week at the diamond bourse, when I announced we had a solution to this crisis, but couldn't say what it was. As a result, no one gave my statements any credence. If we state that a detection method exists, but we don't know what it is, I don't expect that will be any better received. What we need is a real solution."

"We're working hard to find one, Mr. Harrington," Paul said.

"Have you made any progress?" Harrington said.

"We've developed an AI program," Paul stammered. "Tell him about it, Zeke."

"It analyzes diamond composition using machine learning and advanced analytics," Zeke said.

"That all sounds lovely," Harrington said. "But has this advanced-learning gizmo produced anything concrete? If it had, I assume you would have mentioned that at the start of this call. Correct?"

"Yes, but we know a solution exists!" Mimi said. "Can't you give us time to find it? Please." Mimi didn't want to haul out the damsel-in-distress routine again, but she would, if she had to.

"We can't, I'm afraid," Harrington said. "My board of directors is already unhappy that our agreed-upon strategy has been postponed. They feel the more it's delayed, the less effective it will be. They believe it's time to tear off the bandage."

"On the other hand," Mimi said, "once you destroy the industry there's no going back."

Harrington waited a beat before he responded. "You have one more day."

"One more day?" Paul was aghast. "How are we supposed to find an answer to this in twenty-four hours?"

"That's twenty-four more hours than you have now," Harrington said. "You don't have to take it."

Mimi remembered Kabir Mehta saying Vanderklef's attitude was always "take it or leave it." Harrington was strong-arming them, and like Kabir, they had no choice but to accept his terms.

"We'll take it!" Mimi said. "*Mazal!*"

Harrington uttered a noncommittal grunt and clicked off.

Paul looked miserable. "I've been working on this problem all week. How am I supposed to find the answer in a day?"

Paul's defeatism was starting to grate on Mimi. They'd never make any progress if they sat around moping.

"Okay," she declared. "Let's not look at this as a science thing. Think of it as a mystery. We have a clue. The guy who flagged the diamond told me it was 'old.' And he said they tested it with a 'standard' machine. What could that mean?"

"Nothing, probably," Zeke said. "All natural diamonds are old. They were formed billions of years ago."

"Right," Mimi said. "My father always said that's the difference between lab diamonds and regular ones. Mined diamonds were formed before the dinosaurs, and synthetics were grown a few weeks ago in a lab." She thought a bit. "Paul, when you detect lab-grown diamonds, what do you look for?"

"Indicators of the production method."

"Right. You determine *how* the diamonds are made. But do you look at *when* they were made?"

Paul was baffled. "How would we do that?"

"Aren't there devices that determine how old things are?"

"Sure," Zeke said. "There's carbon daters."

Mimi smacked her fist on her hand. "That's perfect! Diamonds are made of carbon!"

"Just a second." Paul thrust out his hands. "It's not that simple. Diamonds are billions of years old. Carbon dating only estimates the date of objects going back a few thousand years."

"Right," Mimi said. "But we don't need the exact time, just a ballpark estimate. The question is, could a carbon dating machine tell the difference between something produced billions of years ago and something produced in the last month?"

Paul and Zeke gazed at each other.

"It's possible," Zeke said. "You'd have to re-engineer the machine so it could tell the difference between a diamond that's recently formed, and one that's—"

"Old!" Mimi called out. "We need a carbon dating machine!"

"Oh, sure," Paul said. "Let's get a carbon dater. I bet they sell them at Home Depot."

"Maybe we can call a research institute," Mimi said.

"I have a friend who can get one," Zeke said.

Mimi and Paul turned their heads.

"You know somebody who could get us a carbon dating machine?" Paul stared at Zeke like he was insane. "We'll need it by tomorrow."

"Probably," Zeke said. "He can get almost anything. He's gotten me tons of stuff over the years. Should I ask him?"

"Why not?" Mimi said.

Zeke typed on his laptop. A minute later, he received a response. "He said he can get you a carbon dater tomorrow if you Venmo him twenty-five thousand dollars."

"He can?" Paul's eyes looked ready to pop out of his head. "Who is this guy?"

"Just someone I met on a subreddit," Zeke said. "MisterBoogerEater."

"His name is MisterBoogerEater?" Paul said.

"That's his Reddit handle," Zeke said. "I don't think it's his real name."

"I got that," Paul said. "You think I should send twenty-five thousand dollars to a guy named MisterBoogerEater?"

"Don't worry!" Zeke said. "I've done tons of deals with him. He and I go way back. We're like the court jesters of that subreddit. Whenever we start up, people say, 'there goes MisterBoogerEater and Yarmulkedude again.'"

"Your Reddit name is Yarmulkedude?" Mimi asked.

Zeke flushed and he looked at his shoes.

Paul aimed his eyes at Zeke. "Let me be clear. If I send this guy twenty-five thousand dollars, that'll eat up most of the lab's remaining funds. So if this doesn't work, I'll have to let you go. Are you okay with that?"

"I guess so," Zeke said quietly.

Paul paced the floor, his face creased and anxious. Mimi tried to remember if he was this tightly-wound and neurotic as a child.

"Mimi, do you think I should do this?" Paul asked. "Give twenty-five thousand dollars to the booger guy?"

"That's up to you," Mimi said.

Paul let loose a long sigh. "I already took one totally insane risk today, when I gave you the one-carat diamond."

"True," Mimi said with a satisfied smile. "And that turned out okay."

"Yeah," said Paul. "I got lucky once today. I shouldn't press my luck. Zeke, tell the guy weren't not interested."

"No!" Mimi screamed. "Zeke, do not tell him that. Send him the money. We need that machine."

"You just said it's up to me!" Paul protested.

"That was when I thought you were going to make the right decision. Not the wrong one."

Paul threw up his hands. "I've had one longshot gamble pan out today. People don't win the lottery twice in a row. How many times has that happened?"

"I don't know," Mimi said. "But—"

"Sixteen times!" Zeke said, lifting his face from his laptop.

Paul turned to him. "What?"

"I just checked. At least sixteen people have hit the lottery twice."

"Where'd you read that?" Paul asked.

"It's on Quora. The source is—" Zeke checked his laptop. "UselessFactsTony."

Paul smacked his forehead. "Great. My business' fate is in the hands of MisterBoogerEater and UselessFactsTony."

"Think about it," Mimi said. "If you don't do this, what's the likelihood of you and Zeke coming up with a detection technique in twenty-four hours?"

Paul's mouth turned into a semicircle. "Zero."

"Right," Mimi said. "Either way, the odds are against you. What have you got to lose?"

"Twenty-five thousand dollars!" Paul exclaimed. "Which I actually need right now. And, as I made super-clear to you at lunch, I don't like taking risks. My biggest gamble was starting this lab."

"That turned out well," Mimi said.

"Until last week, when it collapsed!" Paul said.

"Think of all the work you put into this place," Mimi said. "All the late nights, all the stress. You told me you'd have done anything not to fire your staff. This could bring them back. Come on. We have no choice."

"It's amazing, Mimi. I never have a choice except to do exactly what you want." Paul plopped into his chair, wiped and defeated. "All right. Send the money!" He reached into his wallet, pulled out a credit card, and handed it to Zeke. "This is completely insane, you know that? And Mimi, I'm insane to listen to you."

"The most important thing is that you listened," she said.

Zeke typed on his iPad. "Okay. The carbon dater's been ordered. It should arrive tomorrow."

Paul turned to Mimi. "What will we do until then?"

"Wait," Mimi said.

CHAPTER TWENTY-EIGHT

T HE NEXT MORNING, MIMI WAS BACK at work, listening to her
father grumble that no one was buying the diamonds he'd
posted online. "I'm offering them at such stupid prices," he griped.
"The problem is everyone else's prices are stupider."

"You haven't sold anything?" Mimi asked.

"I did make one nice-sized sale to a dealer in Florida," Max said.
"His business is okay because his customers are rich old ladies who
don't watch the news."

Just then, Mimi received a text from Paul. "We got it!"

Mimi was so excited, she started typing a reply, then decided
it would be better to just call. "You figured out the detection
technique?"

Paul laughed. "No. Not even close. But we did get two things.
Yesterday, I got my diamond back, which was nice. And this
morning we received the carbon dating machine. So hooray for
MisterBoogerEater!"

"Great!" Mimi said. "Does it work?"

"I think so. The instructions are really complicated. For twenty-five thousand dollars, you'd think they'd make this thing easier to use. We're still figuring it out, and haven't tested if it can
detect synthetics. We have a few lab-growns here. Do you have any
others?"

"Sure." She opened her desk drawer. Four lab-grown D Flawlesses stared up at her. "I'll bring them over."

"Okay," Paul said. "Though if Channah comes with you, it could be a problem. I need Zeke focused."

Mimi chuckled. "How about I wait until Channah's on the phone and sneak out of the office then?"

"Perfect!" Paul said. "And don't tell Zeke you came from your father's office. Just tell him you came from—" He thought for a second. "—anyplace else."

"Okay," Mimi laughed.

Before she left, she remembered she'd found another diamond in Dr. Shranka's hotel room—that odd-looking green. She stuffed it in her purse.

WHEN MIMI ARRIVED AT THE LAB, she found Paul and Zeke crouched before the carbon-dater. It was about the size of a file cabinet, and towered over them both. Its translucent top showed a mess of tubes and multi-colored wires. Under that was a sea of buttons, which Paul fiddled with while consulting the manual. Zeke's eyes were glued to the laptop perched on his knee.

"How's it going?" Mimi asked.

"Not bad," Paul said, turning away from the machine. "It can tell us if a diamond was formed under the Earth, or 'old,' as Diamond Superior put it. But we still don't know if it'll give a different reading for the synthetics. We're about to test that."

"Here's some samples." Mimi took out her parcel of D Flawlesses.

Paul picked up one of the diamonds, and with trembling hands, passed it to Zeke. "This is the moment of truth."

"Yes, the moment of destiny," said Zeke, as he took the diamond and placed it under a lens. "The fate of the diamond industry depends on what happens next."

Paul gave him an exasperated look. "Zeke, please!"

Zeke flicked a switch. He consulted the bare-bones program running on his laptop which showed a continually updating stream of numbers.

"What's it say?" Paul asked impatiently.

Zeke beamed. "That it's recent."

Paul's brow wrinkled. "That's what we want, right?"

"I think so," said Zeke. "All the natural stones read as older. That means the machine can tell the difference."

Paul cried out, "woo-hoo!" and gave Zeke a high-five. Mimi cheered, too. Then the room turned quiet, as the three of them absorbed what just happened. The past week had been filled with chaos and uncertainty. Now they had a chance to return things to normal. That was a massive accomplishment. It barely felt real.

She stared at the synthetic diamond lying in the machine. Now that it could be identified, she no longer found it threatening. It was, in fact, beautiful—a miracle of science, in the same way regular diamonds are a miracle of nature.

Paul quickly sobered up, and his innate nervousness took over. He insisted they test the entire parcel. It was only after he tested each and every Shranka diamond—and another six naturals—that he finally exhaled.

"My God," he said, gripping his skull. "This works. We cracked it. Zeke, can you write some software that will turn this thing into a simple synthetic detector?"

"Sure. It might take a while."

Paul's face tensed. "How long?"

"I don't know," Zeke said. "Six hours, maybe."

Paul burst into a delighted grin. "Six hours! That's nothing!"

Paul called John Charles Harrington, who was just as excited.

"Wonderful news," he said. "You should give a presentation on this as soon as possible. I'll arrange with the Jewelry Expo to have you deliver one tomorrow." Harrington even pledged to stand on stage introducing him—a huge vote of confidence.

"All right," Paul said to Zeke and Mimi. "We have about a day to put this presentation together. Just to be clear. We've tested all the synthetics, right?"

"Hold it," Mimi said. "I have one more." She reached in her purse and pulled out the strange green.

Paul was riveted by it. "Wow. That's the oddest-looking green stone I've ever seen." He examined it with a loupe. "There's no question it's man-made. You'd never find a color like that in nature." He passed it to Zeke. "All right. Test it."

Zeke placed it on the machine. He squinted at the readout.

"It says it's synthetic, right?" Paul asked.

"No." Zeke blinked at the screen. "It came back 'undetermined.' It's made from a different material from the others. It has a mix of carbon, instead of a single source. That makes it harder to judge."

"All the other diamonds passed the test," Mimi said. "One 'undetermined' is no big deal, right?"

"No! It's huge!" Paul said. "It can potentially disprove our whole hypothesis. A system like this is only as strong as its weakest link. This brings us back to, well, not exactly square one, but close. Because all Diamond Superior has to do is make diamonds using this different material, and then—"

"The machine will say 'undetermined,'" Zeke said.

Mimi marveled at how Zeke and Paul finished each other's sentences. They were like a geeky married couple.

"There's something different about this green." Paul took it out of the machine and stared at it. "Shranka might have been testing a new recipe. He made those other diamonds from peanuts, which is why they registered as new. But the device says this one includes other organic material."

"Maybe you shouldn't mention the green in your presentation," Mimi said.

"I could," Paul said. "But I'm a scientist. I have to be honest about what I've found. Whether people like it or not."

Mimi's heart swelled. She loved that answer.

Paul settled back in his chair, clutching the green. "I don't want to underestimate what we've discovered. We've made a significant gemological breakthrough. Unfortunately, it doesn't tell us how to spot every last one of these stones. Still, we'll have plenty to talk about tomorrow."

Paul and Zeke began preparing the presentation. Mimi enjoyed watching them type on their laptops, so focused and intent, their fingers dancing on the keys. She was glad Paul was announcing this publicly. That might help "smoke out" Dr. Shranka. Though—

Crap. It all came back to her. She had to tell them.

"Um, guys," she said. "About the presentation tomorrow. There's something you should know."

"Is it important?" Paul said, not happy about being interrupted.

"Very. Remember I told you I spoke to Dr. Shranka in his virtual factory? He told me anyone who tries to find a detection method for his diamonds will be—" She gulped. "Killed."

Zeke and Paul stopped working and stared at her.

"What did he mean?" asked Zeke.

"I think we know what 'killed' means, Zeke," Paul said. "Was he serious?"

"I don't know," Mimi said. "Probably not, but—"

Paul's eyes stretched open. "But this guy actually killed someone, right?"

"Yes, he did," Mimi said, flustered. "Just one person, though."

"Killing one person is a lot!" Paul said. "That's more than most people! Do you think he'll try and hurt us?"

"I don't know," Mimi said softly.

"If you don't mind," Zeke said, "I'd rather not participate in tomorrow's presentation. Not because of me. Because of Channah. We all know what happened to her first fiancé. I wouldn't want anything like that to happen to her again. Not that I think it will, but I can't take the chance. I'm sorry."

"That's perfectly understandable," Mimi said. She turned to Paul. "And how about you?"

"I don't know," Paul said. "What do you think?"

"It's up to you," Mimi said.

Paul rolled his eyes. "All right, Mimi, let's not play this game. Seriously, what should I do?"

"I can't say. Really! I can't make decisions about your personal safety. I don't think you'll have a problem, but I can't guarantee it.

Maybe someone else can give the presentation. Do you know any gemologists who are good at self-defense?"

"Oh yeah," Paul said. "Gemology's full of black belts." He kneaded his temples. "No. I have to give the presentation. I already told John Charles Harrington I would. It's the only thing that will save my lab." He shook his head ruefully. "I've already made two stupid decisions in the last twenty-four hours. I might as well make three. It's amazing what you get me into, Mimi."

"How about this?" said Mimi. "I'll call Michael. He can act as security during the presentation."

"That should help," Paul said. "And if it doesn't, say nice things about me at my funeral."

MIMI LEFT PAUL'S LAB, EXCITED AND anxious. They'd discovered a way to detect the Chrysalis diamonds—most of them, anyway. Yet she still worried about Dr. Shranka. His threats were probably bluffs. If he was logical, he'd be far away. Mimi wasn't sure he was all that logical.

As she walked to her father's office, she called Michael, and asked him to serve as security for the presentation.

He agreed to do it, though not without grumbling. "If it's during the day, it won't interfere with my schedule."

Relief washed over Mimi. "Great. It's being held tomorrow, two p.m., at the Omnichannel Hotel."

"I'll be there. With my gun."

This brought Mimi up short. "You don't need a gun."

"If someone's making threats, I'm bringing a gun," Michael asserted, like he was eager for this argument. "How do you expect me to stop this guy? By pulling his hair?"

"No, it's just—" When Mimi and Michael started the detective agency, he'd advised Mimi to buy a gun and take shooting lessons. She refused. She didn't grow up around guns, and had seen one too many during her investigations. She couldn't imagine owning a firearm—never mind using one. She wondered if Michael had suggested that to test her, to see if she really had what it took to be a detective. Eventually, he dropped the subject, as it was clear the agency wasn't going anywhere anyway.

Mimi had never liked Michael carrying a gun when he was a police officer, and was relieved when he stopped post-retirement. Now, he wanted to bring a gun back into their lives. She didn't think he needed one at Paul's session, but knew he'd insist on it, and it wasn't worth arguing about.

"Do what you need to," she said.

"I will," Michael said. "It's been a long time since I carried, but—" He paused. "It'll be fine. Hopefully, there won't be trouble. Oh, and they just delivered the things Shranka left in his hotel room. There's some diamonds, some machines, and a lot of clothes."

"Okay, good," Mimi said. "Can you ship the diamonds and machines to my friend Paul?"

"No problem."

"All right. Then we're set." Mimi had reached her father's building, but paused before she entered. "So, what do you think? Will it be okay tomorrow?"

"Look, a threat's a threat. You can't just blow it off. You know this case and the people involved. What's your sense?"

"I don't know. I *think* it'll be okay, but I've learned not to underestimate Dr. Shranka."

"There's your answer," Michael said.

CHAPTER TWENTY-NINE

After Mimi returned to the office, she received an Instagram message from Raj Shranka's sister, Vashti. Last week, Vashti Shranka had blocked Mimi. Apparently, the ban had been lifted.

"I just got a call from the New York City police," Vashti wrote. "They said my brother is missing and wanted for murder. They even showed me an article about it. Is that true?"

"I'm afraid so," Mimi replied.

Vashti didn't write back, so Mimi tried to restart the conversation. "We should talk."

Again, there was no response. Mimi figured she shouldn't push it. That turned out to be the right call. A half-hour later, Vashti wrote back, "ok."

That night, over Zoom, Mimi met Vashti.

She had long black hair, smooth skin, and well-situated cheekbones. She was dressed in a business suit, and was accessorized with dangling earrings and perfectly-applied makeup. It was five-thirty in the morning in India, and Mimi wondered if Vashti had dolled herself up for this call. There was a little bit of her brother in her face, particularly her eyes, which radiated a fierce intelligence. She told Mimi she worked as a financial analyst.

"So this police officer from America told me that Raj is a—what did he call it? A 'person of interest' in a murder. Is that true?"

"Unfortunately, yes," Mimi said.

Vashti looked mystified. "They said a witness saw him push somebody off a roof. I told them, that person is either lying or crazy."

Mimi decided this was not the time to mention that she saw Raj Shranka toss Eugene Thorble off the Chelsea Piers T-Pod.

"Raj was not the kind of person to hurt anyone. Even if he wanted to, he couldn't."

"Why not?" Mimi said.

Vashti took a sorrowful breath. "This isn't something that Raj likes me talking about, but I guess I have to. When Raj was a boy, he had this beginner's science kit. He did every project in it. Then he started doing experiments using household products. And he wasn't always careful. What do you expect? He was nine.

"Anyway, one time, he mixed two chemicals together, and they blew up. He lost two fingers on his left hand and damaged the nerves in his left arm and leg. Even now, he moves very slow. He's certainly not strong enough to throw someone off a roof."

What Vashti said made no sense. The person on the roof had no issues with his arms or legs.

"Really?" Mimi asked.

"Yes, *really*!" Vashti snapped. "What do you think, I make up things about my brother losing fingers? The police were surprised, too. They have this idea that he attacked his boss in his hotel room. They said no one saw him leave the hotel, so they think he went down the fire escape. I asked, 'how could he do that, with his bad arm and leg?' They had no answer, of course.

"I believe he was kidnapped by one of the other lab-grown companies. They all know how good he is, and they keep trying to hire him, and he always blows them off. So lately, they've been bothering me.

"I tell them, they're wasting their time. Raj is done with diamonds. He's worked for KM for nine months and accomplished everything he set out to do. He told his boss he was quitting after this conference."

"Interesting." Mimi wrote this down. "Do you have any sense of where your brother is? Have you heard from him?"

"No."

"Has he talked to any other members of your family?"

"There is no other family. It's just me and him. Our mother died when we were young, and our father died last year. That's why we have always been so close."

"And he has no girlfriend, or—?"

"No," Vashti said. "I wish he did. But he doesn't. As far as I know, he doesn't have any friends. Unless you count his computers and his chemicals."

"I've heard he was quiet," Mimi said.

"Yes, always," Vashti said. "Since he was a boy. It got worse after our mother died. He was just eight years old and they were very close. And then after his accident, he became even more withdrawn, because he was so embarrassed about his hand and slow walk. It's been—" She turned her eyes down. "Very difficult. For him, and for me.

"Basically, his whole life is science. He's always tinkering and making things. He built me a television. I mean, who builds a television? Our father used to say that he loved his engineering projects so much one day he'd turn into one. He's so shy it comes off as rudeness sometimes. But he isn't. He has a good soul. It's just hard for him to connect with people."

Good soul? The person Mimi spoke to didn't seem to have a soul, never mind a good one.

"Anyway," Vashti said, "if you find him, let me know. I'm getting worried."

Mimi inhaled. "I spoke to your brother a few days ago."

"You did?" Vashti sat up in her chair. "Why didn't you tell me? Is he still in New York?"

"I don't know. He didn't say where he was. We didn't talk face to face. It was on a virtual reality headset."

"And what did he tell you?"

"That he was on the run because of the murder."

"He said that to you? Seriously?" Vashti narrowed her eyes, like she was trying to assess Mimi through the computer screen.

"Yes. It was a very unsettling call. He wanted my help getting money for his formula. And he threatened to kill anyone who tried to detect his diamonds."

Vashti's face curdled. "That doesn't sound like Raj at all. My brother would never hurt people, and he doesn't care about money."

"Are you sure?"

"Completely sure!" Vashti said. "People would give Raj checks, and he'd forget to cash them. The person you're describing wasn't my brother. I know it."

"I understand you might think that," Mimi said, choosing her words with care. "But people are complex. I've been close to certain people in my life, like my ex-husband, and later discovered I didn't know them as well as I thought." She waited while Vashti absorbed this. "I know you love your brother. But maybe he has facets you don't know about. I found him extremely intimidating."

Vashti's eyebrows rammed together and she leaned into the camera. "Listen to me. There's no one in the world who knows Raj better than me. He would never threaten anyone, he would never hurt anyone, and he would certainly never kill anyone. I'm one-hundred percent sure of that."

Vashti could be lying. She may also be protecting her brother. She might even be in cahoots with him. Yet the way she declared her confidence in her brother's character—with zero hesitation and fire in her eyes—made Mimi sure, too.

CHAPTER THIRTY

MIMI WOKE UP EARLY THE NEXT morning, having barely slept the night before. Paul's presentation was scheduled for two p.m. that afternoon. Mimi was so nervous, she barely ate breakfast.

On her morning commute, Mimi wrestled with whether to tell her father about yesterday's breakthrough. She decided to let him learn about it that afternoon, with the rest of the industry. He'd already taken too many rides on this rollercoaster.

Still, Mimi wanted to tell him. She hadn't lost that reporters' instinct to blast out news as soon as possible, watch people's reactions to it, and luxuriate in the fact that she found out first. When she got to the office—and saw Channah sitting at the front desk with an unmistakable frown—she knew that keeping this secret would be a burden.

"Are you okay?" Mimi asked Channah.

"Not really," she replied. "Zeke slept at Paul's lab last night, because he was working on their presentation. I know you think that we're codependent or whatever, but that's the first night we've been apart since our wedding, and—"

"No, Channah. I get it. I believe this will be over soon. I don't think he'll be pulling many more all-nighters."

"I hope not. I need good news. You haven't been around here much lately. It's so depressing. Everyone is walking around, like they're at a *shiva*. Even the delivery guys look sad. And your father is so upset. He tries to act like he isn't, but I've worked with him for a long time. I can tell."

"Really?"

"How could he not be? He's closing his business after fifty years. And now he's speaking to a real estate agent about selling his house."

Max had said he wanted to put his home on the market, but hearing he was talking to a real estate agent still shocked Mimi. "Channah, buzz me in, right now!"

Channah did so and Mimi rushed to Max's desk. "Dad, are you talking with a real estate agent?"

"Yes," Max said. "That's generally what you do when you sell your house."

"I know." Mimi felt a sudden rush of emotion. "I'm just surprised. That's where I grew up."

"No kidding. You think I want to sell that place? I've lived there forty years. That house is filled with memories. All those good times with your mother. I can still picture you girls running down the halls."

Max's face sagged. "But my business is closing and I'll need the money. Honestly, I should have closed this place years ago. I had considered retiring before your mother got sick. But after she passed, I thought, I gotta keep working. What else am I going to do?"

"Well," Mimi said, "I'm glad you kept it going. I've enjoyed working here."

"You did?" Max suddenly looked sheepish. "I always thought you only came in for the salary."

"At the beginning, sure. But I wouldn't have worked here three years just for the money. You don't pay that well." Mimi smiled to make sure Max knew she was joking. "Anyway, this is a nice place to work."

"Yeah, it *was*," Max said.

Max looked so down when he said this, the dam just burst. "Dad, I wasn't going to say anything," Mimi said, "but Paul Michelson's giving a presentation today, where he'll announce a solution to the Chrysalis crisis."

"Yeah, I heard something about that," said Max.

"Dad, aren't you excited? They can detect these diamonds. The crisis is over."

"I guess. There's been so much back and forth on this thing, I don't know what to believe. And Paul Michelson doesn't have the best reputation."

"That's because of things that happened a long time ago. I know for a fact, Paul's a person of complete integrity."

"I guess we'll see."

"I can't believe you're not more excited about this," Mimi said. "If there's a way to detect these diamonds, you can stay in business. You won't have to sell your house."

Max squinted at her. "Mimi, do you really think, after all this chaos, all this craziness, everything will go back to normal?"

"It could," Mimi hedged.

"Take it from an old man," Max said. "Life doesn't work that way."

A LITTLE LATER, MIMI RECEIVED A CALL from Paul. He sounded shaken.

"Last night, they delivered the diamond maker from Shranka's hotel room to my office," he said. "And we discovered it was rigged. We're wondering if Dr. Shranka did that deliberately, to hurt us."

"What do you mean, 'rigged'?" Mimi asked.

"There was a hole in one of the tubes," said Paul. "If we tried to produce diamonds by pumping methane through that tube, we could have been killed. Methane is not only toxic, it's odorless. Luckily, we caught it before it caused any problems, but it looks like it was done deliberately, to hurt us."

"That's crazy," said Mimi. "But that might not have been aimed at you. That diamond maker has been sitting in Shranka's hotel room for at least a week. I guess he could have snuck in and made a hole in one of the tubes, but he'd be taking quite a risk."

"Well, however that hole got in there, it's got me and Zeke pretty shook up."

"I'm sure. Are you still going to do the presentation?"

"I have to," Paul said. "Vanderklef expects a huge audience. And don't get me wrong, we're happy we got that device, it's given us a ton of insight into Shranka's production process. I've had to rewrite the entire presentation. Again!"

"Did you figure out the issue with the green diamond?"

"No," Paul said. "It still comes up 'undetermined.' And John Charles Harrington told me to not talk about the green during the presentation. He thought it would undercut our main message. So we're leaving it out."

Mimi was surprised to hear that, given Paul's passionate ode to "scientific honesty" the day before—which sparked her equally passionate defense of his character that morning. "I thought you were mentioning it," she mumbled.

"I *wanted* to," Paul said. "I argued strongly that we should. But Vanderklef is paying the bills. They're even reimbursing me for the carbon dater. So I can't really buck them on this. Besides, it's not like I'll be lying. I just won't mention it. It's more of a white lie, or a lie of omission.

"Anyway, I'm risking my life giving this presentation. I'd rather not risk my livelihood, too." He paused. "You get that, right?"

Mimi forgot how defensive Paul could get. She understood where he was coming from, but couldn't help but feel disappointed. "Yeah, sure," she said. "And don't worry about your safety. We'll have Michael standing guard, and I'll be coming over soon. You'll be fine. You're not nervous, are you?"

"I wouldn't call myself relaxed," Paul said.

As MIMI WALKED TO THE HOTEL, she spotted a small black blip moving across the sky. She initially considered it a random object that had nothing to do with her, until it moved lower. It was a drone, like the one that visited her apartment. It had the same glass eye, the same propeller hands.

She tried to ignore it, but then it moved lower again. It was now hovering a few feet over her head, close enough that she could hear it buzz. She began to walk faster. The drone sped up, too. When she crossed the street, the drone crossed with her. As she stood waiting for a traffic light to change, it lingered overhead, in perfect sync. Whatever eye it had, was trained on her.

What did it want? To make another delivery? She'd heard about drones that assassinate people, and didn't know if this one could. She didn't want to find out.

Her heart clanged in her chest, her throat grew tighter, and the back of her shirt became bathed in sweat. She thought about calling the police, but what could they do? Shoot it down?

Mimi ducked into a Starbucks, panting and out of breath. The drone couldn't follow her inside, but loitered patiently outside the door, her own flying stalker. She went to the counter and bought a granola bar, hoping the drone would go away. When she returned, it was still there. She gobbled down the granola bar, then checked her watch. Paul's presentation was in fifteen minutes. She needed to get to the hotel.

She walked outside, and called to the drone, "what do you want?" It flew directly over her. A panel opened and a small box dropped out and landed at her feet. Mimi stared at it, not sure what to do. The drone hovered over her, until Mimi picked up the package. Then it flew away, again becoming a small dot.

Mimi took the square brown box into the Starbucks. She knew she probably shouldn't open it, but given its size, she had a pretty good idea what was inside.

As before, it contained an oversized lab-grown diamond and a loupe. She put the loupe to her eye, and peered into the diamond. And there, through the magic of holography, was Dr. Raj Shranka, standing in front of a fuzzy background.

"I'm recording this because I need to apologize," he said, speaking haltingly. He sounded very different from the nerdy scientist on the instructional video, or the threatening psychopath on the VR headset. He didn't show any signs of limited mobility or missing fingers, though it was hard to tell.

"In my desire to get credit for my accomplishments, I went too far. I never intended to kill people. Now I must pay for what I've done. Shortly after you get this, I will end my life. Do not search for me. I cannot be found. Tell my family I'm sorry. Goodbye."

Mimi watched the video several times, then stuffed the diamond in her purse and left the Starbucks. She hurried to the hotel, sneaking occasional glances at the sky, which was refreshingly drone-free. She was disturbed by Shranka's video, but also puzzled by it. Shranka had mentioned "people" that he'd killed. From what Mimi knew, he'd only killed one—Thorble. He also mentioned his "family." Vashti said she was his only living relative.

Maybe those were just mistakes made by a man under pressure. But what made Mimi truly uneasy was the way the video wrapped up everything in a neat little bow. It felt too neat. As her father said, life didn't work that way.

CHAPTER THIRTY-ONE

P AUL'S SESSION—TITLED "THE CHRYSALIS CRISIS IS OVER!"— drew a huge crowd, enough to fill the several-hundred-seat auditorium where Diamond Superior held its presentation. Except this time, when people entered, there was no thumping techno or throngs of media—just a jittery nerd typing on a laptop, putting the finishing touches on his presentation. John Charles Harrington stood nearby, keeping a close eye on Paul. His company's future was riding on this presentation.

Conrad Vanderklef sat in the audience, tense and fidgety. He also had a lot on the line.

Mimi spotted Kabir Mehta and his nephew Andy. Mimi made her way to Andy. "I just got a message from Raj Shranka," she told him.

"I got that, too," Andy said.

"Really?" Mimi asked him. "Was it delivered by drone?"

"Yeah, I think so," said Andy. "Isn't it awesome? Shranka confessed to everything, and now we don't have to worry about him anymore."

Mimi was speechless. Shranka's message wasn't "awesome." It was horrific: it showed a man confessing to murder, then vowing to kill himself. It was an ugly end to a promising life.

She thought about how shocked Vashti would be, when she

learned the truth about her brother. Mimi still struggled to square that circle.

"By the way," Andy said, "I've decided to take your advice. I'm quitting my uncle's company and striking out on my own."

"Okay," Mimi said absently.

"Aren't you happy for me?" Andy smiled. "The little bird's leaving the nest."

"Sure," Mimi said, still in a fog. Before she could say more, Andy vanished into the crowd.

As Mimi searched for Andy, Paul waved to her and she walked to the stage.

"How are you feeling?" she asked him.

"A little tense," Paul said. "Both about the presentation and, you know, the other stuff."

"I don't think you have to worry about Dr. Shranka. He just sent me a video. He apologized for everything and said he planned to kill himself."

"Really?" Paul said. "How awful."

"Yes." Mimi nodded. "But at least he's no longer a threat."

Paul glanced at Mimi. "Are you sure about that?"

Mimi sighed, exhausted. "I don't know. I wouldn't consider Dr. Shranka one-hundred percent honest. But you'll be fine. Just focus on giving a great presentation."

"I will. Even if it's not—" He lowered his voice to whisper level. "One-hundred percent honest." Paul tilted his head toward Harrington.

"You mean the green?" Mimi was still sorting out her feelings on that subject. "As you said, you have no choice."

"Right." Paul leaned over to give Mimi a hug. She tried to keep it short and businesslike. It still went on longer than she expected.

Afterward, Mimi went into the audience and sat next to Kabir Mehta.

"Did you see the video that Raj Shranka sent?" she asked him.

"Yes," Kabir nodded soberly. "Hrundi showed it to me after he got it on his phone." Kabir was still using his nephew's birth name.

"Andy got it on his phone?" Mimi asked. "I thought he received it by drone."

"Maybe I misheard," said Kabir. "I found the video very shocking. Even knowing what Shranka had been accused of, he never seemed the type."

"I've heard that," Mimi said.

"Of course, I don't know him well," Kabir said. "He was very quiet. One of the quietest people I've ever met. But he struck me as honest. Mostly, we communicated through Hrundi. And Hrundi, I don't trust."

"Mr. Mehta," Mimi asked, "why do you say such terrible things about your nephew?"

Kabir folded his thick arms and shot Mimi a scornful look. "I hired you as my private investigator, not my family therapist."

"But I don't get it," she said. "You know Andy just told me he's so unhappy working for you, he's going to quit?"

Kabir snickered. "I should be so lucky. Hrundi isn't going anywhere. No one will do business with him without me backing him up."

"Why do you say that? He built a successful lab-grown diamond business for you."

Kabir shook his head with obvious disdain. "I thought you were a detective! There are things that I wasn't able to say with Hrundi present, but I assumed you'd learn yourself. You know how to Google, right?"

"Sure. I Googled both of you," she said, though it's always embarrassing to tell someone you've Googled them.

"Did you search for 'Andy Mehta'?"

"Yes."

"That was your problem!" Kabir said, in his familiar bellow. "There's a pop star with that name. That's why he chose it. His real name is Hrundi. Google 'Hrundi Mehta,' and see what you find." He stared at her. "Go ahead. Do it."

Mimi lifted her phone and searched for "Hrundi Mehta" while Kabir looked over her shoulder. The first page was social media posts and an article about his lab-grown business. Nothing too exciting.

"He used search tricks to push away the bad articles," Kabir said. "Keep going."

She clicked to the next page and found Indian newspaper stories about a Hrundi Mehta who'd gotten into scrapes with the law, including arrests for hacking and identity theft.

"My God," Mimi said. "Is this him?"

"Of course it is," said Kabir. "Why do you think he goes by a different name? He's burned so many bridges. He's lucky he's not in jail right now. Fortunately, I knew the judge at his trial, and I told him I would give Hrundi a job, turn him into a respectable citizen. I knew if Hrundi went to jail that would devastate my brother and be a blot on our family name. Hrundi swore to me he'd turned over a new leaf."

"And did he?"

Kabir's big shoulders moved upwards. "I have my doubts. There were rumors he sold some Chrysalis diamonds on the market undisclosed. But I could never prove that. I wouldn't be surprised if he came up with the idea of developing an undetectable diamond. That's how his mind works. He's clever, that one.

"There was a reason I insisted Dr. Shranka and Hrundi stay in the same hotel room. It wasn't just because I wanted Hrundi to keep an eye on Shranka. I also wanted Shranka to watch Hrundi. But now that I've seen the video, I guess Shranka was the bad potato in the bag."

Mimi had more she wanted to ask, but the auditorium lights were flickering. It was showtime.

CHAPTER THIRTY-TWO

A S THE SESSION KICKED OFF, MIMI'S phone buzzed with a characteristically terse text from Michael—"I'm here." She turned around to see him standing at the back of the auditorium, his arms crossed, his head continually moving side to side—a conspicuous demonstration he was standing guard.

Mimi wanted to run up and kiss him, but he was in policeman mode, which didn't involve kissing. She gave him a wave and a smile. He nodded, but didn't wave back, and his face stayed stern.

John Charles Harrington opened the session by reciting Paul's credentials and praising his service to the industry.

"But nothing he's done matches what he'll do today," Harrington declared. "Ten days ago, Diamond Superior announced they had developed synthetic diamonds that couldn't be told apart from natural gemstones. That has caused considerable unrest in the market. Now, thanks to Mr. Michelson, we can end this unfortunate but thankfully brief chapter in our industry's history."

Paul came to the lectern. "Good afternoon, everyone," he said, his voice verging on a squeak. Paul was usually a natural, fluent presenter. But today, his nerves were noticeable.

He started by summarizing the events that led to this point. He admitted his laboratory had been duped last week by the Chrysalis diamonds—for which he again apologized. He detailed the novel method that produced these new stones, incorporating insights gleaned from inspecting the machine found in Shranka's hotel room. He showed off the newly-acquired carbon dater, noting that his lab—meaning Zeke—had developed software that uses carbon-dating technology to detect the Chrysalis diamonds.

"So let me reiterate, we believe that all the colorless Chrysalis diamonds can be identified as synthetic, and soon that will be relatively easy to do," Paul said.

The audience applauded, all except Conrad, who sat scowling. Mimi had mixed feelings as well. Paul hadn't technically lied—he'd said, "colorless Chrysalis diamonds," instead of "all Chrysalis diamonds." But he hadn't exactly told the truth either.

After that, Paul called for questions—and Mimi found she wasn't the only person who noticed his tell-tale use of the word "colorless."

"Just to be 100% clear on this point," the first person asked, "you specified colorless diamonds. Are colored diamonds, like browns and greens, just as detectable?"

Paul stood, frozen. If he answered, "yes," he wouldn't just be approaching the edge of dishonesty, he'd be stepping over it.

Mimi could see him wrestling with himself, until he blurted, "we see no reason why not."

Harrington was pleased. "So just to reiterate, all the Chrysalis diamonds are detectable. Correct?"

Paul looked like a deer in headlights. If Harrington expected a quick "yes," he didn't get one. Instead, Paul turned his head down, and muttered, "it certainly appears so."

"That is wonderful news," Harrington said with a wide smile. "And I hope those who want to destroy our business for their own enrichment are properly humbled right now."

"Actually, John," Paul interrupted, "let me amend that. Scientific honesty compels me to say that we did find a green diamond that was likely produced with the Chrysalis method and has so far been identified as 'undetermined' origin."

Paul pulled the green out of his pocket and set it on the lectern.

"The color of this green diamond doesn't resemble anything found in nature. And while it doesn't register as natural, we can't currently prove it's synthetic. It was likely produced with a different carbon mixture than the other stones. So that's one exception we've found. I wish I could say we have a perfect one-hundred percent success rate. But we don't."

Mimi smiled and sent Paul a quick text: "I'm proud of you."

A look of shock flashed on Harrington's face, but it was quickly replaced by a tight smile. "Thank you for that clarification, Paul," he said. "I understand you're a stickler for accuracy. That's why we have you here."

Harrington was acting like he wasn't angry. That meant Paul was truly in trouble.

"While hearing this news about the green diamond is disappointing," Harrington said, as if he'd just learned it, "the fact remains that the vast majority of these diamonds can be detected." He proceeded to drive that point home, over and over, while Paul stood by, nodding.

Meanwhile, the green sat on the lectern. Its color was so unusual—yet so beguiling—Mimi was mesmerized. Paul had said that diamonds can "speak" to you. This one clearly had something to say. Mimi leaned her head back, and tuned out Harrington, like he was background music.

Then Paul started talking, and Mimi began to listen again. "John is correct," he said. "We've made tremendous progress detecting these stones in a short period of time. When I first started looking for evidence these diamonds were lab-grown, I remember telling someone, 'it's like looking for a ghost in the stone.'"

At this, Mimi's brain began to whir, like a computer that was booting up. She made one connection after another, until everything clicked. Once she'd solved the mystery of the green, the rest fell into place. Yet, as with her past cases, uncovering the truth didn't bring any great sense of relief—just an overwhelming feeling of sadness, because of how tragic and needless and sick it was.

As Paul took more questions—all centered on the green—Mimi

texted Michael, spelling out her theory, but he'd stuffed his phone in his pocket, and had likely turned it off, since he didn't react to anything she sent. She gestured at him to get his attention, but like the rest of the crowd, he was transfixed by the awkward spectacle on stage.

Mimi decided she shouldn't just tell Michael her theory. She should tell everybody.

As the presentation lumbered to its uncomfortable conclusion, Paul said he had time for one more question. Mimi's hand shot up, but Paul called on the increasingly insistent Conrad Vanderklef. A man with a mic ran up to him.

Conrad began by introducing himself—"I used to work for my family company, and now I'm CEO of Diamond Superior, the originator and exclusive distributor of the Chrysalis diamonds and the Delphine V jewelry line." He didn't appear humbled at all.

"I'm afraid I must disagree with the pile of tosh offered by my former colleague John Charles Harrington. This presentation has utterly failed to deliver what was promised on the tin. Unless a detection method is one-hundred percent, it has little practical value. As Mr. Michelson astutely pointed out, that green diamond was manufactured from different material than the others. So all we—or really any lab-grown diamond producer—have to do is make diamonds from the same material as that green gemstone, and that would put the industry in the same situation it was previously, with no ability to distinguish our diamonds from their mined counterparts.

"So while I appreciate the effort, I'm afraid, in the final analysis, it was all for naught. Which was predictable. The technology developed by our company is so innovative, we knew it would be near-impossible for the industry to detect it." He sat down, a smug smile on his face.

Harrington and Paul didn't respond, but grimly conferred with each other. Mimi decided she'd answer for them.

"Can I say something?" she yelled out.

"Not now, Mimi," Paul said, sounding like an annoyed parent.

"Actually," she responded, "now's the perfect time." She flew out of her chair, ran into the aisle, and approached the man with the mic. "Give me that."

The man looked to Paul, unsure of what to do. She yanked the mic from his hand, then moved a couple of steps away so he couldn't get it back. She spun around to face the crowd and held the mic to her mouth. The entire room was staring at her.

"It is important to explain why Conrad's remarks are false. First of all, Diamond Superior didn't invent the Chrysalis formula. They purchased it. It was originally developed by a scientist, Dr. Raj Shranka."

It was now Conrad's turn to ignore decorum. "Oh please," he stood and shouted. "You keep making that claim. Regardless of its veracity, it has nothing to do with Paul Michelson's failure to develop a reliable and credible detection technique."

"Actually, it does," Mimi said, without skipping a beat. "That information is crucial to understanding how that green diamond was produced. Diamond Superior will never be able to make a diamond like that green. At least I hope not."

Mimi braced herself for what she was about to say.

"Last week, Dr. Raj Shranka was killed in his hotel room by a methane leak. A tube in his diamond growing machine was deliberately cut, and he lacked the mobility to fix it. After he died, his body was burned in his bathtub with sulfuric acid, which turned his remains into carbon. Then, they were placed in the diamond-making machine he'd invented, and used to create that green diamond.

"That's why you won't be able to create a diamond like that green. Because it was created with the remains of a murdered man."

An auditorium full of stunned faces tried to absorb what Mimi just said. Even Michael looked dumbfounded.

Mimi knew her theory was hard to believe. She had a tough time accepting it herself. Yet, it was the only thing that made sense. It explained so much.

It explained why no one saw Raj Shranka leave his hotel room. It explained the dark spots in the hotel bathtub. It even explained the diamond's strange color; it had been hastily produced by an inexperienced grower.

It was why Thorble told Mimi Dr. Shranka wasn't on the roof, and why Raj's sister couldn't believe her brother did those things he was accused of. Because he hadn't done them.

And it explained why the person who did do those things, Andy Mehta—otherwise known as Hrundi, the experienced hacker skilled enough to impersonate Raj Shranka—had sprung from his seat and was sprinting toward the door.

"Stop him, Michael!" yelled Mimi.

Michael stepped in front of the exit. He put his hand in front of Andy's chest. "Don't move. I'm calling the police."

Most of the crowd scurried away from Andy, but Mimi moved closer to hear what was happening.

"I've already texted Detective Brill," Mimi shouted to Michael.

"Okay. Just stand there and stay calm," Michael told Andy. "The police should be here soon."

Andy's eyes darted around the room. "I don't have to listen to you," he shouted at Michael. "You're not a cop!"

"Correct," Michael said. "But I used to be. And I'm providing security for this presentation, which means I can ask you to stay here until the police come, which should be any moment now. Stand back, and we won't have any problems."

"This is crazy!" Andy exclaimed. He turned toward the audience and pointed at Mimi. "How could any of you believe what that woman said? She's nuts! She's lying! This guy only believes her because she's his girlfriend." He pronounced the word *girlfriend* like a mocking schoolboy. "I want everyone to witness this. I'm being held against my will."

No one rushed to protect his civil rights—not even his uncle, who had stood up, and was staring at his nephew with horrified fascination.

"What did you do, Hrundi?" Kabir shouted. "Give yourself up and spare our family further shame."

Andy had been acting innocent, but when he heard his uncle

say this, the mask dropped and his eyes turned dark. "Give me a break! You're the one who shamed our family by humiliating yourself before Vanderklef all those years. How long have they been torturing you? Well, I tortured them back. It's a new world now, where Vanderklef is no longer king. And I brought them to their knees, with just these cheap rocks."

Andy removed a cluster of glittery stones from his pocket. This alarmed Michael. "I am asking you," he said, "to stand still, with your hands at your sides, and not take anything out of your pockets. Whatever you have in your hand, drop it!"

Michael still projected the gravelly authority of a veteran policeman, but he was clearly growing anxious. He shifted his weight from one foot to another as he waited for the cavalry to come.

"I'm not tossing diamonds on the floor!" Andy said, sounding more assured. He closed his fist around the gems.

"I'm warning you!" Michael screamed. "Drop what's in your hand!" The situation appeared ready to explode.

Michael removed his gun from its holster, and raised it to his waist—so Andy could see it. "I am asking you politely, one more time. Drop what you're holding."

Andy didn't move, though the sight of the gun made him step back. Mimi angled her head to see what Andy was clutching in his hand. It didn't look like loose diamonds, more diamond rings, which he was slipping on his fingers. *Why would he do that?* When Mimi figured it out, she screamed. "Michael, watch out! He has diamond knuckles!"

Andy cocked his hand back and swung his fist at Michael's face. But Andy no longer had the benefit of surprise, and Michael swerved away in time. Andy still landed a blow on Michael's shoulder, with enough force that it sent Michael crashing against the wall.

Andy darted out the door. Michael lifted himself up and chased Andy out of the auditorium, red-faced and grunting, blood dripping from his shoulder. Mimi ran toward the exit to follow them both. Before she reached the door, she heard a gunshot. She froze and panicked.

Oh my God. Michael's shot Andy. Her mind swam with the legal trouble Michael might face—the investigations, the questioning, the lawsuits.

When she crashed through the door into the lobby, she saw something far worse: Michael, lying on the floor, surrounded by blood.

CHAPTER THIRTY-THREE

FOUR DAYS LATER, MIMI WAS BACK at what was now her official Least Favorite Place in the World—New York-Presbyterian Hospital.

From the minute Mimi entered Michael's room, she could tell how much he hated being laid up in bed, doing nothing. He shifted his bulky frame when she came in, and continued to do so the entire time she was there.

A pile of bandages was wrapped tightly around his leg, covering the sewed-up bullet wound. For the first few days after he was shot, the hospital gave him so many pain meds that he was groggy and uncommunicative. This was the first day they could really talk.

She brought him an iPad and a bouquet of roses—even though his room already had enough flowers to fill a greenhouse. She also had a bag full of his favorite food: several bags of chips, a bottle of Coke, and a freshly-cooked meatball sub, which he greeted like a long-lost friend.

Mimi bent over him and they shared a long intense kiss—though that's not easy to do with someone with limited mobility. Mimi gripped him tight. She remembered feeling that she might lose him, and wept into his shoulder. When she finished crying, she wiped her tears and they kissed again. Mimi pulled up a chair next to his bed, and took his hand. He unwrapped the sub and took a bite. A wide smile formed as it bounced around his mouth.

"How are you doing?" she said.

"Been better," Michael said. His hair was greasy and he had deep lines etched in his face, but otherwise he looked—not great, but decent, given the circumstances.

"I'm just relieved you're okay. You have no idea how scared I was. But we don't have to talk about that."

"Actually," Michael said, putting down the sub, "I want to talk about what happened at the hotel. If that's all right."

Mimi gave a weak shrug. "Sure."

"I've gone over it a million times. And I'm still trying to understand what happened. After that kid hit me in the auditorium, I pulled out my gun and started chasing him. I aimed my gun right at him and said, 'stop, or I'll shoot.' He froze and I walked up to him.

"But instead of giving up, he panicked and swiped at me with those knuckles. I still had my gun pointed at him. I could have shot him right there. But I didn't. He must have sensed I was hesitating, because he took a second swing at me, and hit me so hard the gun fell out of my hand. He picked it up and, well—" He took a sip of Coke. "Here I am. I'm just lucky he was a lousy shot.

"The thing I keep coming back to is, why didn't I shoot that kid? He certainly deserved it. He was just as dangerous and stupid as any of the thugs I dealt with as a cop. You want to know why I didn't shoot him?"

"Sure." Mimi answered, though she preferred they drop the subject.

"It wasn't a legal issue. I would be acting in self-defense. There was a million witnesses. I would have been fine.

"When I pointed my gun at him, I looked in his eyes, and saw a scared little boy. I've seen that look before. I used to see it all the time on the people I arrested. I got used to it. But I hadn't seen it in so long. And for some reason, it really affected me this time. It was kind of—" He searched for the word. "Shocking. Because I was looking at another human being. A total piece of crap, mind you, but still a person. Maybe it was because I'd met him in that conference room, but for some reason, I couldn't shoot him. I choked. I hesitated. And you can't do that. Or you end up like this."

Mimi stroked his hand. "That's fine. It happens."

"It shouldn't, though. Not when you've been doing this for twenty years. Not when your life's on the line.

"I spent years dealing with people who acted like animals. And sometimes when you do that, you become—I wouldn't say you become an animal yourself. But you develop a shell. It makes you tough. Because in those situations, it's either kill or be killed."

He took another bite of his sub, which he washed down with some Coke.

"I've shot people before. And every time, it was the right thing to do, because it saved people's lives. So I never regretted it. But I hated it. I don't want to do that anymore, not if I don't have to. And it turned out—I didn't even save that stupid kid."

After Andy shot Michael, he sprinted through the hotel. When a contingent of police closed in on him, he leapt over a balcony wall to escape. That wall was thirty feet over an atrium, and he fell straight down to the hotel lobby. He was pronounced dead at the scene.

"It's horrible," Mimi said, lacing her fingers through his. "The good news is, you'll be fine. They said you'll go home soon."

"There's no good news here," Michael frowned. "I'll be fine physically, but mentally I'm a mess. I came this close to never walking again. I could have died. After I was shot, the most horrible thing wasn't the pain. It was the fear. I worried I would die and it would crush the people in my life. I kept thinking about my daughter. She's still a kid."

The corners of his eyes grew red, and before long, he was crying. Mimi fought the urge to look away. She had never seen Michael cry before—not even when his mother died. His weeping didn't last long, but it still felt endless. She got out of her chair and held his hand and stroked his head until he stopped.

"I'm sorry," he said, grabbing a tissue. "It's just—"

"Don't apologize. It's okay. You've been through a horrible experience."

"Anyway," he said with a sniffle, "you have a right to say it. I know you hated it when I said it to you."

"Say what?"

"That you're tired of running to my rescue. If you hadn't warned me about those knuckles, that kid could have killed me."

"Come on, Michael! I would never say that! We're a team. We're in this together."

Michael didn't respond. Instead, he gazed into space. At first, Mimi thought they'd hit a natural silence, but something was on his mind.

"I suppose you're wondering what will happen to the detective agency," he said.

"That's not my main concern." Mimi sat down.

"Before you came here, I checked its voicemail. It's been over-flowing with inquiries since you fingered that kid. Some of them could be great cases. If this was six months ago, I'd be overjoyed. But not now.

"I know you don't have your P.I. license yet, and you can't run the agency on your own. But I can't do it anymore. I can't."

"I understand," she said. "We can talk about it later."

"We can. But I'm firm on this."

"Okay," Mimi whispered.

"I've been thinking about a lot of things," Michael said. "This was supposed to be my last two weeks managing the club. Obviously, I can't do that now.

"I told the guy who runs the club if a similar position opens up, he should let me know. And last week, he told me he'll be coming back to New York, and he needs someone to run his place in London, and if I want it, the job is mine. And I thought, no way am I living in London. But this morning—" He turned his face to the wall. "I called and told him I'd do it."

"You're moving to London?" Mimi asked, in disbelief. When

he didn't reply, she blurted, "that's great, honey," though she wasn't sure how great it was.

"I can't do it now, obviously, but the doctor said in a month or two, I should be able to go. Catherine starts her junior year abroad in France in September so I'll see her a lot more if I'm living in London than if I stayed here. I agreed to do it for a year, and then, who knows?"

"Okay," Mimi said. Her voice sounded distant to her, almost robotic.

"It's a pretty big step," Michael said. "England may be a bad fit for a Brooklyn kid. I don't know much about it, except they drive on the wrong side on the road, eat lots of meat, and like to hang out in bars. So we'll see. I'm looking at this as an adventure."

"Okay," Mimi repeated, though she was having a hard time not crying.

"I want you to come with me," Michael said.

"You want me to move to London?" Mimi felt like a weight was being dropped on her. She was receiving an awful lot of information at once.

"Sure. We'll explore it together. What do you think?"

"I don't know," Mimi said, feeling put on the spot. "It's a big move. I'll be uprooting my life. I'll be leaving everything here behind. My friends. My family."

"Not everything. You'll have me. And you can stay in touch with your family. You can Zoom."

Mimi was about to say, "my father hates Zoom," but that wasn't really the point. "It'll be different for you. You'll have a job. Your daughter will be nearby. I'll just have you. And if your new job is anything like the one you have now, you'll never be around."

"I'm not worried you'll have nothing to do," Michael said. "You'll get involved with *something*. You're a smart cookie. Hopefully you won't try and solve any murders."

"Do they have murders in London?" Mimi asked.

"Sure. Don't you watch PBS? That's half their programming. But they're very genteel. After the murder, the killer drinks tea."

That brought on a chuckle. "But isn't London expensive?"

"No worse than New York. And the owner said he'll put me up the first year in his flat, which I guess is a small apartment. I'm excited about it. I enjoyed managing the club over here so hopefully I'll like it there, too."

Mimi fell back in her chair. Tectonic plates were shifting beneath her. She took a deep breath to prepare herself for what she was about to say. "If I go with you, will we get—" She couldn't get the word out.

"Get what?"

Dammit, Mimi thought. *Why must I say it?* "Married."

Mimi saw the shock in Michael's eyes.

"You want to get married?" he asked.

"I guess," she responded, with a surprising tremble in her voice. "It's not something I think about all the time. But if I'm uprooting my life, I'd want some stability."

"I don't know," Michael said. "I've been married before. It's a big commitment."

"No kidding. I was married too, remember? They let you do it twice."

"Honestly, I haven't really thought about it. You know how much I care about you. But getting married, I don't know. I'll be really busy."

Mimi almost groaned. That had become Michael's all-purpose excuse. "So you don't want to get married?"

"No! I didn't say that! I don't know. You just raised that out of the blue. I thought we'd go to London. We've never really lived together. I figure we could try that, then decide." His detective eyes bored into her. "Do *you* want to get married?"

"I don't know. Maybe." She fiddled with her purse strap. "I guess we both need to think about it."

Michael wet his lips. "We shouldn't be discussing this now, when I'm lying in a hospital bed. I'm on these meds and they tell you not to make big decisions on them."

Mimi almost said *you just accepted a job on those very same meds,* but didn't. "We can talk later. You need to rest up."

Mimi stood up, and leaned over Michael's bed. She picked up a tissue and wiped up the tomato sauce from the meatball sub that had dribbled onto his chin. Then, they shared a sweet, tender, extra-long kiss—which, Mimi knew, would be their last.

CHAPTER THIRTY-FOUR

THE NEXT DAY, JOHN CHARLES HARRINGTON of Vanderklef called Mimi, and asked her to come to his regular table at the European Club. When Mimi arrived, he was so ebullient that Mimi wondered if he'd loaded up on Old Fashioneds.

"Given you helped us resolve this sordid little drama," he said, as he smoked his standard cigar, "please let me know if there's anything I can do for you."

"Well, for starters," Mimi said, "I'd prefer you not smoke."

Harrington's eyebrows arched, then he quickly regained his composure. He snuffed out his cigar in an ashtray and muttered, "no problem." He was still adjusting to this new world where he couldn't always do what he wanted.

"In any case," he said, "I called you here because we're keen to acquire the detection technology that was developed at Paul Michelson's lab. Mr. Michelson stipulated that any payout must be split evenly between him, you, and his associate, Zeke Kotek. Mr. Kotek has signed off, and now we need you to as well."

Paul insisted we split the money. Mimi thought. *He is an honorable man.*

"We are willing to pay one-hundred thousand dollars—thirty-three thousand for each of you," Harrington said, as his hands fluttered about, in the absence of a cigar.

Mimi nodded. "Thank you. I appreciate the offer. However, the three of us saved your billion-dollar company. We deserve one-hundred-and-fifty thousand dollars. At least."

Harrington's head jolted back. "That's a little beyond our budget."

Mimi put on her sternest poker face. "One-hundred-and-fifty. Take it or leave it."

Harrington smirked. "You've learned the business well. *Mazal.*" They shook hands.

"So," Mimi said, "this solves the Chrysalis problem, right?"

"It should. Our scientists have inspected Shranka's diamond maker, and we're hopeful that, in relatively short order, they can develop a detection device that doesn't rely on carbon dating. And we no longer have to worry about Diamond Superior dumping stones on the market. We've acquired the company."

"Really? I thought Conrad would never sell."

"He didn't want to, but the investors forced his hand. They didn't see any future in the business, now that Diamond Superior's name has been tainted by that diamond made out of Dr. Shranka. People are already weary of blood diamonds. They're not going to buy murdered-people diamonds." This normally would be the point where Harrington would take a contented puff on his cigar. He had to settle for drumming his fingers on his chest.

"How did Conrad take the news?" Mimi asked.

"From what I heard, not well. But don't feel too badly for old Con. He was able to fulfill his lifelong desire to be a CEO. Granted, it was only for two weeks, but he did get that title.

"Mind you, if Conard had stayed at Vanderklef, he would have remained a high-ranking executive. Not CEO, of course, but better than the title he just negotiated with us—'non-executive director emeritus.'"

"What does that mean?"

"He gets to use our fifth-floor washroom."

"That's it?"

"It's not nothing. It's quite a nice washroom. He also retained the rights to his daughter's jewelry line, so he'll still be able to waste his family's money."

"I'm surprised," Mimi said. "Conrad told me his investors would back him, because they were mission-driven."

"In the end," Harrington said, "his investors were driven by the real mission of every investor." He rubbed his fingers together, the universal sign of money. "We just saw Diamond Superior's factory—the one in India, not the VR version. It wasn't exactly eco-friendly, but then, few factories are. The late, unlamented Mr. Thorble was good at telling people a story they wanted to hear. Even his employees believed Thorble and his billionaire backers were underdogs, fighting the establishment. When they heard Vanderklef was buying the company, almost half of them quit."

"Wow."

"Yes." Harrington said. "We were quite pleased. We don't have to pay them severance. We've had to fire the rest. About one hundred people. Bloody shame."

Mimi stared at him, shocked. "You fired one hundred people?"

Harrington shrugged his broad shoulders. "We no longer had a need for them. We have our own diamond distribution system. We don't need theirs."

"But still—"

"Their whole mission statement was putting us out of business. They wanted to disrupt us, so we disrupted them first. That's how business works. In any case, we'll retain a small crew in India, to keep the factory going. We'll need their help with our lab-grown line."

Mimi wasn't sure what she just heard. "Hold it. Vanderklef is going to sell lab-grown diamonds? I thought you specialized in precious objects."

"Traditionally, we have. But now that we've seen the profit margins on that business, it's hard to resist. They produce them for a dollar a carat, and sell them for five hundred. You rarely see business models like that." His face almost glowed. "Ultimately, our mission is the same as Diamond Superior's." His fingers made the money sign again.

"We're announcing it in a few days. We have to be careful with our messaging. We'd like to limit the industry to one nervous breakdown a month."

Harrington stroked his chin. "If I'm not mistaken, you're running a diamond co-op in the African Democratic Republic. I'm a little hesitant to ask, now that I've witnessed your negotiating savvy, but would you be interested in selling it?"

Mimi was stunned. "We don't own the co-op. We're just its distributor. You'll have to talk to Reverend Sulaiman Kamora. He runs it. But I'm a little surprised you're interested. It doesn't give you much of this." She rubbed her fingers together.

"Well, as you might have heard, Vanderklef has a bit of an image problem. All due to things in the past, of course. But getting involved in a project like that could be in our corporate interest."

"PR interest, you mean," Mimi said.

"You could look at it that way. We're not a charity. It's also not a bad business model."

"Because you don't have to build a big industrial mine."

"Bingo."

Mimi had long sought better funding for the co-op. At one point, she considered approaching Vanderklef, because of their deep pockets. Now, they wanted to buy it. Mimi didn't totally trust them, but given all Reverend Kamora had been through, he'd probably jump at their offer—especially if his village would be guaranteed income for the next few years.

"If you do buy it," Mimi said, "promise me you'll take care of the people there. They've been taken advantage of for years. Don't just look at them as dollar signs. See them as people."

"I promise," Harrington said, "hand on my heart, we'll do our best."

Mimi sighed. "Their best" was probably all she could hope for.

"Remember," Mimi said, "I'm a reporter. If you don't do right by those people, let's just say it would not be in your corporate interest—"

"Message received." Harrington glanced at his watch. "Anyway,

I probably should reach out to Reverend Kamora. It was lovely chatting." That was her cue to leave.

"Before I go," Mimi said, "I'm wondering, how did you know I ran that co-op? I've always heard that Vanderklef had this vast intelligence network—"

"Ah yes. That talk about us having a massive web of informants is, I'm afraid, a fiction. I discovered you were involved with that co-op because you told me about it, when we met after Thorble's funeral."

"Right. But speaking of Thorble's funeral, you found out where it was. And I know for a fact, that information was difficult to find."

"Let me just say this—" A smile crept across Harrington's face. "You're not the only person who knows how to reach out to disgruntled ex-employees."

It was only after Mimi left that it hit her: How did Harrington know she'd spoken with a disgruntled ex-employee?

A FEW DAYS LATER, CHANNAH AND MIMI were having lunch in Bryant Park, when Channah looked around conspiratorially, then declared with a grin: "I have news. I'm pregnant."

"What?" Mimi asked. "I thought you didn't want a baby yet."

"I didn't. At least I didn't before. I wanted to wait. And so every time that Zeke and I, you know—we—you know—" Channah's face turned pink.

"It's all right, Channah. You don't have to give me details."

"Anyway, when Zeke found out how much money he was getting for that Chrysalis thing, he said we'd use it for a trip around the world. I mean, we probably won't see the whole world. That would take years. But we'll see a lot of it. Maybe seven or eight countries. Which is seven or eight more countries than I've seen now. Anyway, I was just so excited to hear that, that we had a little celebration and weren't careful. I mean, we didn't—"

"Got it," Mimi said.

Channah giggled. "What can you do? You can't fight nature. We can plan all we want, but in the end, our fate's in the hands of

Hashem. I'm just happy I'll get to travel before I have the baby."

"So how do you feel about everything?" Mimi asked.

"It's not what I planned, but now that it's becoming more real, I'm excited about it."

Mimi gave her a long hug.

"Think about it, Mimi!" Channah laughed. "We're getting a new codependent."

A few days later, Paul called Mimi. She thanked him for insisting she receive an equal share from the sale of the detection technology.

"No problem." He cleared his throat and launched into what sounded like a pre-prepared speech. "Recent events have prompted me to re-evaluate my life. I've been running my lab nonstop for three years. Even before all this, I needed a break. But when you have your life threatened, it makes you stop and think.

"I've been very inspired by what Zeke is doing, traveling the world before his baby comes. I've never actually travelled for pleasure. I've always done it for business. I usually just go in and out of a country, without really getting to know it. So now that the lab's doing well again, I've decided I'm going to travel as well."

"Great," Mimi said.

"Yeah." He cleared his throat again. "So how is your boyfriend, the policeman? Is he okay?"

"He's doing better, thanks," Mimi said. "The doctors say he'll make a full recovery. Though honestly, I'm not sure he's still my boyfriend. We're figuring that out."

"Yeah, Zeke told me that." Paul took a breath. "So, my question is, would you like to travel with me?"

Mimi was too stunned to respond.

"I know this is out of the blue," he said. "And I apologize if it makes you uncomfortable. You said I should take more chances, so I figured it wouldn't hurt to ask. The worst you can say is 'no,' right?" He let out an unconvincing laugh. "So, any thoughts?"

Once again, Mimi was at a loss for words.

THE END OF THE CHRYSALIS CRISIS was great news for the diamond business. Having survived a near-death experience, it now had a new lease on life. Max and his friends suddenly had more business than they could handle. Prices kept rising, in a seemingly endless spiral. The rally went on for weeks, with buying and trading growing ever more feverish.

Channah said she had never seen Max so happy. Mimi warned her father to take it easy, but she, too, was heartened by his high spirits. Until one afternoon, he began complaining of chest pains.

CHAPTER THIRTY-FIVE

A FEW DAYS LATER, MIMI WAS BACK at New York-Presbyterian Hospital, walking down its ammonia-scented halls until she got to her father's room.

Max was sitting up in bed. He was clad in a hospital gown, and had his *yarmulke* on. He'd just had his lunch delivered; it came in a specially sealed container, with a sticker on top attesting it was *glatt kosher*.

As Max covered his chicken sandwich in ketchup, he said his doctors had told him that his second "heart episode" was more serious than the first.

"They think I'll eventually need a pacemaker. So I guess I'll be part-machine from now on."

"You'll always be all you," Mimi said. "When are you coming back to the office? We've missed you."

"Well—" Max said, dragging out the word. Mimi knew she was about to get bad news. "The doctor told me work is causing me too much stress. I said that didn't make sense, because things were going well. He said that sometimes good news can be just as stressful as bad. Anyway, he said that after this episode, I should seriously consider retiring."

Mimi sat forward on her seat. "So will you?"

"I think so," Max said in a small voice. "It's funny. I used to joke that the only way I'd leave the office was feet first. I didn't mean it literally.

"Anyway, I'm making a deal to sell all my inventory. It's good timing, because the market's now as strong as it's ever been. I'll be getting my nest egg back, and then some. And then I'll shut my office. That'll be it, after fifty-two years." He paused for a moment. "How do you feel about that?"

"You have to do what you think is right."

"I thought you'd say that. When you used to come to me for advice, that's what I used to say. I never meant it. How do you really feel?"

Mimi smiled. "Dad, I'd love for you to keep the business going, but not at the expense of your health. It's fine. I'll be fine." Mimi wondered if she was trying to assure her dad or herself.

There was a brief moment of silence. "What about the detective agency?" he asked.

"It's closing. Michael's leaving for London."

"And you're not going with him?"

"No." That word brought on a twinge of pain.

The week before, Mimi had told Michael she wouldn't move to London. She'd spent the past few nights crying and wondering if she'd made the right decision. Michael had sent her an email, thanking her for giving him a "new life" by getting him involved in the jazz club. "I owe you a lot," he wrote. "I hope you know that." Mimi read it a dozen times before deleting it.

She also phoned Paul, and told him she wouldn't be going with him either. She wanted to figure things out herself.

She did agree to house-sit Michael's place and take care of his dog while he was away. Mimi was finally ditching her crappy apartment and moving into Michael's. The catch was, Michael wouldn't be there.

"So what are you going to do?" Max asked.

"I don't know. I have a little money."

Actually, by Mimi's standards, she had a lot of money. She'd received the fifty thousand dollars from Vanderklef for Paul's technology, and was getting another twenty-five thousand from Kabir Mehta. He'd raised his final payout to the detective agency to fifty thousand, because he felt so bad about Michael's injury. Michael told Mimi she should take it all, since she did all the work. Mimi countered that Michael did the really hard part—getting shot—which netted them the extra cash. So they split it.

Mimi had a financial cushion that would last a while, depending on how frugal she was. Still, she was on the verge of being unemployed, and wasn't sure what she'd do next.

"Reverend Kamora has asked me to be a consultant for his co-op," she said. "He wants me to be their monitor. Make sure Vanderklef is paying them fairly."

"Good," Max said. "They'll need someone like you watching out for them."

"I'll have to learn a lot more about diamond grading and valuation. I'm sure that will take a while."

"Yeah," Max said, chewing on his sandwich. "Try your whole life."

"I may have to call on your expertise once in a while. I'm sure you'll be okay with that."

Max nodded. "Of course."

"Anyway, that'll just be part-time. I might also start writing again. I have a friend who works in publishing, and she heard about my investigations, and thinks there might be a book in them. I was going to tell her no, because it always felt wrong to write about these things. But for the last few nights, I've been jotting things down and I really enjoyed it. I've missed writing. So, maybe I'll do that."

"You should," Max said. "You have a great story to tell. Stories, actually."

"I thought you never liked me investigating."

"Of course, I didn't," Max said. "You had guns pointed at you. What father would want that? You know how many years I spent worrying about you girls? I'm not going to stop now."

After that, the conversation shifted. Between bites of his sandwich, Max relayed "big news"—Channah was having a boy. In line with the Jewish custom of naming children after the departed, she was naming him Yosef, after her former fiancé.

Channah had told Mimi that the day before; Mimi tried to act surprised, but she also got choked up when she heard it again.

"Well, Dad," Mimi said, "I have something good for you." She pulled a two-carat yellow oval from her purse.

"Is that 'The Yellow'?" Max was amazed when Mimi produced the diamond his wife wore. "I can't believe you got that. I was so stupid to sell that thing. I called the guy I sold it to, and told him I was willing to pay any amount of money to get it back. But he'd already sold it to someone who sold it to someone else, and this market's so crazy, he lost track of it. How'd you find it?"

Mimi had to tell him the truth. "I asked the people at Vanderklef to grow it for you."

Max recoiled. "They grew it for you? You mean it's—"

"Yes," Mimi said. "It's synthetic. I remembered what you told me about the original's color and clarity. So I had them make one just like it."

Max brushed it aside. "I don't want it. It's an imitation. It's not the same."

"I'm not saying it is. It doesn't have the same memories attached. Just think of it as a memento of a memento."

Max gazed at it. "I'm not interested. You know how I feel about synthetics." He pushed it away. But he kept staring at it, and about a minute later, he picked it up and placed it in his hand. "It's nice, I guess."

"You don't have to keep it," Mimi said. "Vanderklef made it for me for free."

"I just heard that Vanderklef will sell lab-grown. I can't believe that."

"It's crazy. What do you think will happen to the business? To everyone on Forty-Seventh Street?"

"I don't know." Max put the lab-grown "Yellow" back on the tray table. "It'll be a different industry, that's for sure. Where it ends up—" He shrugged and left it at that.

"Do you think they'll ever make synthetic diamonds where you can't tell the difference?"

"It's possible," Max said. "They came close this time. If there's money in it, they'll try again. I was just reading, they think soon you won't be able to tell the difference between a regular human voice and machine imitation. You won't know who you're talking to." He frowned. "I'm not sure I want to see that."

"I'm not sure I want to see it either," Mimi said. "When I speak to my journalist friends, they're all convinced they're going to be replaced by AI. The future seems so scary."

Mimi expected her father to agree. He was always complaining that the world was going to hell. Instead, he frowned at her.

"*Bubela*. Don't be that way. There's no point. The world's always been crazy. Life's full of uncertainty. You never know what will happen. You just have to do your best.

"I know I sometimes complain when things change. But the past wasn't perfect. Trust me; I was there. A lot of things are better now. When I was a kid, women couldn't do half the things you do now. I had relatives with numbers on their arms. So yes, things could definitely be worse. Way worse."

"Is this your attempt to cheer me up?"

Max shrugged. "Just thoughts I had. You lie around all day, it makes you think." He pointed to the window. "It's a nice day outside. Take some time and enjoy it."

"I don't know, Dad. We've kind of screwed up weather, too."

He glanced out the window. "It looks nice today. I'd love to be out there but I'm stuck here in this *verkakte* bed. I hate to say it, but someday, many many decades from now, you might end up in a bed like this. Then, you'll wish you were outside, enjoying the nice days."

Mimi took her father's hand and her voice broke. "Dad, I can't tell you how much I appreciate all you've done for me. I mean, you've always helped me, but these last few years, I don't know what I would have done without you. You helped me get back on my feet, when I had nothing. That meant so much to me."

Max smiled, and the ghostly sheen that was covering his face melted away. "Of course I helped you. You're my little girl. I was happy to do it. It made me feel like your father again. And don't think you didn't do a lot for me. I probably would have packed it in a long time ago if it wasn't for you. Anyway, if you ever get in a bad way again, you can always count on me."

"It's okay, Dad. I'll be fine."

"I know you will. You've accomplished a lot. I could never understand how you figured out those crazy mysteries."

Mimi shrugged. "I've always done puzzles, and I looked at the cases that way. I'd spend a lot of time thinking about them until the answer came."

Max laughed and finished off his sandwich. "Amazing. You're going to be fine, kiddo. You've had a good impact on people, whether you realize it or not. Anyway, whatever happens, remember your father loves you and is always on your side."

They talked a little longer, and eventually Max said he was feeling tired and needed to take a nap. Mimi kissed him on the head and left.

MIMI CALLED BRENDA FROM THE HOSPITAL lobby. "I just visited Dad. He seems okay. I guess he'll be staying with you after he gets out."

"He'll be here while he recuperates," Brenda said. "Then, he might move back to his place, or keep staying with us. It's up to him. He has a decent nest egg now."

There was a short pause, and then Mimi blurted, "Brenda, I want to thank you for all you've done for Dad."

"Of course," Brenda said. "I'm his daughter. Thank God we were able to. And you know, I appreciate you working with him all that time. It meant a lot to him. And when Dad moves here, he's going to miss you. A lot. So make sure you visit him, okay? At least once a month. And call him at least twice a week. He'll be happy to hear from you. Actually, you should probably call him every day." Brenda was back to older sister mode. "And by the way, I'm your sister. I wouldn't mind hearing from you once in a while, too."

Mimi smiled. "You will."

"Listen, I know Dad closing his company may not be what you want, but he had to do it."

"It's okay," Mimi said. "I understand. I'm fine with it."

"That's good, because when I talk to him, the main thing he's worried about is you. Do you know what you'll do?"

"No. But I'll be fine."

A FEW WEEKS LATER, MIMI WENT TO her father's office to gather her belongings. Max and Channah had already cleared out their stuff, but Mimi kept delaying taking hers home. When she finally did, the office was so empty it was eerie. She threw away most of what she had there, but kept a few souvenirs—an article about her co-op in the ADR, and an invoice commemorating the first diamond it sold. On her father's desk, she found a picture of her mom, looking young and vivacious, showing off her newly-acquired engagement ring in front of Max's first office. Her smile covered her whole face. Mimi wondered if her father had deliberately left that there for her. She stared at it for a while, gave it a kiss, and dropped it in her purse. Then she turned out the lights, one last time.

As Mimi waited for the elevator, she remembered the first day she went to work for her father's company. At the time, she felt like she'd hit a new low. But at some point, working for her father stopped being something she felt forced to do, and became something she enjoyed. She'd spent three years at a workplace where people truly cared and looked out for each other. Before this, she'd doubted offices like that existed.

She remembered something else about that day. Back then, she was unemployed and single, and petrified about the future. Now she was unemployed and single again. But she wasn't scared. She was a tough cookie. She'd figure something out.

The elevator delivered her to the ground floor, and she stepped out onto Forty-Seventh Street. It was a beautiful day. The sky was blue and dotted with clouds. The gems in the windows sparkled in the afternoon sun.

Mimi had always considered the Diamond District a disgusting mess—and well, she still did. Today, though, it was full of familiar faces. One of them waved to her. She happily waved back. She saw Zeke and Channah walking across the street, hand in hand. She thought about saying hi to them, but decided to let the two parents-to-be enjoy the moment.

Mimi marveled how this one block contained so many people, so many cultures, so many worlds—and so many mysteries. Mimi spent a moment drinking it in. Then she strode to the subway, eager and excited for whatever came next.

GLOSSARY

of Yiddish/Hebrew/Diamond Industry Terms
(But Mostly Yiddish)

Alter kaker—*Yiddish.* An old person, though not a particularly vibrant one. Roughly translates to "old fart."

Baruch Hashem—*Hebrew.* Translates to "blessed be the name," or "thank God."

Blood diamonds—*Diamond industry.* A term that has no specific definition, but generally means *conflict diamonds*, which are diamonds used to finance civil wars.

Bubela—*Yiddish.* Sweetheart. A term of endearment.

Carat—*Diamond industry.* The unit that measures a diamond's weight. It is believed to have been derived from the carob bean.

Chemical vapor deposition (CVD)—*Diamond industry.* One of two commonly used diamond-growing processes. (The other is HPHT.) With CVD, a diamond seed is placed in a chamber, and the chamber is filled with carbon-rich gasses. As the gas is heated, it releases carbon atoms, which bond with the seed, forming a diamond.

D color—*Diamond industry.* The highest color grade a diamond can attain. A D-color diamond is colorless, meaning it has no body color under ten-power magnification. The people who devised the grading scale made "D" the top grade, instead of "A," so it wouldn't be used commercially. That plan failed.

Einikel—*Yiddish.* Grandchild.

Flawless—*Diamond industry.* The highest clarity grade a diamond can attain. A flawless diamond has no visible flaws, even under ten-power magnification.

Ganef—*Yiddish.* A thief, crook.

Glatt Kosher—*Hebrew/Yiddish.* Generally refers to food being prepared to an even higher standard than regular kosher food.

Hashem—*Hebrew.* Translates to "the name." It is used by Orthodox Jews who don't wish to utter the word *God* out of respect.

Hock—*Yiddish.* To bother, nag.

Hawker—*Diamond industry*—A person who stands in the Diamond District—Forty-Seventh Street between Fifth and Sixth Avenues in Manhattan—and tries to lure passers-by into a store, to either buy something or trade in their used jewelry. Many people find them annoying, this author included.

High pressure-high temperature (HPHT)—*Diamond industry.* The second diamond-growing method. With HPHT, carbon atoms are subjected to intense amounts of heat and pressure, then bond together to form a diamond. This method mimics how diamonds are formed in the Earth's mantle.

Kibitz—*Yiddish.* Make small talk.

Lab-grown diamonds—*Diamond industry.* Diamonds that are produced in factories and laboratories, rather than under the Earth. Also known as "man-made," "lab-created," and "synthetic" diamonds. "Synthetics" are different from diamond simulants like cubic zirconia, which resemble diamonds but have a different chemical composition.

Loupe—*Diamond industry.* A small handheld magnifying glass that lets dealers examine diamonds at ten-power (10x) magnification.

Mazal—*Hebrew/Diamond industry.* The shortened version of *Mazal u'bruche,* which translates to "luck and blessings." It is used, along with a handshake, to seal deals in the diamond industry.

Mishigas—*Yiddish.* Craziness, nonsense.

Mitziah—*Yiddish.* A good deal or bargain.

Mitzvah—*Hebrew.* Translates to "command." It generally means a good deed.

Olev ha-shalom—*Hebrew.* It translates to "may peace be upon" the person's memory. Similar to saying "rest in peace."

Oy—*Yiddish.* An expression of dismay. Also: *oy vey.*

Pepper spots—*Diamond industry.* Little black specks in a diamond, caused by uncrystallized carbon. They are considered flaws.

Pisher—*Yiddish.* An insignificant person, a nothing. This book pays tribute to the *pishers* of the world.

Schlep—*Yiddish.* To move very slowly, to drag.

Schmooze—*Yiddish.* To engage in friendly talk.

Schmuck—*Yiddish.* A jerk, an idiot.

Schnook—*Yiddish*. A fool.

Schnorrer—*Yiddish*. A beggar or moocher.

Sheitel—*Hebrew*. A wig worn by some married Orthodox Jewish women, out of a desire for modesty.

Shtetl—*Yiddish*. A small town, generally in Eastern Europe, comprised of mostly Jewish residents. Immortalized in *Fiddler on the Roof.*

Shiva—*Hebrew*. The prescribed seven-day mourning period in Judaism.

Shul—*Yiddish*. A synagogue.

Tachlis—*Yiddish*. Bottom line.

Tsuris—*Yiddish*. Anxiety, fears, problems.

Tzedakah—*Hebrew*. Charity or acts of charity.

Verkakte—*Yiddish*. Ridiculous.

Yarmulke—*Yiddish*. A skullcap worn in public by Orthodox Jewish men, as well as by less observant Jews during prayer and visits to synagogues.

Yenta—*Yiddish*. A gossip.

Zei gezunt—*Yiddish*. Farewell, be healthy, be well. An excellent phrase to end this book.

Rob Bates has written about the diamond industry for three decades. He is currently the news director of *JCK*, the leading publication in the jewelry industry. There, he has won 12 editorial awards, and been quoted as an industry authority in *The New York Times*, *The Wall Street Journal*, and on *National Public Radio*. He is also a comedy writer and performer, whose work has appeared on FuseTV, comedycentral.com, and Mcsweeneys. He lives in Manhattan with his wife and son.

www.ingramcontent.com/pod-product-compliance
Lightning Source LLC
Chambersburg PA
CBHW011513100726
47899CB00010BD/3341